Land of Shadows

Books by Priscilla Royal

The Medieval Mysteries
Wine of Violence
Tyrant of the Mind
Sorrow Without End
Justice for the Damned
Forsaken Soul
Chambers of Death
Valley of Dry Bones
A Killing Season
The Sanctity of Hate
Covenant with Hell
Satan's Lullaby
Land of Shadows

Land of Shadows

A Medieval Mystery

Priscilla Royal

Poisoned Pen Press

To Sharon Kay Penman
Inspiration, mentor, and friend
With love and gratitude.

Acknowledgments

Patrick Hoi Yan Cheung, Christine and Peter Goodhugh, Maddee James, Henie Lentz, Dianne Levy, Paula Mildenhall, Sharon Kay Penman, Barbara Peters (Poisoned Pen Bookstore in Scottsdale, Arizona), Robert Rosenwald and all the staff of Poisoned Pen Press, Marianne and Sharon Silva, Lyn and Michael Speakman, the staff of the University Press Bookstore (Berkeley, California).

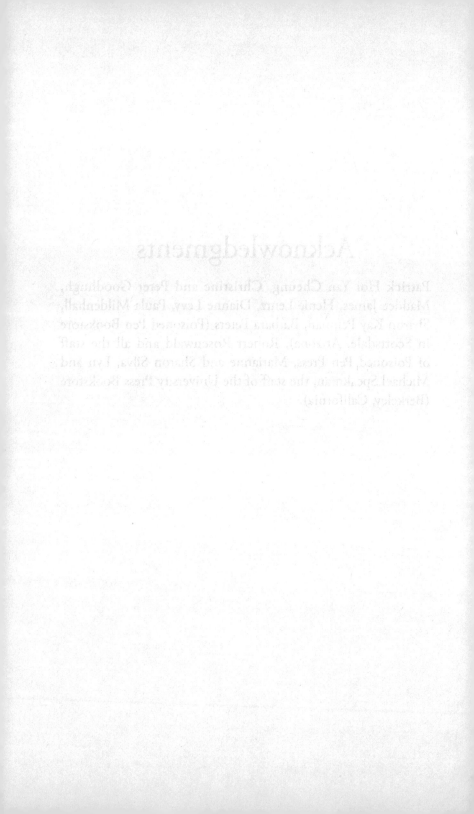

Acknowledgments

Patrick Hoi Yan Cheung, Christine and Peter Goodburn, Matthew James, Merle Levin, Diane Levy, Paula Mildenhall, Sharon Kay Ramsell, Barbara Lucas (Pioneer Pet Bookstore in Scottsdale, Arizona), Robert Rosenwald and all the staff of Poisoned, Pat Frost, Marianne and Sharon Silva, Lyn and Michael Spe..., the staff of the University Press Bookstore (Berkeley, California).

Every way of a man is right in his own eyes: but the Lord pondereth the hearts.

—Proverbs 21:2 (King James version)

A voice was heard in Ramah, lamentation, and bitter weeping; Rachel weeping for her children, refused to be comforted for her children, because they were not.

—Jeremiah 31:15 (King James version)

Chapter One

Baron Adam of Wynethorpe opened his eyes.

How long had he lain in this bed? Time had an unnatural feel. He no longer had any sense of it.

A tall nun leaned over and smiled at him.

Although her features were indistinct, he was certain he knew her. A memory flickered. Was it she who had come with his daughter and saved his grandson's life many years ago?

He struggled to speak, but his words were unintelligible. Trying again, he failed and grew angry with frustration. Had he been bewitched?

"I am Sister Anne, sub-infirmarian from your daughter's priory at Tyndal," the nun said.

Adam tried to smile, but he could not feel one side of his mouth. That she had understood what he wished to ask was a miracle, he thought, for he was only able to utter grunts and gasps.

"I am here, Father." This woman's soft voice was at his ear. "Hugh should arrive soon, but the snows have kept Robert at Wynethorpe Castle."

It was his youngest child, and he was relieved she was beside him. As much as he loved all three of his children, it was his daughter, Prioress Eleanor, who gave him the greatest joy. If he could not reply with speech, at least he was still able to nod.

His daughter took his hand and placed his palm against her cheek. "You have suffered apoplexy," she said. "Sister Anne,

Brother Thomas, and I came to Woodstock Manor as soon as we received word."

In acknowledgement of what she just said, he blinked. His eyes were heavy with fatigue and he let them remain shut for a moment. It was then that the memory of what had happened to him returned.

King Edward, Queen Eleanor, and chosen members of their court had gathered at this manor in Oxfordshire before traveling on to Gloucestershire where the royal couple spent every March. Baron Adam was one of the few who always accompanied them to their secular retreat at Quenington, a manor actually owned by the Knights Hospitaller. One evening, while the king was in conversation with him, the earth inexplicably rose to smite Adam. His last thought, before all went black, was to wonder how this extraordinary event could even occur.

When he awoke from a strange sleep and even more peculiar dreams, he was lying in this bed. His grandson, Richard FitzHugh, was by his side. The youth smiled, then bent closer to say that Prioress Eleanor, her talented sub-infirmarian, and Brother Thomas had been summoned from Tyndal Priory.

Before he drifted back into an uneasy slumber that day, Adam felt relieved that his beloved daughter would be accompanied by Brother Thomas. If he was going to die, he wanted to confess and receive the comfort of the Church from a man of God whom he respected. Not only had Brother Thomas proven his loyalty to the Wynethorpe family, but he had become an advisor and confidant to young Richard when the lad's own father was fighting in Outremer and Wales. Sometimes, Adam thought, his grandson was closer to Brother Thomas than he was to his actual father.

A chill struck him. Was he dying now? He opened his eyes wide.

The world he knew was still there.

Sister Anne lifted his left arm and ran something along it, then looked down at the baron.

He felt nothing. Assuming she had reason for this, he shook his head.

She gently laid his arm down and smiled, but her eyes lacked brightness.

Now he was certain he would not recover. Sister Anne's smile was meant to convey hope, but her eyes betrayed her. Had he not learned to read a man's true thoughts behind the public expressions, Adam would never have survived the court of kings, let alone won victories to benefit his family's fortunes.

"Are you able to eat some soup?"

Looking at his daughter, he saw she held a bowl. Despite the crackling fire not far from him and the bright tapestries hanging from the walls, the room felt so cold. A light steam rose from the food. He managed to utter something that almost sounded like *yes*.

Sister Anne draped a cloth under his chin and over his chest. Eleanor sat on his right and dipped a spoon into the thick meat broth. "Sip it, Father," she said. He could hear her tears even if she did manage to hide all other evidence of them.

As he drew the warm soup into his mouth, he felt a sudden panic. Could he swallow it?

"If you cannot eat, spit it out, my lord," the sub-infirmarian said.

Once he relaxed, he was able to do so. After a third spoonful, he grunted.

His daughter understood he wished no more and gave the bowl to a servant to remove.

The soup tasted like metal, even if the smell suggested the broth had been made with fresh meat and pungent spices. If he could not taste food, he no longer cared to eat it. And the effort to suck up the three spoonfuls had exhausted him.

Although he slept, the rest never chased away fatigue. When he awoke, he felt as weary as he did when he fell asleep. Now, as he faded again into his world of curious dreams, he looked around the room one last time.

In the corners, there were odd shadows he hadn't noticed before. Glancing at the window, he knew it was daylight. Perhaps, he thought, the sun is too weak to chase away all hints of Satan's hour?

But his eyelids grew heavy as iron, and they closed against his will. There were people in the room, and he knew they must be speaking. Most assuredly, his daughter was praying, but he heard nothing except a distant mumbling. The hush weighed down on him like a great tapestry. In the past, this would have been frightening. Instead, it brought him a curious tranquility.

Yes, he decided with relief, I am ready to die. I shall not fight against Death when he takes me by the hand and leads me to God's judgment.

With that thought, Baron Adam of Wynethorpe fell into a sleep that some would call the harbinger of the eternity for which he now longed.

Chapter Two

The sun tried to erase the memory of the great storm that had just passed through, but it failed despite the now-dazzling light.

During the early morning hours, black clouds had turned the land dark with pelting rain, and winds howled like the damned in Hell. Outside the walls of Woodstock Manor, large branches lay scattered across the road like dead soldiers on a battlefield, and a few trees leaned sharply, victims to a fierce wind that rarely struck this part of England.

It also left foul mud, Brother Thomas thought with disgust, as he watched his feet sink into the tan muck. Looking over his shoulder, he saw Richard FitzHugh trudging back and forth with undefined purpose. The lad seemed oblivious to the mud covering his boots.

"I doubt your father will arrive this soon," the monk said to the nervous youth. "The roads on which Sir Hugh will travel may not be passable."

Richard looked down at the ground. They were standing in the middle of what was, only yesterday, a byway to the manor. Now a stream of rushing water gouged a path where horses and wagons must pass. As treacherous as the journey would be through this, it promised to be even worse when the earth dried into a surface so rough it might break a horse's leg.

With a sheepish look, the youth nodded to the monk and turned back to the gates of the manor house.

Brother Thomas followed. If I had had a son, he thought, as he climbed with Richard up the slight incline to the manor, I would have wanted the boy to be like him. Sir Hugh was rarely with the lad, and the monk had become like a father to him, a situation Thomas relished.

He loved Richard's cleverness. At fifteen, the youth often thought like a boy, but he showed evidence of becoming a thoughtful and capable man. As a child, Richard had visited Tyndal Priory and delighted Prioress Eleanor and Brother Thomas with his harmless antics and surprising wit. He was also eager to learn, asking endless questions of the adults. Some might have found this habit annoying. Neither aunt nor monk did.

Richard was now grieving over the impending death of his grandfather, a man who might have frightened him at times but one whom he admired. Baron Adam was like a mythological knight to his grandson: loyal counselor to his king, brave in battle, faithful in both body and heart to his dead wife, generous to the Church, and fiercely devoted to family.

But something else was also troubling the young man, and Thomas did not know the exact cause. Baron Adam's mortal illness did not completely explain Richard's pale countenance and obsessive restlessness. These signs developed only after he learned that Sir Hugh was traveling to Woodstock Manor.

"Your father is traveling as quickly as he can," Thomas said, concluding that the youth's reaction might be fear that Sir Hugh would not be here in time for the baron's death.

Richard shuddered and wheeled around. His eyes were dark with unmistakable terror.

Although the lad looked like Sir Hugh, with his height, broad shoulders, and muscular build, Thomas had never seen a fear so profound in the father's eyes, even when he was facing death in a cave from an angry sea rising to drown him. There must be more worrying Richard than the need for a father's comfort in the face of his grandfather's death.

"Aye, Brother, he will." Richard wrapped his arms around his chest.

Others might assume he felt the chill in the air. Thomas knew he was trying to calm himself.

"Since my Uncle Robert cannot be here, and Sister Beatrice is too frail to travel from Amesbury Priory to be at her brother's bedside, my lord father will be here if he has to propel himself and his men through a great mud sea to do so."

There was much pride in those words, but the monk also sensed a hint of disdain. Youths longing to attain the status of manhood often grew unsettled under the rule of fathers, but the monk hoped there was no possibility of conflict now between sire and lad. Hearts were bruised enough with sorrow over the baron's pending death.

At the same age, Thomas had felt obliged to win his father's high opinion. Since he was only his father's by-blow, he knew from boyhood that he must earn his security. He succeeded and was sent to cathedral school so he might gain a fine position in the Church. Never once had the monk uttered a disparaging word or tone of voice when he spoke of his father. He knew how tenuous life could be for one born out of a brief tryst. Did Richard? Like Thomas, Richard was illegitimate.

A crow flew overhead and landed on a nearby tree limb. Clinging to the swaying branch, the bird cawed with braying sharpness as if determined to remind all living things that he was considered a harbinger of death.

The young squire looked up at the creature and trembled.

Thomas had counseled the boy in discretion when the youth was ready to leave his grandfather and Wynethorpe Castle for a position as a page in the king's court. Since then, the lad had never shown any inclination to disregard this counsel. Had something happened recently to make him grow less amenable?

Richard stared at the crow for an instant longer and then continued on to the manor entrance.

Try as he might, the monk could not think of anything that had altered, other than Richard's position from page to squire. When had he first noticed the change from shyness around Sir Hugh to this thinly masked discontent? Although Thomas had fallen from grace when he was caught in the arms of a man he loved deeply, he knew Richard did not suffer this particular torment. The youth had always confided his fears to the monk. Why had he remained silent about whatever was troubling him now?

Thomas stopped at the gate and found a rock against which he could rub his boots. The result did not make him happy. The anticipation of having to clean them thoroughly later did not please.

As they entered the courtyard, Richard stopped to talk to a young man of his own age who was surrounded by several playful young hounds.

Thomas raised his face to the sun. It had now grown surprisingly warm for the end of March, especially after that brutal storm. Opening his eyes, he realized that the windows of Queen Eleanor's lying-in chambers were immediately above.

The young men gestured with enthusiasm as they began a debate over the merits of various hunting dogs.

Thomas turned his thoughts to the health of the king's wife. He had heard that she was recovering apace.

By the grace of God, the birthing of a baby girl had gone well. The king had waited, pacing outside the chamber where his beloved wife was struggling to preserve her own life while bringing forth another. He refused to leave until he could see her and the child. From all reports, King Edward had looked down on little Mary in his arms with besotted adoration, suggesting she would be favored, as his daughters always were.

Considering the royal couple's fondness for the tales of King Arthur, Thomas was surprised the little one had not been called Guinevere, in hopes that she would be the means by which the legends would be fulfilled. And wasn't this bright sun an omen of a glorious future? He realized he was grinning over his idle musing.

"Shall you share the joke with me, Brother?" Richard's eyes were twinkling.

This was the boy the monk knew best, one who enjoyed a bit of gentle mischief. "I have decided that the sun might foretell the return to England of King Arthur and Queen Guinevere."

Richard gestured at the departing *varlet des chiens* with his bounding pack of dogs. "My friend has recently become the assistant to the Master Huntsman and concurs with his master that the earth is growing warmer. As a consequence, our queen's hunting dogs may be shifted soon from their higher beds to the oaken ones on the ground. Now which event do you consider more likely, Brother? The return of the legendary king or imminent arrival of summer?"

"You trust this young man's reasoning?"

"When he was still the page to the kennel, and let me sleep with the dogs on occasion, he taught me how to heal their feet with salted water. I would trust my own feet to him before I would the court physician. Considering how much you walk, Brother, would you not have confidence in such a man?"

Thomas looked down at his booted feet, bearing the evidence of his march through the dense road mud, and then glanced back up at the sun. "As difficult as it is to believe your friend now, I suspect he is more likely to be right than those who talk of King Arthur returning from Avalon."

The two laughed heartily as they walked into the manor where a warm fire and a fine mulled wine with honey and ginger awaited them in the dining hall.

Perhaps, Thomas thought, the youth would confide in him now.

◇◇◇

Richard warmed his hands around the cup of wine. "I grieve over my grandfather dying."

"He will have a good death," the monk replied, noting the youth's moist eyes. "All mortals are flawed, but your grandfather has been a far better man than most. God will surely be kind to his soul."

"It was he who arranged for me to become a page in the king's court." Richard sipped at the cup, then put it down on the table, and gazed into the distance.

"It was also your father who…"

"He was with our current king in Acre. It was my grandfather who did this. I have tried to be worthy of his kindness." The tone was brusque, but his smile softened it.

"And you are now a squire," Thomas replied. "I have heard that King Edward will take you into his own service. That brings great honor to your family." He had never tried to hide his pride in the lad's accomplishments and did not do so now.

Richard stared at his cup with an expression of uneasiness he did not disguise.

"If you are thinking of your birth, you need not. Your father acknowledged you soon after you were born. Your grandfather could not have done more for you, had you been the child of a lawful wife. Prioress Eleanor, your uncle, and Sister Beatrice have taken you into their hearts. You are a Wynethorpe."

"And you, Brother, what do you think?"

Thomas blinked. Should he ask Richard what had happened to cause this apparent unease or was the youth about to tell him? He chose to let the young man speak further if he wished. "My own father was of high rank, but my mother's station was not," he continued. "I do not even know her name, yet he educated me for the Church as he might any younger son. You have met others of similar birth who have proven themselves and received a father's welcoming embrace into the family. That place is yours already. What cause do you have to doubt it?"

"That is not what I meant. Do you think I serve the family well?"

"Yes." Thomas was emphatic.

"And should I now fail?"

"We all must in some way. Even though we were created in God's image, we are imperfect creatures. But if you adhere to honorable principles, remain humble to God, keep a kind heart, and obey your worthy father, you will bring honor to the family and repay the gifts bestowed upon you by your sire and grandsire."

Frowning with his thoughts, Richard picked up his cup and drank.

Before any more could be said, a servant emerged through the doorway and ran to Richard. "Your lord father has arrived and expects your attendance!"

Sweat broke out on the young squire's forehead, but he thanked the man and sent him back with word to Sir Hugh that he would come as required.

Thomas could no longer bear not knowing what Richard was suffering. He rested his hand on the youth's arm to keep him seated a moment longer. "What is troubling you?"

The young man sighed. "I wish I could lie to you, Brother, but I cannot. Please wait until tomorrow before urging me to speak. I beg this favor of you." His eyes filled with tears. "I own a secret that will make my father hate me and sever all contact between us."

With that, the youth rose and walked swiftly away to meet the man he dreaded to see.

Chapter Three

As he gazed down at the scene in the courtyard, Father Eliduc smiled with great amusement.

Sir Hugh of Wynethorpe stood next to his bastard son, Richard. The youth had rudely turned his back to his father and was watching a huntsman's assistant exercise several young dogs. The heir of the dying baron was talking to the sodomite monk, Brother Thomas, but edged away while he did.

What a splendid trio, the priest thought. Stroking the small gold cross hanging on a silken cord around his neck, he savored his hope that he would soon own the loyalty of all three men, not just the monk whom he had once saved from death.

In name, Father Eliduc served a man of high rank in the Church, but his true function was to collect patronage, create debts, and discover information that would help the Church in its struggle to gain victory over secular power. More than one pope had promised him a place in heaven for his many successes. Soon he would add the Wynethorpe family to his list of those who were obliged to support the Church above the demands of any earthly king. Since Sir Hugh had the reputation of being a man especially disinclined to do so, this feat would only enhance Father Eliduc's reputation.

Some of his success was clever planning, but the priest believed that much was a sign of God's pleasure in his work. A man less attuned to His desires might not have chosen to stay in Woodstock Manor after apoplexy struck Baron Adam, the queen had given birth, and the king had left for Gloucestershire. But he sensed that he must, and God opened his eyes to how he could expand the power of the Church by increasing his own influence with the royal couple and in the court itself.

Once Prioress Eleanor arrived with her precious monk, Eliduc humbly relinquished his duty to cleanse the baron's soul. Brother Thomas could take care of that matter while the priest turned his efforts to serving the needs of Queen Eleanor who longed for God's comfort throughout her travail. For once, her beloved Dominicans were not close by.

He had chosen words as soothing as the taste of honey to her before and after her painful labor. Indeed, it had been his subtle suggestion of the Virgin's name that caused the royal parents to call the baby Mary. For these devoted services and healing prayers, he would be amply rewarded, gifts he would wisely direct into the Church's coffers. His faith demanded he do so, but the Church provided him with comforts enough for his invaluable services.

As for the dying baron, his soul would receive a proper cleansing. Brother Thomas might be a sodomite, but he had always served the Church and his prioress well. Under his auspices, Baron Adam would die the good Christian death for which he longed.

What had especially pleased Father Eliduc, however, was the arrival of Baron Adam's heir, Sir Hugh. The priest had plans for this knight's bastard son, a scheme that would please the lad, if not the father, and place the family in Eliduc's debt.

The priest shivered with pleasure. God's plans were being realized in splendid ways!

As for Brother Thomas, Eliduc decided the man needed to be reminded that his foul sins had not been forgotten. Although the monk believed he had finally completed his penance for sodomy after Father Eliduc saved his life, the priest was aware of the growing affection between Thomas and a certain wine merchant from Norwich.

After all these years of chastity, Eliduc feared the monk might have grown complacent and be faltering in his vows. Although he would not go back on his word to Prioress Eleanor that her monk was free now of obligations to spy for him, he believed Brother Thomas should be reminded of the growing intolerance of the Church for wickedness. Eliduc rubbed his hands together in delight.

He turned away from the window and walked into the dining hall. A cup of honeyed *hippocras* would be pleasant with its gentle warmth from pepper and ginger.

But he had no sooner found a suitable place by the fire and raised the cup of mulled wine to his lips than he heard men shouting, then a woman's scream.

"The queen must rest," he muttered. "How dare anyone cause a disturbance that might upset her?" Slamming the cup down, he rushed to the scene of the commotion.

Several soldiers surrounded an older woman who held two young girls close to her breast. One soldier grasped the woman by the shoulder and arms, while another tried to drag the girls away from her. As the girls were wrenched away, the older woman screamed again. The captured girls reached out to her and wailed piteously.

"Stop!" Eliduc shouted as he ran toward the man he believed to be the leader. "What is happening here? Do you not know that the queen's chambers are close by? She will hear you and fear for her safety."

The captain pointed to the older woman. "Arrogant Jews," he sneered. "The crone says she came to see our queen." He mockingly crooked his fingers to form horns. "How dare she think anyone would allow it? Look at the filthy creature!"

Eliduc had already seen the large piece of yellow felt cloth, which all three bore, cut into the shape of the tablets carried by Moses from Mount Sinai. Since 1275, King Edward had demanded strict enforcement of the law requiring all of Jewish faith, over the age of seven and regardless of gender, to wear this badge.

As for what else brought out the captain's disdain, the priest noticed the disheveled appearance of the trio, and his nose wrinkled at the sour odor of unwashed bodies. But the captain had not recognized the original quality of the robes the women wore, Eliduc thought. Stained and rumpled as the clothes might be now, they had begun life as well-made, expensive garments.

"I shall speak with them," the priest said.

The captain's expression betrayed reluctance to allow this, but he was not a fool. Father Eliduc was no ordinary priest. No one with his wits about him would thwart the desire of this man, so high in the favor of England's king and queen. Waving his men back, he bowed to the priest and allowed him to approach the huddled trio.

"Why have you come to trouble Queen Eleanor?" Eliduc stroked his golden cross.

None of the women spoke. The elder was comforting her young charges.

Eliduc did not stand too close to the women. His own chastity was cause enough, although lust for coupling had never been a struggle, but he also believed that distance bred respect. Except when King Edward performed that sacred act of touching sufferers of scrofula, the king's evil, he kept himself away from common hands. Eliduc believed all high-ranking men of the Church should as well.

He waited, with evident impatience, for an answer to his question.

The girls had ceased their sobbing, although the younger one continued to hide her face in the older woman's shoulder. The elder now glared at the priest, her brown eyes aflame with anger.

Eliduc shivered in spite of himself. The Devil is close, he thought.

The older woman laid her chin against the top of the head of the frightened child and grasped the hand of the other. "I have come to beg mercy for my granddaughters from Queen Eleanor. Their father, my son, was hanged for coin-clipping, a crime of which he was innocent." Her speech was educated. Had she been a Christian, her accent would have proven her birth to be one of high rank.

"None of the executed was innocent," the priest replied. "Evidence of the crime was found in the houses and displayed at the trials of those later hanged. Their offense was a treasonous act."

"I have no wish to plead for my dead son. Of those executed, some were surely guilty, although I can swear to at least one innocent. No, I have come because these two children, daughters of Lumbard ben David, no longer have a roof to keep the wind from bruising their tender flesh nor enough food to sustain them. No matter what the king's justice concluded about my son, his children are without fault and do not deserve to starve."

"Lumbard ben David?" In spite of his resolve, Eliduc stepped closer and stared down at the woman who spoke. "What is your name?"

"Chera, widow of David of Oxford, a man also known as *the kind*."

Despite his usually iron self-control, Eliduc gasped. He knew this family and had good cause to take an interest. Why had he not been informed that this man had been arrested and hanged for coin-clipping? "You say that you no longer have a roof or food?"

"When the king's men raided our quarter, Sir Walter Clayton took my son away that night after finding evidence he deemed proof of guilt. Since the crime was, as you have said, one of treason against King Edward, all our property was confiscated. We three were thrown into the street with no more than the clothes we wore." Her eyes grew dark, not with anger but from grief. "These babes have suffered the death of a father, not more than a year after the death of their mother, and they now must beg like paupers."

Eliduc shrugged. "You have the option of casting aside your ignorant faith and receiving adequate food and lodging in the king's House of Converts. With no possessions left, you would benefit from Christian charity. Of even greater merit would be the instruction you and your granddaughters would receive for salvation of your souls after baptism."

Chera said nothing. Her stern expression was response enough.

"You say that your house was seized along with all your belongings?"

She nodded.

Eliduc's smile was not a pleasant one as he faced the captain of the soldiers. "Let them stay the night here," he said. "This woman's son may have been a felon, but I know their family. Until now, they have been loyal to our kings and have always paid their assessed tallage to the Lord Edward without delay." He bent his head in the direction of the women. "As Christians, we may offer the charity of a few hours by the fire before they are sent back to Oxford."

He folded his hands in a prayerful manner when he looked back at the distressed supplicants. "One of these soldiers will take you three and clear a place near the fire in the dining hall." He nodded to Mistress Chera. "Do not speak to anyone there. If someone demands to know why you are allowed to stay here, you may tell them that Father Eliduc has permitted it for one night." His lips twisted into a thin smile. "The queen has recently endured Eve's curse by giving birth to a child and shall not be disturbed. Of course, your petition to speak with her is denied."

Chera bowed her head.

Eliduc marched off. The news he had just heard upset him terribly. Another cup or two of mulled wine was needed to calm his nerves, but he would order it brought to his chambers. This small comfort of privacy was needed. His head ached. He wished to be saved from the lewd jests of soldiers, the trivial joviality of courtiers, and the sight of unrepentant Jews who stubbornly denied the true faith.

Chapter Four

The woman's laughter cut through the din of those gathered in the dining hall like the screech of a trebuchet.

Eyes widened and mouths froze in mid-sentence, but once she was recognized, a titter fluttered through the hall before the usual chattering din was restored.

Hawis, wife of Sir Walter Clayton and one of many ladies attending Queen Eleanor, clasped the arm of her brother-in-law more firmly as she looked around for a cup of fine wine and a cold supper.

"I am chilled," she sighed into Maynard Clayton's ear.

He looked uncomfortable but seemed unable to distance himself from the nearness of her soft breast. "Wine?" His voice was hoarse.

"Something to warm me." She gave him a flirtatious look.

Her words had felt like a hot caress on his cheek. He gazed around for a servant.

She pinched his arm, and then shoved him gently away. "Seek refreshment for me. I shall wait for you—but not too long."

There were fewer than usual in the dining hall. Many had traveled on with the king, but those most in favor with the queen and her ladies had remained while she recovered from the birth of a daughter.

When her water unexpectedly broke and the queen knew the birth was imminent, she had entered the darkened lying-in chamber which was swiftly prepared for her ordeal. The doors had been firmly shut against all but God, a priest, and those women experienced enough to help her safely through the suffering. The king had remained until after the birth, but Queen Eleanor then urged him to travel on to their planned destination. Being an avid hunter herself, she understood his longing for his hawks and the chase. Most of the court had joined him.

Hawis was grateful she had not been chosen for enclosure in the stifling room with the laboring queen, or to wait upon her once the bloody cloths and basins had been removed. She and her husband did not have children, a failure most believed cause for grief, but Hawis was secretly pleased. She did not like brats but, in the presence of Queen Eleanor and King Edward, pretended otherwise.

Now Queen Eleanor was resting until the day she could be churched, although there was a rumor that she was already in communication with her agents on property matters. Eleanor of Castile was not a woman to lie idle when rents could be increased. Nor was she inclined to let severe reproofs wait if one of her attendants offended.

As Hawis fell into musing over her recent and rather unpleasant conversation with the queen, a bellow came from the direction of the kitchen.

A man emerged, face red and bald head sweating as he franticly looked around the hall. Then he saw what he was searching for. "Stop him!" he roared, pointing toward the floor. "Stop that water rug!"

A medium-sized dog, with curly silken ears and a white coat spotted with tan, flew through the gathering with what appeared to be a large chunk of venison in its mouth.

As he sped passed her, Hawis drew her robes back so the purloined meat would not bloody them.

No one stopped the creature. Some laughed. The man from the kitchen wiped his brow and retreated, concluding that any attempted pursuit was pointless.

"What just happened?" Maynard asked, handing Hawis a cup of wine.

"The queen's water spaniel," she said, sniffing at the wine. "His name is El Acebo. You haven't seen him before?"

"I have never hunted with Queen Eleanor," he said. "My brother's generosity to me does not extend to such pleasures."

"The wine is nice," she replied. "Was there no bread or meat?" Her tone hinted at her disappointment.

Sighing, he left to find another servant.

A sharp draft from an open window or door chilled Hawis, and she edged her way to the fire.

Some courtiers left, allowing her access to the warmth. Looking for a place to wait that was neither too hot nor too cold, she stopped abruptly as if God had struck her motionless.

A bedraggled trio sat on one side of the snapping flames. As the older woman turned her head, Hawis' face turned deep red. "How dare you befoul this royal manor?" She rushed to the group and raised her cup with a threatening gesture.

Chera looked up and pushed the two girls behind her. "We were allowed to sit here for the night. My intent was to leave, but a member of the court granted us this charity."

"Who?"

"A priest who called himself Father Eliduc."

Hawis stepped back and lowered the cup of wine. Others she might have been able to overrule. This priest was untouchable. "He is an exemplary Christian," she muttered, "but how dare you come here with the spawn of a scoundrel, who was hanged for treason against the king?" In contempt, she used her chin to point at the girls.

"My son was neither traitor nor rogue," Chera snapped.

"Our lord king does not hang innocent men."

Chera bowed her head with the requisite meekness. "There is only One who never makes a mistake," she said under her breath, but the soft retort was lost in the crackling of the fire.

"I asked you why you came here."

"When my son's house was seized by your husband, you saw us thrown into the street. You know we have neither food nor shelter. I came with my granddaughters to beg a small mercy from our queen."

"You think she would deign to speak with traitor spawn?" Hawis raised the cup again. Drops of red wine slopped over the rim to the ground.

"Jacob of Oxford, a man of our community well-favored by the queen, was a friend of my dead son."

Hawis looked surprised, and then smirked. "Our lady does receive some of her queen's gold from the debts he sells her. Perhaps she shall learn, when she rises from childbed, that this man was friends with a traitor. That news would not please her at all."

Chera paled. "My son spoke up in his defense when others in our community railed against his dealings with the queen."

"Indeed?" Hawis rolled her eyes. "The Jew is lucky to have our queen's favor. He would be wise to take note that Christians have offered him an honored place in this court when stiff-necked Jews wished to reject him for his loyalty to the crown."

"I have no desire to argue these matters with you or with our queen. My only purpose here is to beg enough charity to leave this land with my granddaughters and travel to France without hindrance where my family has offered us shelter."

"Leave? And deny our king some of the levy required of your people?"

"I have nothing to give. I have no husband or son. All was taken from me."

"Surely your community will feed you until you can arrange for your granddaughters' marriages. They will breed sons who must contribute to the cost of protections King Edward offers you."

Chera began to speak but chose not to. Her expression was sad as she glanced up at the woman standing over her.

"But perhaps no one will offer you charity. You people know little of that, do you? Money-lenders? Coin-clippers? You steal from good Christians, deny the Christ, and then wonder why godly people shun you."

One of the girls mumbled something, but Chera hushed her. "My lady, please leave us in peace. We are permitted to remain by this fire one night. Tomorrow morning we will be gone."

"One night only. If I find you here past daybreak, you will have good cause to rue your delay. Do you understand me?"

Chera nodded.

Hawis strode away, stepping around the spaniel munching on the filched meat.

The dog growled softly.

Maynard approached and offered her more wine. "A servant shall bring you food."

She held out her cup and glared back at the trio, expressing her dismay at what Father Eliduc had inflicted on the queen's courtiers.

"Why be so angry with them?" He squinted as he looked at the grandmother who clasped her girls close.

Hawis spat. "They are descendants of those who killed Christ."

He frowned. "But two are children and one an old woman. They are no danger to us. Why not let them sit by the fire and even have some scraps to eat?"

She looked at him as if he were a small boy lacking all understanding of a grown man's greater wisdom. "Let us speak no further of the stink of unbelief they bring with them. They must be gone by the time the sun rises or they shall feel the hard blows of my displeasure." Reaching out, she rubbed her hand lightly over the hair on his arm. "Instead, let us depart this hall and find a private place where we may enjoy more pleasant matters. The food may be brought to us there."

Maynard nodded, rendered speechless with longing, and followed her from the hall.

Chapter Five

All buildings, whether manor, tradesman's house, or peasant's hut, speak when night chases God's light below the edge of the earth. In those hours of Satan's rule, wood groans as it holds the weight of floors, stone rasps against stone when the earth moves under walls, and rushes on a roof whisper with the wind and restless rats. Although the spirits that take possession of houses in darkness may be impish rather than malign, mortals shrink from them.

To Richard FitzHugh, the sounds were terrifying.

"Why can't I pray?" he murmured, but the question was only intended to mute the eerie voices. To pray for salvation when he would never change his plan would be lying to God, and that was a worse blasphemy than the transgression he was going to commit. Tonight, he would sin both willfully and grievously.

Another soft moan reached his ears, and he cupped his hands over them to still the murmuring of demons who, he feared, were dancing within the stones under his feet.

For all his height and man's strength, Richard owned a child's heart in this moment. Tears wended their way down his cheeks. He was shamed by them.

Until now, he had rarely suffered humiliation. As a page, he had learned to serve his lords and their ladies at table. It was a humble duty he found appealing. With other boys, he laughed as he tilted at a target, sometimes festooned with a silly face, while his companions pulled him along on a wooden horse. When he took a tumble, he made a jest and leapt to his feet. Only once had he wept when he played at war. That was when one of his friends was blinded in a mock battle with a wooden sword.

A few years hence, he was expected to become a knight, after he learned to cut off a man's arm with his sword or spill his brains with a blow from a mace. When he looked at his father, he saw someone who glowed with delight only when he was about to shed blood. Richard knew it was his father's wish that he also become a soldier and walk by his side as castle walls crumbled and blood mixed with rubble in the streets. Tonight he would force himself to perform one last test to see if he could transform himself into a man like his father.

As he pressed his back against the rough stone wall, he groaned. Of all the things learned in his years at the king's court, it was the study of religion under the instruction of Father Eliduc that pleased him most. Father Eliduc, if Richard had sought his advice, would have urged him to turn back from his vile intent tonight and spend the darkest hours on his knees in one of the many chapels in Woodstock Manor.

And Brother Thomas? He had chosen not to seek his counsel. Although he felt closer to the monk than he did to his own father, Richard had hesitated because he was not sure the monk would understand. Despite his illegitimacy, Brother Thomas was of far higher birth than Richard. He might have been a bishop or even gained a secular title, but there was a rumor that he had committed a dishonorable crime many years ago and had chosen the life of a simple monk as penance. If so, he had never been faced with the questions Richard was now.

But Thomas' father had concurred with his son's new vocation, in spite of other hopes he might have harbored for his bastard boy, and eased Brother Thomas into Tyndal Priory. In truth, according to Prioress Eleanor and Baron Adam, it was a vocation for which the monk seemed quite suited. Brother Thomas served God well.

If Richard found himself in similar circumstances, would Sir Hugh as easily pick up the cross instead of the lance for his own bastard child? His father was a man who cared little for men of faith. His only creed was knighthood and dedication to the laws of chivalry.

Chivalry was an almost holy principle, yet Richard had seen a far different version during his life at court. Out of courtesy and convenience, it retained its nobility, but men befouled it with scheming, lust, and slaughter.

Or am I simply bitter? he thought.

In any case, he was alone and scared.

He shook off the feeling, stiffened his resolve, and edged toward his rendezvous. Part of him longed for what he was about to do. Part of him was horrified and disgusted. He swallowed bile and strode around the corner into the adjacent hall.

But what he saw brought him to a halt.

A short distance in front of him stood a figure. Frightened, Richard backed against the wall and slipped around the corner again to hide.

He was not naïf. Men and women made secret trysts, whether married to others or not. Plots were formed, and revenge often sought. None of that mattered, but this shadow was in the shape of a man he thought he knew well.

Was that his father outside the door he himself was about to enter, and, if so, why was he there?

Cautiously, he peered around the corner.

The shadow looked back in his direction, then swiftly fled down the hall as silently as a ghost.

Richard shivered. Maybe this was not his father. Had he seen a spirit? Was this an imp waiting to make sure he was firm in his wicked resolve?

Taking a deep breath, Richard FitzHugh bit back his terror, strode to the door, and knocked.

It opened softly. Only a flicker of light from within suggested a difference between deathly black and enticing shadow.

"You are late," the voice said, then opened the door further.

Richard slipped inside.

Chapter Six

Prioress Eleanor opened her eyes.

Where was she?

The dream had unsettled her. Her spirit was depressed, her throat sore, and her neck ached with stiffness. As she pushed herself upright, she realized that reality was more upsetting than any dream. She had fallen asleep at her father's bedside in the midst of prayer. Frightened, she reached out to grasp his hand.

"He sleeps, my lady." Sister Anne stood beside her and put a comforting hand on her prioress' shoulder. "Not well, but he sleeps."

Eleanor bowed her head, ashamed of her weakness. How could she fall asleep when she had sworn to keep vigil and pray for her father's soul?

"Your brother has arrived." The sub-infirmarian gestured at a kneeling man, his head bowed but his lips firmly shut. He had chosen to grieve at the foot of the bed, as if he was not worthy of a place nearer his father's side.

Was he praying? Eleanor feared not. The state of his soul had long troubled her.

Her brother was older than she, and they had never been as close as she was with Robert, their middle brother, but she remembered the high-spirited, pink-cheeked young man who had gone to Outremer with their prince. Years later, he returned gaunt, a man lacking mirth and owning fewer words.

She had changed as well. When they first met, after his voyage home, they approached each other with the memory of childhood but soon departed, confused and uneasy with the transformation each found in the other. In time, he learned to accept that his little sister now ruled a priory, and she, less successfully, gave this wounded soul the place in her heart once occupied by a brother she had secretly called Sir Bedivere, one of the most loyal of King Arthur's knights.

Every day, she begged God to bestow peace on her brother, a calm he had lost in Outremer. In time, she grew familiar with this stranger. She learned not to approach him from behind without speaking first and at some distance. Once she forgot, and he had swung a fist at her, his eyes wild with undefined fury. He had not struck her, but she discovered caution. Neither spoke of this incident afterward.

Anne whispered in her ear, bringing Eleanor back to the unhappy present. "You need sustenance," the sub-infirmarian said. In the company of others, Sister Anne was formal in her address. In private, she spoke as the close friend she had become to the prioress.

Eleanor silently looked at her father. His breathing was labored.

"Come with me. I expect no change but will leave an attendant. Your brother will summon us if needed." Anne bent her head in the direction of the silent man.

◇◇◇

Even with the fire roaring in the dining hall, the air was raw with dampness. The prioress shivered. The storm might not have brought snow, and the next day had promised greater warmth, but she felt as if today's wind had driven icy rain deep into the stone walls. At least her father lay in a room with walls blanketed in tapestries to keep the chill away. One even lay on the floor, an odd practice brought by the queen from Castile.

When the servant brought the weak ale, steaming loaf of bread, and fragrant cheese, Eleanor stared at it. A queasiness rose from her stomach, and she looked away.

"Please," Anne begged, "a few bites."

The warmth of the caring friendship drove away the nausea for a moment, and Eleanor began to pick at the food. It tasted like dust, although she knew that was not the fault of the meal, and then she drank some ale. As she did, her gaze fell on a sad group huddled near the fire. "Who are they?"

"I do not know, but they are Jews. See the yellow tablet emblem visible on the older woman's robe?"

"I wonder why they are here," Eleanor said, the cup paused near her mouth. "The two with her are young girls." She studied them for a moment as they rose. The older woman's expression grew frightened when she looked up at the light in the hall and saw that it came from the sun, not candles.

"Their clothes are stained and torn," Anne said.

"And they are hungry," Eleanor said, rising. "The one girl is pressing her hand to her stomach." She picked up her bread and cheese from the table. "No one is offering food. I shall take them this."

Anne nodded and gave her a brief smile.

As the prioress approached the trio, one of the girls grasped the older woman's sleeve and whispered in her ear. The other girl drew back, her eyes narrowed and her fist clenched.

Eleanor ignored the gesture. "Have you broken your fast?"

Chera brushed her granddaughters behind her like a mother chicken protecting her chicks. "I beg pardon, my lady. It is long past first light, and we shall quickly depart this place."

Eleanor offered the cheese and bread. "You must not travel without food. Please take this. As guests in this manor, hospitality demands it."

One of the girls looked at it longingly.

Chera closed her eyes as if weary of arguing. "We are not guests, my lady. We came as supplicants, told our plea would not be heard, and were granted a roof for one night until the sun rose. We have slept too long and have no right to expect further charity."

"This is not charity," Eleanor said abruptly. "You have two young girls in your company. If you are not hungry, I know they are."

Chera glanced behind her, and then looked back at the prioress. From her expression, it was evident she was struggling with a decision.

"Please take this for them," Eleanor said in a gentle voice. The way the woman was looking at her eyes, the prioress guessed she was trying to read her soul for any malign intent.

Flushing slightly, Chera took the food, passed it to her girls, and murmured instructions.

"Thank you for this gift, my lady," the two replied, almost in unison. The angry one had softened. The other kept her head bowed.

"If I am not being rude, what was the boon you came to beg and from whom?" Eleanor gestured to Chera to follow her a short distance away so the girls might eat in peace.

The woman shook her head. "My heart grows weary of the futile tale, my lady, but I had hoped to see the queen on my granddaughters' behalf."

A servant walked by, close to the girls. The timorous one drew back with a cry.

"There is nothing to fear, child," Eleanor said.

The girl blinked but said nothing, then bowed her head again over her bread and cheese.

"Ah, but they do have good reason for concern, my lady," Chera replied in a quiet voice. "They watched as their father was accused of coin-clipping and dragged away in the middle of the night by soldiers. He may not have been hanged before their eyes, but they know how he was killed."

Eleanor covered her mouth in shock.

Chera closed her eyes as her cheeks reddened with emotion, but the gesture failed to hide her fury.

The prioress felt a stab of empathy for this woman's anger. It did not matter now why the man had been hanged. Even a guilty father is still a father, the prioress thought, and grieved for the children's fear and pain.

"But we have heard that Queen Eleanor has just given birth. Had I known before, I would never have wished to trouble her in her weariness." Chera bowed to the prioress. "I am grateful for your compassionate gift to my granddaughters, my lady. We shall soon depart, but I must beg one more favor from you, if you would be so kind?"

"Tell me what you desire."

"If we are approached by soldiers or other members of the court because we have stayed beyond the permission granted, may I say that you gave us leave to sup first?"

"Of course!" Eleanor said. "They may come to me for confirmation if they wish, and I shall attest to it."

Chera thanked her, then bent down to urge her girls to follow her. The rest of the food, she advised, was best saved for their long walk back to Oxford.

For a moment longer, the prioress watched the trio, then returned to where Sister Anne sat waiting, her eyes darkened with sorrow.

"She is the mother of a man hanged for coin-clipping," the prioress said, sitting close to her friend so others might not hear her words. "The girls are the man's daughters. I grieve for them even more than the mother. They are too young to understand the gravity of their father's crime and should never have seen him dragged away in chains in the middle of the night."

"The raids were swift, and many were hanged with little concern for justice." Anne made a ball of the small piece of bread and crushed it in her hand.

Eleanor was surprised at her friend's statement. "Surely you are not suggesting that some were innocent!"

"They are a hated race. Many are gold or silversmiths and money-lenders, thus belong to professions where money clipping is both possible and a temptation. Although I believe the evidence proves guilt amongst them, I wonder that so few Christians, who engaged in the same professions, were arrested. Of those, few were hanged and more paid bribes to gain their freedom. Hundreds of Jews have been executed, my lady, both men and women. If anyone in the Jewish community protested his innocence, he was not heard even if he offered to pay a fine to be released."

Eleanor sat back with a frown. "Why kill the innocent?"

"You know the wickedness of men better than I. Remember the Jewish family caught in Tyndal village and condemned as murderers by the crowd because it was convenient to do so? Had you and Crowner Ralf not taken their plea of innocence seriously, they would have been butchered by the mob."

"Your words remind me of the story of Abraham who begged God to save Sodom for the sake of the innocent who lived there."

"It does me as well. He feared asking God to save the city for fewer than ten honest men." Anne put down the ball of crumpled bread. "Have you ever wondered if there were nine innocents who died in the flames for wont of someone to plead for them?"

Eleanor looked shocked, then closed her eyes and pressed her fingers into the corners to relieve the weariness. "I do not know if this woman's son was innocent or not." Then she looked over her shoulder and watched the weary trio departing. "But I felt no evil in the older woman. She loves her granddaughters. Perhaps she did raise a good son."

Anne followed her prioress' gaze and sighed.

"Why do the Jews refuse to convert?" Eleanor rested her chin in her hand and frowned with the perplexing thought. "The family, accused of murder in the village, were good people. In this woman and her granddaughters I sensed no harm." As she looked at Sister Anne, her brow furrowed. "Some say they are a wicked race, but I have not seen evidence of evil. Surely Satan is not so clever that he can transform a wicked person into the shape of a virtuous man?"

Anne said nothing, then reached over and squeezed her friend's hand.

Chapter Seven

Brother Thomas stole a look at the sharp-featured man walking beside him with a determined gait. With the death of her father imminent, he grieved that he must trouble Prioress Eleanor with the violence of evil, yet he was unable to prevent this intrusion by the king's justice. Now, of all times, her burdens should be lightened, but God had always demanded her service when He believed it was needed.

The men entered the dining hall where they were told the prioress and her sub-infirmarian had gone.

"My lady." The monk bowed his head, as did the man next to him.

Sister Anne looked at the men and sighed. Her face revealed surprise over this interruption. Glancing at the monk, she then lowered her gaze. It was clear from his expression that he had been unable to stop this.

Turning to greet her monk, Eleanor saw his black-haired companion, a man whose gray eyes studied her with curiosity and respect. Then she read the reluctance in Thomas' eyes. Briefly, she begged God in silence not to place another weight on her heart, a plea she feared He would not grant.

"What has happened? I assume you did not come because my father has slipped closer to God, Brother."

The monk introduced his companion as Alan FitzRoald, High Sheriff of Berkshire.

"With profound regret, my lady, I am here to beg a favor," the man said. "I know of your father's illness and would not ask this boon if I could do otherwise."

She smiled at the man, hoping the gesture conveyed warmth and not the uneasiness she felt. "If your honorable request is within my power to grant, I will be happy to do so."

"Hawis, one of our queen's attendants and wife of Sir Walter Clayton, a king's man, has been found hanged in her chambers." The words had been spoken, and he seemed relieved, but it was also evident how loath he was to have uttered them.

Eleanor looked at her sub-infirmarian, then at her monk, and knew both were waiting for her to speak. She longed to send this sheriff on his way, but realized, as did her friends, that she would not. The sadness in their eyes was joined by an equal longing to comfort her. That gave her the strength she needed.

"I am hesitant to leave my father's side," she replied, "but tell me what you need from us." She indicated that she included her companions.

FitzRoald knelt. "My lady, our queen has suffered the pains of birth. One of her women is dead, whether by her own hand or another's. I dare not disturb the queen at such a time with the turmoil of an investigation, nor request the assistance of her midwife. The king would never forgive me if his wife weakened as a result." He raised his hands in a pleading gesture. "We have no physician here, and the corpse is a woman's body. Your reputation and discretion in similar matters is known throughout our land…"

Eleanor thought she saw the trace of tears in the man's eyes. She liked this sheriff for his willingness to seek help in a delicate situation as well as his apparent reluctance to involve her when she was suffering her own anguish. "You cannot keep all knowledge of this matter from our queen," she said.

"I may still hope to discover the cause of this death before others spread the tale with idle speculation. If I can confine the news to those closest to our queen, they will keep it from her until after she is more fully recovered from the child's birth. When the facts are known, I can soften the blow of her attendant's death." He remained kneeling.

The prioress glanced at Sister Anne. She knew she need not ask the question. Her friend always understood what was needed.

"With your permission, my lady, I will examine the body," the sub-infirmarian said. "The inspection should not take long."

"And I shall attend your father, my lady," Brother Thomas said. "He expressed his desire for confession and forgiveness. That should be done soon. If there is any change in his condition, I will come for you."

She shut her eyes and nodded. Granting this requested favor by the sheriff was difficult. At other times she had hesitated to take on the burden of seeking justice as God demanded of her, but she had always obeyed. Today, her heart protested loudly at this cruel invasion of her grief. It tore her from her father's side when he was still aware of her presence and she might find a last comfort in the pressure of his living hand on hers.

But the prioress also knew that her father, even on his deathbed, would tell her to do what she must for their earthly queen. She could hear his voice in her heart, reminding her that this was the duty of a Wynethorpe. Brother Thomas would bring solace to Baron Adam's soul as he faced death, and she would order prayers for him once she returned to Tyndal. Now she had no choice but to obey the commands of God, and her father's wish, to serve King Edward's queen in this tragic matter.

Lost in the silence of her thoughts, she had forgotten that the High Sheriff of Berkshire remained a suppliant on her knees before her. She gestured for him to rise.

"Sister Anne and I shall follow you to the place of the woman's death. Like you, we believe the queen must be left in peace until the time is right for her to be told of this misfortune."

The tears in FitzRoald's eyes flowed with relief. "My gratitude is beyond measure, my lady. I vow to make a donation to your priory...."

The prioress looked up at him, her gray eyes as somber as a wintry day. "We are all loyal subjects of King Edward. Let us not speak of gifts until this matter is satisfactorily resolved. If it is, then God must be thanked."

Brother Thomas bent to ask if there was something he could do to assist before returning to Baron Adam.

She assured him that cleansing her father's soul was the greatest service he could give. "I know you will summon me if need be, but my father does have his eldest son by his side," she murmured.

He bowed. "As much as he loves Sir Hugh, the baron will not die until you are holding his hand, my lady."

Her expression blended sorrow with relief, then she turned to Sister Anne. "Let us go," she said.

◇◇◇

As the trio left the dinning hall, no one noticed Father Eliduc lurking in a nearby corner.

Watching them leave, the priest folded his hands into an attitude of reverent prayer. Although his expression suggested he grieved over the news that a mortal had died without the comfort of the last rites and a priest to murmur into her ear, his narrowed eyes suggested his troubled thoughts were of a more worldly nature.

Chapter Eight

The naked corpse of Hawis twisted slowly. A thick rope looped over a low beam near the ceiling and was knotted around her neck. Her dead eyes bulged, and a scattering of vivid but small red marks dotted her throat. From the angle of her head, an observer might wonder if she was looking askance at heaven or even listening carefully to a sound no living creature could hear. The chambers reeked of overripe feces from loosened bowels.

"Cut her down," Sister Anne said.

The sheriff grabbed a stool that was turned over near the woman's feet. As he stood on it to saw through the rope, Eleanor called out to him, "Stop! Please step down for a moment."

When he did, she took the stool and placed it under the feet of the corpse. There was a gap of several inches between the two. "Do you see anything else she might have stood on in order to hang herself?"

The three did a brief search but found nothing.

FitzRoald finished cutting the rope and lifted the corpse down, placing it gently on the floor. "Badly knotted," he said with a frown. "I am surprised it withstood any thrashing if she tried to save herself from her sinful intent."

Sister Anne knelt and began her examination.

Eleanor was touched that this man had treated the corpse with rare tenderness. His expression also suggested remorse as if he feared insulting the dead woman by handling her naked body. Yes, she decided, he is a good man.

"Who discovered her?" she asked.

"A servant noticed an odd smell. Her door was slightly open and he saw the body. He sent for me immediately and did not enter the room."

"Has anyone been in here after you?"

Although it was clear from his frown that he was very unhappy with what the three of them had found so far, he answered honestly. "I left a man outside, telling him to linger by the door but pretend he was not on guard. I hoped to delay the rumors as long as possible." He smiled briefly. "The lad is one of the clever ones in my company. A few stopped to talk with him. He complained that I had kept him waiting, then said he hoped I had forgotten the meeting because he feared the task I planned to assign him would be unpleasant."

Eleanor turned to her sub-infirmarian. "Have you found anything of interest?"

"As if the stool were not proof enough, my lady, I am sure she did not hang herself," Anne replied.

The sheriff raised an eyebrow.

"Few women strip before committing self-murder," the nun said. "The soul might be naked, but no woman would want strangers to see her mortal body in that state."

"Anything else?" he asked.

"Come closer and I will show you."

Eleanor knelt beside her. The sheriff remained standing and kept a respectful distance from the two religious.

"Here is the rope burn, but it is a light mark, not a deep one." She moved the rope aside. "These marks suggest two thumbs have been pressed into her throat. When I touch her under her chin, the bulge in her throat is loose and soft as if crushed. My conclusion is that she was strangled first, then hanged from the rope." She looked up. "The rope could have been slung over the beam from below. This woman was not fat, but it would have taken some strength to slip the noose around her neck, raise her that high to make this look like self-murder, and secure the loose end of the rope."

"Forgive the question, Sister, for I mean nothing ill by it. Could you have committed this crime?"

"Nor am I offended," Anne replied with a quick nod. "I could strangle her, if she did not fight too hard, but raising her, even with the rope, and tying the loose end would be difficult." She lifted one of the woman's hands. "As you can see, her nails are not broken or bloody. She did not struggle to loosen the knot around her neck. She was dead or unconscious when she was hanged. This is not self-murder. As you suggested, most who try to hang themselves quickly realize the sinfulness of their act. They thrash and claw to loosen the knot. Mistress Hawis' hands were free, yet they were not bloodied by the rope. As you also noticed, the loose end of the rope was not tied well. Had she struggled, she could have freed herself."

"My prayers have not been answered," FitzRoald said with reluctance. "I had hoped it would be self-murder, even an accident, although that I knew the latter to be unlikely. Murder paints this tragedy a far darker hue." He muttered something incomprehensible but sharp enough to be a curse.

"I must return to your father soon, my lady." Anne went over to the basin on top of a table and splashed water over her hands.

"As must I," the prioress replied and then quickly circled the room, looking for anything that might suggest who had done this. If only the murderer left something behind, she thought. Like the sheriff, she longed for this crime to be solved with no delay.

Instead of joining her, FitzRoald stared at the sub-infirmarian cleansing her hands.

Turning around, Sister Anne saw his expression. "I do not want to bring the smell of earthly violence to the room of a man who is making his peace with God," she explained. Her father had taught her this practice, but she rarely chose to explain that to the curious.

He nodded and asked her a question about the corpse.

Meanwhile, Eleanor had found nothing helpful. She studied everything again more slowly and then noticed the bed. The sheets were stained, although they would have been changed the day before. Virgin though she was, the prioress was not unworldly and had her suspicions. She called for the pair to examine what she had found. When the sheriff blushed, she knew she had been right.

"Someone, I assume Mistress Hawis, lay with a man before she was killed," Anne said. She turned to FitzRoald.

His mouth had dropped open in shock.

"I did not take vows as a young girl," she said. "I was married before I entered Tyndal Priory."

"Forgive me," he replied. "I did not know you were a widow."

Anne turned away to study the rumpled linen and said nothing. He might think what he wished about the reason her marriage had ended.

Eleanor slipped to her knees by the bed. She had kicked something with her foot and now saw it glitter on the floor in the hesitant light. When she picked it up, she gasped as she recognized the object. It was a gold cross with a unique design, a gift she had sent to her nephew, Richard, when she received word that he had become a squire.

"What is it, my lady?" Sister Anne knelt beside her friend, and then saw what was in her hand. She had been with Prioress Eleanor when she had sent it to Richard. Turning pale, she opened her mouth to speak but chose silence as the wiser choice.

Eleanor fought with her loyalty and love for her nephew. But the battle was quickly lost. Although she wished it were otherwise, she must tell this king's man what she had found.

The shadow of the High Sheriff of Berkshire fell across the kneeling women and dimmed the shining gold of the cross.

With a trembling hand, she passed the cross into the hand of FitzRoald. "This belongs to my brother's son, Richard FitzHugh. I know because it was my own gift to him."

"I am sorry that you had to find this, my lady," the man murmured, but the cross disappeared into his fist.

"Someone else would have done so," she replied.

Anne helped the prioress to rise. "We must leave," she said as gently as possible but squeezed her prioress' elbow to show her sympathy.

"You shall question the boy." Eleanor regretted she had called Richard that, but, in her heart, he was still the child who rode up and down the corridors of Tyndal Priory on the hobbyhorse Brother Thomas had made for him. "My only plea is to have his father by his side when you do."

FitzRoald bowed. "Of course. Will you summon your brother and explain why the lad must be questioned, or shall I?'

"I shall explain it all to both," the prioress replied, then she led the way out of the chamber of death with all the dignity of one who heads a successful priory. Only Sister Anne knew how hard it was for Eleanor to hold back the tears.

Chapter Nine

FitzRoald, Prioress Eleanor, her brother and nephew, as well as Brother Thomas gathered in a smaller chapel at Woodstock Manor. Of the many places set apart for prayer here, this one was rarely visited. It afforded more privacy for the grim proceedings.

Eleanor glanced at her dour brother, then back to his equally solemn son. Richard's face had turned the color of a corpse as he stood before the High Sheriff of Berkshire.

Her heart broke. This was a nightmare, surely, and she would awaken soon to find her nephew, still a child, laughing at something Brother Thomas had said.

"We have found this object next to the bed of Mistress Hawis." FitzRoald opened his hand to reveal the cross. "Do you recognize it?"

Richard stiffened. "It is mine. My aunt, Prioress Eleanor, gave it to me."

"Might someone have stolen it?"

"No. I was wearing it when I entered the woman's room last night. I know because I grasped it in my hand as I shut the door."

"She was murdered last night."

Richard shut his eyes tight, uttered a soft cry, then took a deep breath. "I grieve to hear this news."

Hugh's brow furrowed and his eyes narrowed as he directed his fierce gaze at the wall between his son and the sheriff.

Hugh and Richard were so much alike, the prioress thought, with their gray eyes and unusual height. The only difference was that Richard seemed to have forgotten his joy in life sooner than his father had. Even his cheeks had lost the boyish plumpness that did not leave Hugh's until he had been in Outremer.

"Please tell me why you were there." FitzRoald smiled to reassure the youth that any man would understand his purpose there.

"I confess I went to lie with her in sin. She was alive when I left her bed."

The sheriff glanced at the father, hoping he would not offend this powerful family by his questions. He cleared his throat. "If you will, explain what you did after...?"

"Enough." Hugh roughly pushed the sheriff to one side. "My son is a man and need not be questioned as if he were a naughty child or some feeble woman." He stepped close to Richard until their noses almost touched.

Eleanor willed herself not to interfere, but she clenched her fist in anger over her brother's harsh confrontation of his son. At least her nephew had shown courage by not flinching before his father's wrath. She was proud of Richard.

"You coupled with the whore. When did you leave?" Sir Hugh's eyes blazed in the dim light.

"I do not know the hour of night, my lord. I waited until she fell asleep before I left her chambers."

"How long were you there? You know the time. What Office?"

Richard shook his head. "I do not know the time. I was there long enough to couple with her. She fell asleep. I dressed and left."

"There were few clouds that night, and you did not notice the position of the moon, the stars? What kind of soldier does not observe such things?"

"I am not a knight, my lord. I am a squire and have much to learn."

Despite the gravity of the situation, Eleanor was pleased when her nephew responded with spirit as well as courtesy.

"Did she rush you into spilling your seed? Did she say anything that might have led you to believe your time with her was limited? Was she expecting anyone after you?"

Richard blushed. "She did not have to rush me. She was naked when I entered. I took her first on the rushes, then…" He turned away and hid his face with his hands.

Eleanor wanted to comfort him. He might be old enough to know a woman, but he was still a child to her, one who was being pushed too hard by his father. She stepped back to keep from reaching out to comfort the boy who was struggling to be a man.

Hugh did not wait for Richard to recover. "You waste our time with this whimpering. Answer my questions," he snarled.

"She mentioned no one else."

"If you are innocent, you must have left shortly before the murderer arrived. Surely you heard or saw something unusual outside the door. If you claim otherwise, your story rings false."

Turning pale, the youth shut his eyes against his father's angry face. "I noticed nothing, saw no one, and heard not a sound."

"You lie! Either that or you are too lax to enter the king's service as a squire. How could you protect our king if you don't sense danger? Have you learned nothing of survival in battle or in times of other danger? You are not my get if you are so incompetent." Then Hugh stepped back and said in a lower voice, "Or perhaps you killed the woman and do not have the courage to face the hangman for your crime. No son of mine would dare to sully the family name with cowardice."

Eleanor saw her nephew sway as if he might faint. Frightened, she turned to Brother Thomas who stood in silence beside her.

He shook his head, his eyes counseling her to keep her peace.

As much as it hurt her, she knew he was right. This was between son and father, but she was angry with her brother. Richard could not have killed the woman. Not her beloved nephew! Surely Hugh agreed with her? Then she glanced at her monk and read the same thoughts in his worried look.

Richard glared at his father, then strode around Sir Hugh to face FitzRoald. "Arrest me," he said to the sheriff in a voice as brittle as an ice shard. "I killed her. She brazenly flirted with me and then begged me to come to her chambers. When I arrived and my seed discharged before I could mount her, she mocked my virginity, my fumbling and inability to pleasure her. I was no man, she said, but rather still a child who should be suckling at his mother's breast."

FitzRoald gaped at him in horror, and then turned to Sir Hugh. His eyes begged the knight to advise on what must be done with this son.

"I was enraged and killed her." With eyes narrowed, Richard looked over his shoulder at his father.

Hugh looked at his son as if the lad were only a servant who had displeased.

Eleanor knew the story could not be true and longed to ask her nephew for details. It should not be difficult to prove that he did not even know how Mistress Hawis had been killed.

But she did not have the chance.

"Arrest him," Hugh said, and then turned and walked out the door. He did not even glance back.

Eleanor bit her lip and tasted blood.

Chapter Ten

"You are innocent, Richard," Eleanor said, walking to her nephew's side. "Why did you confess?"

Instead of replying to his aunt, the youth extended a hand to FitzRoald. "May I have my cross? I acknowledged it is mine and that I lost it near the bed of the murdered woman. Having it with me would bring comfort. I shall produce it as evidence against me when I am put on trial."

The High Sheriff of Berkshire was sweating, knowing he must take into custody this son of a man so favored by King Edward. The stink of his fear filled the chapel. It mattered not that the father himself had demanded his son's arrest for murder. Men often changed their minds when anger cooled, and the one punished was the man who had obeyed too quickly.

But Eleanor suspected that FitzRoald hesitated for another reason as well. His expression throughout the questioning had suggested that he doubted the truth of this confession. A brief glance in her direction revealed his wish that he could let the youth remain free despite the demands of the law.

Brother Thomas, who had been watching the grim proceedings in silence, wanted to shake sense into the lad, but there was nothing he could say now to convince Richard he was being appallingly foolish.

"Since I am still a squire in the king's service, my oath remains an honorable one," Richard said. "It was uttered in the presence of this good monk, you, my lord, as well as that of my aunt, the Prioress of Tyndal. Although she and Brother Thomas may, out of love for me, long to deny what I have confessed, they cannot lie in the presence of God." He glanced at his aunt with sad affection.

"Please give the cross to him," Eleanor said, her voice uneven. She had hoped to show a manly resolve but, instead, had betrayed the emotions of a frail woman.

FitzRoald handed the cross to the young man.

Eleanor grasped her nephew's arm. "This is a hanging offense, Richard. Do you understand that? Why did you confess?"

His only reply was to look away.

The sheriff bowed to the prioress. "Your nephew will be kept in gentle confinement here until the queen and her court are ready to leave. It would not do to take him away in chains while others stared. You and Brother Thomas may visit him as often as you wish."

She thanked him, but hidden tears kept her from saying more.

FitzRoald led Richard away through the open door of the chapel. The sound of their footsteps faded into silence.

For one of the few times in her adult life, Prioress Eleanor covered her face and publicly sobbed.

"My lady," Brother Thomas said, his voice soft as a tender embrace, "let me try to find ways to ease this unbearable pain you are suffering."

Slipping to her knees in front of the small altar, Eleanor continued to weep.

Her prayers were silent ones, but the monk knew what she begged God for and joined his hopes with hers. Then he waited for her to speak.

Finally, she rose and turned to him, her eyes red with lamentation. Rubbing her face to destroy the evidence of her sorrow, she found the courage to smile at him. "You are kind, Brother Thomas. God gave me a precious gift when He sent you to Tyndal Priory."

He blushed. It was not a gift, he thought, but his own crimes that flung him into her service. But if God could create the world out of chaos, He should also be able to mold a blessing out of folly. With humility, he bowed his head.

"I beg pardon for my tears," she said. "It betrays my fragile faith."

"Jesus wept before God in Gethsemane and begged Him to remove the bitter cup of his coming trials from his lips. Your father is dying. With little regard for your deep sorrow, you have been dragged into another violent crime. Your nephew has just been arrested after falsely confessing to murder. You are not made of granite, my lady, yet even stones must weep over the injustice of all you are suffering."

Her face turned pink at his kindness and gentle voice. "You know and love Richard as much as I, and you also believe he is innocent."

Thomas was about to reply when he felt a light touch on his sleeve. Startled, he bit back a cry.

"I, too, grieve over this failure of justice." Father Eliduc lifted his hand from the monk's arm and smiled at the pair.

In the uneven light of the chapel, his glittering eyes reminded Thomas of the snake in Eden. The man even slithered in comparable silence. How did he know they were even here?

The priest bowed to the prioress. "Forgive the intrusion, my lady. While meditating on what evil perils we mortals face, I was walking through the hall and overheard some of what was said here. Then I watched the sheriff leading young Richard away and noticed that you remained in this chapel to pray."

This meant he was not only spying on them, Thomas thought, but had also witnessed Prioress Eleanor in a rare moment of weakness. Anger burned through him like a conflagration, fueled by alarm and hate. His hand curled into a fist, and he longed to hit the man but dared not. If the priest tried to make use of this discovery to extort something from his prioress, however, Thomas realized he might not be able to keep himself from committing violence against him.

Father Eliduc glanced at the monk's hands and smirked, as if reading his thwarted desire to strike him. Then he turned to

Prioress Eleanor with a look tainted with disingenuous concern. "We share a common desire to save your nephew's life."

The brief interaction between monk and priest had not been lost on Eleanor. The tension between the men dried any remaining tears and cooled her grief. "I would hear this," she said and was pleased with her self-control.

Having gotten the response he planned, the priest continued with more sincere courtesy. "Richard is a good lad. Like you, I have no doubt he is innocent. There are others who have greater motive for killing the woman."

"Name them," Thomas snapped.

Eliduc wagged his finger at the monk. "Remember the virtue of patience, Brother. Having met Master Durant of Norwich, you should have a better understanding of its worth. As a wine merchant, he knows how much patience is needed when it comes, shall we say, to the creation of the finest wines."

Thomas flushed.

The priest turned back to address the prioress. "The killing of Sir Walter Clayton's wife may have many causes. I mention this first. When the Jewish Quarter was raided to bring coin-clippers to justice, Mistress Hawis was present when her husband arrested Lumbard ben David and threw his mother and daughters into the street. I have heard that Hawis urged her crowd of companions to mock the women and then urged them to physically abuse the three. When Chera, ben David's mother, begged for mercy, Hawis slapped her. Do you not find it interesting that this Jewish woman should have arrived at Woodstock Manor just before Mistress Hawis was murdered?"

Eleanor thought of the woman and granddaughters she had met. Were they truly capable of such an act? But she urged him to continue. Logic could wait until all facts had been accumulated.

"Mistress Hawis committed adultery with enough frequency to grant her a special torment in Hell," Eliduc said with a flash of attempted geniality. "Her current and most devoted lover is her husband's brother, Maynard Clayton. He is quite obsessed with her. Rumors abound that she wished to end the affair and repent before her husband came back from London. Indeed, this is what she told our queen when our lady confronted her about her wickedness. Another tale hints that she also told Maynard that she would claim he had raped her if he did not agree to the end of the relationship." He cleared his throat. "Sir Walter is not known to be a charitable man."

"Any other suspects?" With each additional name, Eleanor felt increasing relief.

Eliduc shrugged. "Your nephew was not the only virgin youth to seek her bed. Young men are often possessive about first passions, if they believe they might be in love." He briefly looked at Thomas. "A second love is often required to cure them. Have you not found that to be true in your years of hearing confessions, Brother?"

His anger might have rekindled if Thomas had not felt a deadly chill. He forced himself to nod.

Eliduc smiled at the monk's muted response. "As we all agree, God ought to be our only and certainly our greatest love, but not all mortals are capable of the pure passion of faith."

Thomas made himself look away and face his prioress. "Your father is dying, my lady. Let me speak further with Father Eliduc while you return to Baron Adam's chambers. I shall do everything possible to free your nephew from all suspicion in this crime and will keep you informed."

"There may be things that I can do best to accomplish this end, Brother. You must swear to let me know if this proves to be the case." Eleanor urged Father Eliduc to concur with the same request and was surprised when he nodded his agreement without hesitation.

With that, the prioress left the two men to return to her father's bedside.

Father Eliduc and Brother Thomas turned to stare at each other in wary silence.

Outside, the skies grew dark and rain began to fall as if the heavens themselves had observed these sad events and found cause to weep over the vagaries of men.

Chapter Eleven

Father Eliduc chose to break the silence. "May we speak together without rancor or distrust, Brother?"

"I believe in miracles, Father, but that is not one of them."

"Whatever our disagreements in the past, we are of one heart in this matter. I wish to prove young Richard innocent as fervently as do both you and Prioress Eleanor."

Thomas nodded with a thin smile "I am grateful, but let us not pretend that your motive lies solely in the unsullied concept of justice. You have another purpose of lesser purity."

"Some day we must debate the meaning of justice," the priest replied. "For now, I believe any differences between us in this matter are minor and would not be issues that you or his aunt would find troubling."

Taking a moment to reflect on this, Thomas decided that the priest might own a scheming mind, but, were he to be fair, Eliduc was not purely evil. Although the man had exacted a price for saving Thomas' life and releasing him from a foul prison, he also sent the monk to a place where he had finally found contentment. In retrospect, the penance the monk served was a little thing, had harmed no innocent, and he had been freed from it some years ago. It had also trained him to become a better helpmate to his prioress in her jousts with those who broke God's commandments.

"I cannot agree to the price without the approval of Prioress Eleanor," Thomas said.

"Price? What an avaricious sound that word has! You have been spending too much time with merchants and not enough on your knees in prayer, Brother."

Thomas felt his face grow hot. Did this priest have spies embedded in stone walls and in the gloom of dusty corridors? This was another reference to the innocent hour he had enjoyed with Master Durant at Woodstock after the monk and his prioress arrived to attend her sick father.

When Prioress Eleanor had gone on pilgrimage to Walsingham, the wine merchant, and sometimes spy, had helped them solve a crime of treason. Afterward, Thomas realized he had found in Durant a comfortable companion. During this recent reunion, that bond had grown stronger, a pleasurable thing although the monk sensed there was something more. Only their farewell kiss, seemingly no different than what one brother might give another, conveyed a danger, one which Thomas suspected was understood by Durant as well as he.

He cleared his throat. "Whatever word you choose, Father, you have another interest in freeing Richard FitzHugh from suspicion of murder. Name it."

Eliduc laughed heartily as if they had shared a private jest. "I want to take young Richard into my own service so he might train to become a priest. I ask only that you and your prioress persuade Sir Hugh to allow it. Neither of you should find this vocation for the lad offensive. It is a godly thing."

"I have good cause to know your definition of the word *service* very well. It is rarely voluntary. Richard attends the king as a squire, a position that will lead him to knighthood, wealth, and a good marriage. How dare you try to snatch that happiness from him! And for what reason? Some minor weakness you have discovered in him? And if he has already agreed to your plan, with what did you threaten him?" Thomas began to tremble. The youth had said he had a secret to confide in him, one that would make his father hate him. Was this secret what Father Eliduc had discovered?

Eliduc raised a hand. "Calm yourself, Brother. Richard has confided in me only his sincere longing to dedicate his life to God. Not as a monk, mind you, but as a priest. It seems he has a scholarly bent as well. None of this would be penance, which your assignment to Tyndal was. Indeed, his carnal longings may be more easily dampened with prayer than yours have been." He smiled. "Or so it seems of late."

"I have done nothing…"

"…but sin in your heart. Yes, Brother, I know. We speak, however, of Richard FitzHugh and his desire to serve God, rather than King Edward. What opposition could you or your prioress possibly have to that?" He shrugged. "Now the boy's father is another matter."

Thomas shook his head. In truth, he had no objection, nor, he suspected, would Prioress Eleanor. She might be the one most in favor of it, depending on the path this priest set her nephew upon. If the vocation served God and brought honor to the Wynethorpe family, she would be delighted.

But he also knew this priest had more in mind. Godly vocation aside, penance intended or not, Eliduc would expect Richard to repay him with something of value. The man might find the word *price* offensive, but he surely had one in mind.

"His time with me would be short. I have reason to hope that Richard may find a place with the new Archbishop of Canterbury, John Pecham." Father Eliduc first gazed upward, then bowed his head, and managed to look almost humble.

Against his will and better judgment, Thomas was succumbing to the plan. Who knew how high Richard might climb under the patronage of the Archbishop of Canterbury? If there was a price for this, it might be small in exchange for a future as bright as it would be in the king's service. "I cannot speak for…"

"…but you cannot see how she could deny her nephew the opportunity."

"Surely you can understand why Sir Hugh would not be pleased with this new proposal," Thomas said. "He has always planned and hoped that his son would fight beside him in service to the king, as he has and his father did before him." He was uncomfortable being on the same side as Father Eliduc. Had any other cleric made the same suggestion, he would have been very happy.

"All the way back to the days of William the Bastard, if not before." The priest sighed with a rare show of annoyance. "Baron Adam also had other plans for his daughter but allowed her to serve God instead of a husband. Why, do you think, Sir Hugh would feel any differently about his bastard son?"

"He has always hoped that his son would…"

"Do not waste my time with repetitive and commonplace remarks, Brother. You know, as well as I, that the heir to the Wynethorpe lands is a fornicator, a friend to heretics, a man of little faith, and generally owns a rotted soul. He hates those who pray. He is loyal to King Edward, but our king returned from Outremer an ardent Christian. Look how he hammers the Jews for their iniquities. Sir Hugh, on the other hand, found the company of infidels in Outremer enjoyable and even brought one of them home with him. He has formed a pact with the Prince of Darkness."

"The man, Lucas, converted from Islam and is now dead. Sir Hugh gives generously to the Church."

"To his sister's priory, Brother, only to his sister's priory."

"What are you trying to tell me, Father? If you are so convinced that Sir Hugh is the Devil's spawn, why do you think anyone can persuade him to let his son become a priest?"

Eliduc stepped nearer and grasped the cross Thomas wore around his neck. "Because he is a foul sinner, and you are an unrepentant sodomite. He will listen to one of equal foulness." He moved away and slipped his hands back into the sleeves of his finely woven robe. "But you have served God well, despite your failings, and thus have power over Satan's minions like Sir Hugh."

"And if I fail?"

"Ah, Brother, I think you know better than to consider that a possibility." Father Eliduc waved his hand with a dismissive gesture. "If a man, who longs to serve God, is kept from that holy vocation, I fear His wrath would be terrible indeed against those wicked mortals who allowed that to happen."

Thomas shivered. For an instant, he wondered if God's face bore the likeness of Father Eliduc. Quickly, he shook the image out of his head. God bore no man's face. "You will do all you can to save Richard from the hangman?"

"Do I have your word that you shall get his father's permission for the lad to enter my service? If Richard FitzHugh is allowed to serve God, I have vowed to set him on the path to great preferment."

Whatever the man's other faults, Thomas knew the priest never gave his word lightly. He agreed but warned Father Eliduc that Prioress Eleanor must also agree.

The priest snorted as if that was a foregone conclusion. "Then you have my oath that I will work to save the lad from this unjust accusation of murder."

In silence, the men continued to study each other like two circling cats, each deciding whether it was better to attack or depart with a great show of mutual contempt.

Finally, with a nod, Father Eliduc turned and left the small chapel. His footsteps made no sound as he walked away.

Thomas covered his eyes. There was little doubt that his prioress would support Richard's change in vocation. Sir Hugh's position on the matter was a far greater problem.

Unlike the priest, Thomas believed the knight was a complex and unsettled man, one who had a tortured soul but not an irredeemable one. King Edward may have come back from Outremer a more zealous believer, but Sir Hugh was not the only crusader to return with a weakened faith. Some men chose never to leave the land where their friends had shed blood, as if the closeness of their graves gave them greater comfort than belief in a God who had let them die but not helped them regain Jerusalem.

Sir Hugh did not have that choice. He was his father's heir.

Or was the priest right? Maybe he saw the flaws and weaknesses in the Wynethorpe heir that Thomas could not because he was, as Eliduc often reminded him, an unrepentant sodomite? Sir Hugh's inability to support his beloved son in the face of unjust charges was inexplicable. There might be other signs of unnatural behavior as well.

Thomas groaned. He knew he would have another long night on his knees when he returned to Tyndal, arguing with God about this. As hard as that might be, he feared that the prospect of changing Sir Hugh's mind about his son's vocation might be the greater trial.

Chapter Twelve

Prioress Eleanor knelt by her father's side and grieved. His breathing grated the ear, a sound foreshadowing the end of mortal life. Before he fell into that sleep which mimics death, he had briefly squeezed her hand with remarkable strength. She almost wept but, as had become a necessary habit, willed the tears back. It might be best for a man facing eternity to think only of the joy of seeing God, but her heart was filled with gratitude for that small and comforting gesture he had given her. Surely He would not begrudge such kindness when it eased the sorrow of selfish mortals soon to be bereft of a loved one?

And I am selfish, she thought. I am not ready for him to die. It has been too short a time after we made peace. I need my father to be on earth for a short while longer.

Of course she had prayed that he might heal from this apoplexy, and most certainly believed in miracles, but her heart told her that God intended otherwise. She must face her father's death whether or not she was prepared for it.

She kissed his hand, then stared at it, remembering a time when she was a little girl and her mother was still alive. It must have been summer, for the day was warm, and she recalled the gentle scent of bright wildflowers. He had lifted her up to the sky, saying it was all hers if she willed it. Her mother had scolded him, saying that only God could grant his daughter a place in Heaven. Eleanor no longer kept the memory of his reply, but he had put her down next to her mother, then slipped to the ground beside them both and took his wife's hand. Her last recollection was watching them laugh together and joining in the merriment for no other reason than a child's simple joy.

No, she said to God, I am not ready for him to leave me. Then she pressed her face into his palm and wept as quietly as she could.

Sister Anne knelt beside her and whispered in her ear. "You must seek rest," she said.

Eleanor looked up with no attempt to hide her grief from her beloved friend. "I must be here when he dies."

"It will be soon, but not yet. Hours? Perhaps much longer. Brother Thomas has prepared him for death, but your father is a virile man and his soul must struggle far harder than most before it can free itself of the body."

Sleep appealed more than the prioress wished to admit, but still she hesitated.

"Please take my advice," Sister Anne urged. "When the death rattle begins, you shall be here to pray for your father. I give you my word. But you need the strength to do that for as long as it takes his soul to finally escape."

Knowing her friend was right, Eleanor surrendered and rose.

The sub-infirmarian hugged her. "May God's peace embrace you and give both body and soul ease," she said.

As the prioress left the chamber, she saw Brother Thomas speaking with FitzRoald. Her head might ache as much as her heart, and she longed to escape to her rooms, but she wondered if something had happened and knew she must find out. Walking toward them, she allowed herself hope that her nephew had regained his senses and recanted his absurd confession.

"You have something new to report?"

Brother Thomas looked up. "I was telling the sheriff what Father Eliduc had said about others who might have killed Mistress Clayton."

She listened carefully, and then turned to the sheriff. "What might this mean for my nephew?" Her expression betrayed nothing of her own thoughts.

"My lady," FitzRoald said, "I do not believe your nephew's confession. Some might claim I am swayed by his father's rank and friendship with King Edward, but I have often seen the lad at court. He is a good boy and is growing into a thoughtful man of moderate habits. In my experience, such a crime and such a nature are not compatible."

"I am relieved that you share my belief," the prioress said, "although I might be accused of setting aside his confession out of familial love."

With courtesy, the sheriff bowed his head. "Your vocation and reputation prove you understand the evil ways of men far better than I. I do not think you would allow kinship to blind you to the truth." Despite those words, FitzRoald knew how much she loved Richard FitzHugh. "Yet I may not free him until I have caught the true killer, my lady. He did confess."

After the briefest hesitation, Eleanor nodded. "Despite my sorrow over your decision, I understand and concur."

"At least you are willing to continue searching for the murderer." Thomas laid a friendly hand on the sheriff's shoulder.

"I am a man of faith, Brother, and believe in justice. A hanging based on lies does not please me just because it is someone's desired result, nor do I wish it because it is my easiest solution to a difficult problem."

Thomas grinned. "For a moment, I thought I was hearing the voice of our Crowner Ralf."

"I know his elder brother, the sheriff, well and have heard tales of this younger kinsman."

Neither Thomas nor his prioress need ask his opinion of either brother. His inflection suggested he shared their tolerance for the one and respect for the other.

"Do you have any good reason to suspect that Maynard Clayton might be involved in this murder?" Thomas' expression revealed only curiosity.

FitzRoald shrugged. "He is a younger son dependent on the charity of his elder brother. Although he showed every sign of being besotted with Sir Walter's wife, I am not even certain they were lying together. From what I have heard, she preferred seducing virgin boys to any bed sport with full-grown men. As for killing her because she may have wanted to end some alleged affair, Maynard never seemed a man inclined to violence. A bit of a cokenay, if you ask me."

Thomas was unsure whether to believe the priest's view of this situation or the sheriff's. When it came to seeing weakness in anyone, Father Eliduc was more likely to find even the smallest malignancy in the soul. "There must still remain a possibility that Maynard killed her. Fear of what she might tell her husband, perhaps? Terror that Sir Walter might cast him away from his bed and his board for the sins he committed with his sister-in-law?"

"Of course. But there is an even stronger likelihood that the Jewish woman did it."

"But surely the grandmother is not a reasonable suspect," Eleanor said, picturing the small-framed woman who must be close to three score and ten.

"I cannot disregard her," FitzRoald said. "She and her grand-daughters were seen leaving the manor, and I sent soldiers to bring them back. Until the murderer is found, I cannot let them depart. They are in custody."

"They are no threat to anyone," Eleanor protested. "Have you seen their attire? When I saw them this morning, they were about to leave without eating. I insisted they have something to break their fast. The grandmother gave all the food to her girls but touched nothing herself. This is not a cruel woman, nor one obsessed with revenge. They are homeless, hungry, and weak. How could anyone even think they could have anything to do with this crime? An elderly woman and two girls?"

"Nonetheless, the old woman's son was hanged for treason, and Mistress Clayton's husband was the one to arrest the man. Nor should we forget that they are Jews, a stiff-necked people who refuse to acknowledge Christian truth and are prone to violence against us."

"I pray for their conversion, Sheriff, but they are still under the protection of King Edward. We have spoken of the demands of justice, and that is required here. When I met the trio this morning, I found no arrogance, only a desire to be heard by the queen. Many other petitioners, some with far less need, would not be so meek, nor would they turn away from their errand out of compassion for our lady's recent travail."

"In truth, my lady, I agree that there are questions regarding the ability of the old woman and two weak girls to strangle and hang a woman like Mistress Hawis, but I cannot let them leave the manor. Were I to ignore their motive and possible guilt, many would accuse me of incompetence and with good cause. Caution is required if justice is to be rendered." FitzRoald looked down at his hands and scowled as if they had offended him.

"You sent rough soldiers to turn three ragged women back from their journey?" Outrage was obvious in Thomas' voice.

"I ordered them to be gentle, Brother, and the three are currently being held in a manor root cellar."

Eleanor raised an eyebrow. "Three women, guarded by men, in a root cellar? Held there with no regard to their needs for modesty?"

"What else could I do with them until the details of the killing are clearer or the murderer is caught? Others here will learn of their presence. Many more know of the conflict between Mistress Clayton and these Jews, as well as their relationship to the hanged traitor."

Eleanor stiffened. "You need not treat them as if they were magdalenes being sent to the stocks. One is a grandmother and two are virgins. Bring them to my chambers where they may wash, sleep, and change their torn garments without fear of a man's rude and mocking gaze. I shall provide that protection you require, Sheriff."

"But, my lady…!"

"You may keep a guard outside my door, if you will. I doubt they will try to flee." Nor would the men dare enter my chambers to abuse the women, she thought.

Thomas clapped FitzRoald on his back. "A fine idea!" he said. "Who better to watch over them than the Prioress of Tyndal?"

The sheriff thought for a moment, then nodded. "Perhaps they will even see the error of their beliefs," he said. "I would be happy enough to find them accepting baptism and innocent of the suspected crime."

Chapter Thirteen

Baron Adam slowly drifted out of the strangeness of his dreams, but he kept his eyes shut. Since Brother Thomas shrove him, he had tried to numb his senses to the world but also found the experience of dying less frightening than he once feared.

Stretching out the fingers on his good hand, he felt the warmth on the bed where his daughter had leaned. She must have left, but that did not trouble him. He was confident that she had done so for good reason, one that would probably add to her growing reputation as a godly woman. Deep within him, his soul smiled more fully than his ravaged body would allow. Pride in the virtues of a daughter vowed to God was no sin. Brother Thomas had confirmed that, saying it was a way to worship the God they all served.

His thoughts shifted to Hugh. He was probably still kneeling close by. Before Adam had last fallen asleep, he noticed that his son's lips were not moving in prayer, although his lashes were wet as if he had been asleep in an army camp and his body dampened with morning dew. Adam's heart was still bound enough to this world that he grieved for his boy. As a soldier of the king and a crusader under God, Hugh had served loyally and well. But his soul had been grievously wounded. Would God forgive him for his apostasy? Might He even heal him of it?

Adam wanted to cry out to his eldest child and beg him to repent, but he knew he was no longer able to reach him. If only he had done more while he was an earthbound creature. After all, he had been a soldier himself and counselor to King Henry III. He knew how war and ambition festered inside the heart and infected the soul. And hadn't his own soul grown dark when his adored wife, Margaret, died in childbirth? He had cursed God for years and kept his beautiful daughter far from a father's embrace only because she reminded him of his wife.

But all that he had confessed to the good monk. Now he must turn his thoughts to God and let his daughter and Brother Thomas do what they could to cleanse Hugh of his sins before he died and Satan took his soul to Hell.

As he lay in bed, eyes still closed, he realized that the images of his son, the servants, and even good Sister Anne were slowly growing pale.

Was he dying? Was it now? At last?

No, perhaps not quite yet, he decided. A dying man had some choice, it seemed. He would wait until his daughter returned and took his hand, granting him that touch of holiness to help him on the final journey to God's arms.

Although he could not utter the words needed to express his sins and contrition, Brother Thomas had urged him to think of all his sins and silently beg God for His forgiveness on behalf of his soul. At that time, he had closed his eyes and concentrated on recalling every wickedness he had ever committed. When he was done, he opened his eyes and blinked.

Brother Thomas read his intended message and gave him blessed absolution.

Then Baron Adam of Wynethorpe had closed his eyes, vowing he would not open them again to the world. He might still fear God's judgment, but he believed in His mercy just as fervently.

But if the living had faded, the shadows he had noticed earlier were forming shapes behind his eyelids, although they were nothing he could recognize.

As he now lay motionless, he heard a hum, like the distant sound of men in pleasant conversation. Adam could not hear what they said, but he was as comforted by it as if he were listening to monks in a priory singing an Office.

Slowly he slipped back into a sleep that grew ever more profound, his heart at ease and his soul eager for the future.

Chapter Fourteen

Chera gazed at her two granddaughters lying on a thick straw pallet, a furred blanket wrapped around them. "When I see them sleeping in such peace, I almost believe there is an angel that looks over each of them." She bent to shift a lock of hair from the forehead of the older one. "I observe no mortal flaw," she whispered. A twinkle flickered briefly in her eyes.

"But awake they own less perfection?" Eleanor smiled.

"Never less in my heart, but I do not tell them that. They should not know how my love for them often blinds me." Sorrow deepened the furrows in her face. "Since my son's death, they have become my only reason for living."

"I will keep them in my prayers," the prioress replied.

Chera bowed her head.

"Come and share more of this meal. You made the girls eat but took little yourself. Remember that your strength is needed so your granddaughters may thrive."

Walking over to the food, the elder woman stared at it without enthusiasm, and then broke off a small bite of bread. "I am grateful not only for your charity but also for your thoughtfulness in providing food you thought would not be abhorrent to us." She gestured at what remained of a thick vegetable soup with crusty bread sitting next to a plate of dried fruit.

"The servants here know that Brother Thomas, Sister Anne, and I do not eat any meat from creatures that walk on four feet, nor do we use the fat from the flesh of these beasts for cooking. This is not out of fear of disobeying any ancient law but because their meat heats the blood and leads to sin. We do eat fowl and fish without any prohibition, and the milk and cheese from cows, sheep, and goats grace our table at the same time. I am not aware of most restrictions you might have besides eschewing pork, but I hope I was right in ordering vegetables, fruits, and cheese?"

"You have done all possible to make our incarceration a pleasant one."

"This is not a prison cell." Eleanor turned to the ewer of ale, poured, and offered the grandmother a mazer from which to drink.

Chera hesitated but then thanked her and sipped before replying. "Still we were advised not to leave Woodstock Manor. If we attempted to do so, I do not doubt that a party of sword-bearing men would run after and lead us, not too gently, back to the root cellar."

"I will not lie. There are those who believe you had a reason to harm Mistress Clayton."

"And we are also Jews, my lady. We are often accused of the most horrible of crimes because it is useful or convenient." Her bitterness cut the air like a sharp knife. Then she sighed. "Forgive my rudeness. I meant no ill."

"Nor did I take offense," Eleanor said. "Yet you cannot deny that you were angry with the woman and that your son was hanged as a traitor."

"No, and I freely say to you that I told Mistress Clayton I would happily kill her and her husband for the cruelties they committed against an innocent family. Such vile and insulting injuries can never be undone now that my son has been unjustly executed. You say this woman has been murdered?" She waved her hand as if dismissing the news. "My son was as well, and her husband did all he could to lead him to the gallows."

"You said that you came here to beg mercy from Queen Eleanor?"

"We had cousins who advised her father, the noble King Ferdinand III of Castile and Leon, and were granted olive groves and vineyards for their good service. My son was also the friend of the man who serves the queen in all matters relating to my people." Chera put her mazer down on the table. "Queen Eleanor is known for her charity to those who kneel before her and beg it. Now I would not trouble her, but, before I knew of her recent birthing, I had hoped the love she bore her father would soften her heart enough to give us only what we needed to leave England."

Eleanor took in a deep breath. "You have another solution before you. Faith…"

"My lady, I shall not enter into a debate with you on that matter. My heart is full of gratitude for all you have done, and I would not have dissention between us. You have offered us safety in a perilous time, given my girls a warm place to sleep, food to sustain, water to cleanse, and clean clothes without fleas."

"I have done nothing my faith does not demand."

"And you have performed what He commands us all to do and done so with a good heart."

Eleanor longed to say more but chose to let Mistress Chera continue.

"On my own shoulders, I am willing to accept the weight of suspicion, both whispered and shouted, the need to keep a possible murderer close to hand while the sheriff seeks the felon, and the refusal of anyone to believe that the king may have hanged an innocent man. But no burden should fall on the heads of my tender-aged granddaughters."

The prioress glanced at the two small shapes sleeping so soundly. If this woman was willing to remain until the crime was solved, then so be it, but Eleanor agreed with her about the girls. "Have they no other kin in England? I could arrange to have them sent to them." No matter what anyone else claimed, she could not see either girl being partners in murder.

"There is only my daughter who is married to a man living in Paris. Our community here was devastated with the arrests and hangings. Several families have lost everything. Husbands, fathers, and even mothers have been hanged, while all possessions were confiscated for the king's coffers. Everyone shares what they have, but few were left untouched and all fear that the raids have not ended. We have lived under a different roof every night, but pride forced me to the streets when I believed we might be taking food out of the mouths of babes. I chose to come to Woodstock Manor as a beggar for a small kindness." She raised her hands in a gesture of futility and fell silent.

"Although my heart grieves over your tale, you surely must understand that coin-clipping is a treasonous act. Hundreds were found guilty and rightly executed for the crime. Evidence was found in your house, so your son cannot be innocent."

"My lady, I do not disagree that some were guilty, perhaps even most. I only protest my son's innocence. He was a physician, not a money-lender, and rarely took coin. He accepted payment in any reasonable form from his patients. That was often food, pewter plate, or even jewels. Of all those arrested, he was one of the least likely to have committed the crime."

"But the evidence was found. He would not have been arrested otherwise."

Chera's smile was thin. "I do not expect you to believe me any more than Sir Walter Clayton did when he found what he called *evidence* hidden in the thatch of the roof. My son had let the king's men in willingly, knowing he had never done this treasonous thing as they claimed. When the clipping forceps, bag of coin bits, and a silver ingot were found and shown to him, he was horror-struck. None of us knew how these things had come to be there."

Eleanor felt an eerie chill. "Then you say the evidence was deliberately placed in your house to discredit your son? Why?"

"I wish I could answer that question. I cannot. Even if I knew who desired this evil to befall my son, I doubt I would be believed because of my faith. After all, there are Christians who engage in this treason and also lend money at interest. Yet few were arrested and even fewer hanged. Coin-clipping has been deemed a Jewish transgression, like crucifying Christian children and using their blood to make our bread for *Pesach*."

"Not all Christians believe these ridiculous tales." Eleanor flushed with anger.

Chera touched her arm. "I believe you are innocent of believing the libels, my lady, but mortals sometimes hold irrational assumptions close to their hearts because it pleases them to do so." She hesitated before continuing. "Christians lived in harmony with us in Oxford before these raids. Many of them were shocked when they heard of my son's death."

Eleanor said nothing while she calmed herself. Yes, she was angry with this woman for lashing out at Christians as she had, but the more she talked with Chera, the more she believed her to be an honorable woman. Once again, her heart commanded her to remember that the search for justice demanded God's perfect tranquility. She also knew that the older woman had spoken the truth. Men do believe lies because it gives them pleasure to do so, and, in the tumult of anger and fear, the innocent often suffer with the guilty.

"Try to think of any enemies your son may have had amongst your own community or the Christian. I seek only the truth, wherever that may lead." Eleanor offered her more ale.

Chera shook her head. "My son was well-respected by all. He had patients among the Christians too. Prohibitions against intermingling never last when pain makes life unendurable or cancers eat at the flesh. If a Jewish or Christian physician is noted for cures or relief, we all seek him, no matter what our religious differences."

Eleanor remembered how Sister Anne had helped the young Jewish woman through a terrible birthing. And as she thought more on this, she recalled that Lucas, the convert from Islam, who returned from Outremer with her brother, had sought help from a Jewish doctor when cancer rotted his bowels. "Aye," she murmured without realizing she had spoken aloud. "I know that well."

Chera put a hand to her mouth. "Your brother is Sir Hugh of Wynethorpe, is he not?"

Eleanor nodded.

"He sought help for a friend from my son. A London physician, Master Gamel, recommended him, but your brother's friend came too late for my son to save his life."

If Hugh had met this man, he might be able to tell her more about any enemies or whether he might have had reason to clip coins. "And your son was called…?" Father Eliduc had told her, but Eleanor so distrusted him she needed to hear the woman confirm it.

"Lumbard ben David."

Perhaps Sister Anne knew something of him as well, the prioress thought. She often had contact with other physicians in the course of treating patients from many parts of England.

"My lady?"

Eleanor saw the tears and realized that this strong woman had reached the limits of her endurance. The prioress tried to smile in a futile attempt to chase away the grimness of the moment, but she could not banish horror from the woman's heart. How could one not feel terror when it seemed impossible to prove innocence in a world that denied it was likely?

"Please do not doubt my gratitude," Mistress Chera said. "Our differences have not hardened your heart, nor have they made mine insensitive to the gifts you have given us." Seeing the prioress begin to speak, she begged permission to continue. "I agree to this confinement for myself until we are released from all suspicion. I swear to remain, ready to face the king's justice."

"Your word is honorable," Eleanor replied.

"I do beg one final but great favor." With difficulty, the older woman slipped to her knees and raised her hands in supplication.

"If it is within my power to do so, of course!" The prioress urged her to rise, but the woman refused.

"Should I be taken for hanging, my lady, will you swear to save my girls from abuse and harm?"

"Surely no one would think they were guilty…"

"I have seen babes raised on the point of swords."

Eleanor felt her face turn hot as fire. "I swear to do as you ask," she said.

Chapter Fifteen

The sight of Richard standing before him, head bowed, broke Brother Thomas' heart.

Soft-cheeked youth never lasts long in a world of violence and death, but memories cling far longer. The person before him may have become hollowed-eyed from fear and pale-skinned from lack of sun, but the monk still saw the little boy for whom he had woven tales and made a hobbyhorse at Wynethorpe Castle only eight years ago.

"Why did you confess?"

Richard raised his head but only to stare at the stone wall of his cell.

Thomas waited. "You didn't do it," he said and fell silent, willing to remain so until he got the truth from this boy.

"I killed her for the reason I gave."

"Why do you want to be hanged for a lie?"

Richard shook his head and slid down the wall to sit on the ground. Thomas took it as a good sign that the lad could not look him in the eye. He would take advantage of that hint of frailty to get him to talk and see reason, no matter what had happened that night in the woman's bed.

"Before you go to the scaffold, a priest will come for your confession," the monk said. "Think carefully. Will you die and face your God with falsehood in your heart? Your aunt will spend the rest of her life praying for your willfully tainted soul.

Would you be so unkind to her?" He knelt beside the youth. "She knows, as well as I, that, if you choose hanging, you will have failed to be honest with God."

The youth rubbed his eyes with the heels of his hands. His cheeks were damp.

At least he is struggling with what he should do, Thomas thought, and reached out to touch the lad's shoulder. "I know you have lied for a reason, Richard. If there is someone you are trying to protect, then tell me the circumstances and let us plan together what we must do."

"Will you swear to tell no one?"

"Your aunt must know." That was one exception the youth might allow, although Thomas feared it might be the only one.

Richard gazed at the floor.

A hungry mouse with nose twitching emerged from a tiny hole in the rock, saw the men, and skittered back into the safety of its small cave.

"If I tell you," the youth said, "will you listen to my reasons and respect my desire for continued silence? If I think my aunt will honor that wish as well, then you may tell her."

Fearing what he might learn, yet far more terrified that this boy would die for something he had not done, Thomas reluctantly agreed. "But may we compromise if I find it necessary? Or at least let us discuss it. Allow me to present my arguments."

A slight smile played with the corners of Richard's mouth. "You always said that when I was a willful child and had done something wrong for which I did not want to apologize."

The monk returned the smile. "Was there ever a time we were unable to come to a reasonable solution on what must be done?"

"And you always let me get away with some childish wickedness." Cheeks tinted pink, Richard looked shyly at the monk. "You treated my opinions as worthy thoughts, Brother. A kindness to a boy whose father never…" He fell silent. A tear sparkled briefly in the corner of each eye. Then the moisture vanished as if exiled for committing the crime of weakness.

The monk wanted to hug the child he still recognized in the lad but held back. Richard's desire to become a man must be honored. "Begin with the truth in this matter."

Richard balled his hands into fists.

Was it shame or anger that caused the color to flare in Richard's face as well? Thomas knew the fists were not intended to render violence but rather to keep the lad's emotions under control.

"I did not kill her. Yes, I came to her a virgin and groped at her like a fool. Yes, I tried to take her on the floor, but my seed spilled before I could…" He sobbed and turned away.

"All men suffer humiliation with their first woman. I did."

Richard tried to smile, failed, and continued to weep. This time the monk did pull him into an embrace and held him until the sobbing stopped. "Go on," he said gently, releasing the youth, and sitting back.

"But she did not mock me as I claimed but gently led me to the bed where she undressed me and taught me a slower pleasure." He blinked. "That must have been when I lost the cross that my aunt later found."

"Probably."

"But I left her alive, Brother. On my hope of heaven, I swear it."

"Who are you protecting?" Thomas kept his voice low so the guards outside could not hear his question.

"My father, or so I fear."

The monk had not expected this and learned forward in shock. "Why?"

"I saw him in the corridor before I entered Mistress Hawis' chamber. With the lust I suffered on seeing her, I forgot, but, as I was dressing, I was filled with horror. Had I mixed my seed with that of my father in the same woman? That must surely be a transgression almost beyond a soul's redemption! Unlike my prior testimony to the sheriff, I shook her awake and asked if he had been with her before I arrived." He turned away and held a hand to his mouth as if about to vomit. "Satan is a stinking monster!"

Thomas waited, knowing Richard needed to regain a semblance of dignity.

"She would not say one way or the other, only that she preferred the simple ardor of young men to the predictable coupling of their elders."

"Are you sure you saw Sir Hugh?"

"I could not see the man clearly, but he bore similarities. When the man heard me behind him in the hall, he glanced back at me and then fled. In the dim moonlight, I feared it was my father."

"But you need not protect him simply because he might have been in the hall. You are not certain that the man was Sir Hugh. If it was, and you both did lie with the same woman, your sin of commingling seed is pardonable because you did not know for certain that it was he or that he had ever lain with her. From her words, it appears unlikely that he had. This is not the willful deed of Jacob's son Reuben with the father's concubine."

Richard was listening intently.

"All you have done may be confessed, repented, and pardoned with due penance. Even assuming that your father had lain with Mistress Hawis before you arrived, however, that is no proof that he later returned to commit murder."

The lad took a deep breath, and a normal color began to return to his cheeks.

The monk doubted that the person outside the murdered woman's door had been Sir Hugh. He had just arrived at Woodstock and gone immediately to his father's bedside. Perhaps grief had driven him to seek a woman's bed, but, from what Thomas knew of the man, he preferred married women of a different sort to the brazen Hawis. Nonetheless, the information might be very important. The unknown person might still be a witness or even the killer.

"After I learned of Mistress Hawis' murder, I wanted to protect him from any suspicion of the killing, Brother. I also hoped my silence would save him from the queen's wrath. Queen Eleanor may finally lose patience with him for his wicked ways.

He refuses to marry, as she wishes him to do, and insists on sinfully lying with women at court. She and the king have argued about this. It will no longer be tolerated."

"The women may be banned from court, but I doubt King Edward would banish a man he has learned to depend upon in war. Your father fought by his side in Outremer, and the king has never forgotten the loyalty of his comrades-in-arms there."

Richard laughed without mirth. "Then my wish to protect my father matters not, Brother. He also showed how willing he was to conclude that I am guilty of killing Mistress Hawis. You heard him say that I am not worthy of him. Did you and I not speak of my fears in this regard? Now we know my father holds me in utter contempt."

"He was rough with you, but he is a knight and knows you will enter into the profession of war. His methods may have been intended to toughen you further for adversity, but I know he loves you more than himself."

Richard's eyes narrowed. "You mean that as kindness, Brother, but he does not love me now and, if he ever did before, most certainly he never will again."

Thomas recognized the obstinacy in the son that he had often found in Sir Hugh. It might be a good quality in a knight, one that kept him facing the enemy when a softer nature would urge retreat, but it was not one the monk especially admired. Yet he dared not criticize. His own father had bestowed upon him the same paternal gift. It was what kept Thomas arguing with God beyond the point when most men of faith would surrender.

"You said, before your father arrived, that you had something to tell me. Please do so now," the monk gently urged.

Richard dropped his head into his hands. "My father went to Outremer to fight the Infidel. He followed our king to war with the barbarian Welsh. On occasion, he returns to gift me with his presence. I see a silent, hard man who is scarred by violence and has fallen in love with shedding the blood of his enemies."

Thomas was tempted to defend Sir Hugh but knew he would be wiser to say nothing.

"I have been trained to follow him. He assumes I shall earn land and wealth with my sword, plunging it with joy into men's quivering bowels. In times of peace, I shall be expected to earn the trust of King Edward's heir, Prince Alphonso, as my father and grandsires have done back to the days before the Duke of Normandy became king of this land." He rubbed a hand over his mouth. A thin line of spittle glistened on his knuckles.

"They have been honorable men, Richard, and all served their liege lords well."

The young man thrust out his hand as if begging alms. "And sold their souls for power and other worldly goods! You are a man of God, Brother. You know that God wants us to turn the other cheek to our enemies and give our wealth to those less fortunate that we." He began to weep. "I see my grandfather dying and think of the violence he committed and the schemes he perpetrated for which he must now repent before God sends his soul to Hell for those sins."

Thomas briefly grasped the lad's outstretched and trembling hand. "Your grandfather is a good man. He has been faithful to his wife, even after her death, and worked hard to serve his king and bring honor to the family. There is no wickedness in that. He did not rise in his lord's esteem because he lied or cheated other men. He did so because he was a loyal knight and a wise counselor."

Richard only shook his head.

"There is more that brings you sorrow, lad. What is it?"

"My grandfather was kind to me, despite my bastardy, but he spent years suffering from a battle wound that never quite healed. I honor and love him for his goodness but hate the anguish brought about by an act not done in the name of pure faith."

Perhaps not in the cause of faith, Thomas thought, but he suffered it out of loyalty to God's anointed king. This might be cause for debate later, but he would not interrupt Richard now.

"Then there is my father! He is a cruel man whose scars from battle are lesser ones, but, unlike my grandsire, he only finds pleasure in inflicting pain." Richard hesitated, his expression a mix of confusion and anger. "I both hate and love the man who sired me, Brother. Is that possible?" Then he groaned. "I loathe the world, Brother! It is a place owned by the Devil who mocks our weaknesses and leads us to blaspheme against God."

"At your age, I felt the same about my own father," Thomas replied. Although he thought Sir Hugh cold and unpredictable, he would never say so. As for his own father, he had been a good man, the monk realized after he had reached manhood. He might have paid little attention to a bastard son, but he did so less out of disinterest than lack of time. When Thomas did offer a great service to him, his father responded generously.

The youth smiled. "I knew you would understand."

"Continue. What more need you tell me?"

Richard drooped with weariness but then straightened as if he had no right to the failing. "I have spoken to Father Eliduc, and he has encouraged me in this matter."

Thomas felt a sudden and profound chill.

"I have no wish to follow in my father's vocation and earn my knighthood. I want to become a priest and serve God. My faith is not as strong as yours," he said bashfully, "and I do not want to become a monk, but Father Eliduc said he might find me a position with a high-ranking cleric where I could avoid the scheming evil and violence of the secular world."

"This truly is a desire that will not please your father."

"As I said, he will loathe me the more for it."

Not hate you, but he will grieve, the monk thought. Nor was the Church innocent of all the evil Richard wished to escape. "Chastity is required," he said, hoping to remind the lad that vows were not easy, as the lad had surely learned in Mistress Hawis' bed.

"I went to that woman to test myself. My lust overwhelmed me, yet I was disgusted by the filth and reek of my sin and hers that night. Did you not lie with women, Brother, before you took vows? Did you find pleasure in it?"

"I did," Thomas replied but found it impossible to explain why he found the pleasure of coupling with women so easy to reject. His flesh sought a different and more profound comfort in the arms of a man, a far worse sin than committing unsanctioned sex with women. After the hesitation, he said, with sufficient honesty, "I enjoyed the release it gave me."

"Do you miss lying with them?"

Thomas shook his head. But he had suffered a far worse torment. After Giles had been taken from him, he entered into hellish darkness, a time of impotence except in dreams. But the devilish imps that came to pleasure his body at night were all male. Satan knew him well.

"Then I shall conquer lust as well!" Richard pounded his fist into his open hand. "Women have tempted men since Eve corrupted Adam. They destroy men with their lusts and rot our male power. Only holy virgins like my aunt are worthy of respect."

Thomas was taken aback by this vehemence, which sounded like it might have come directly from the mouth of the abhorred priest. Did this youth truly hate women or simply blame them for what all young men suffered until they learned to control themselves? He would never forgive Father Eliduc for taking advantage of a boy's confusion and implanting this hatred in his heart.

Richard looked hopefully for a response.

This was not the time to argue over whether either gender bore the greater blame for lust, Thomas thought. When all danger that the youth would be hanged had passed, he would try to undo Father Eliduc's malignant influence. "Tell me how your desire for a religious vocation permits the sin of self-murder, if you insist on dying for a crime you did not commit and with a lie tainting your soul?"

Richard's eyes began to glow with a maniacal light Thomas had seen once before in a youth at Tyndal Priory. "Because I would rather be a martyr to my faith than follow the path my father wishes I take! I confess I was angry with my father for failing to believe I was innocent of killing Mistress Hawis. Indeed, my heart cried out when he said I was no son of his, being only a coward and a laggard, but I am now convinced that Satan will blind him completely and he will reject my wish to become a priest. He is like those pagans who sent Christians to the lions for failing to deny their beliefs."

As the youth went on to cite holy virgins who rejected marriage, choosing horrible deaths to keep their virginity, Thomas swore oaths against the priest. Finally, he raised his hand for silence. "I wish you had told me of your desires earlier, Richard. It is a subject that requires prayer as well as discussion."

"I have debated it with Father Eliduc."

Thomas tried not to shout a warning that this was the last man from whom he should seek advice. Instead, he forced himself to nod. "Surely he would not counsel you to let yourself to be hanged because Sir Hugh proved difficult on the matter of your vocation."

Reluctantly, Richard agreed, and the light of zeal dimmed in his eyes.

"Then agree that I may tell your aunt about your desire to enter the priesthood and your fear that your father will deny your request. I suspect she may be able to convince her elder brother that he should grant permission once you are found innocent of this crime. He honors her, and her word has weight with him."

For the first time, Richard looked hopeful. "Then tell her, Brother, with one restriction."

The monk nodded, albeit with reluctance.

"She must not tell my father any of this. I shall choose the time and place for doing so. That is what a man must do. Once I have done so, she is free to act fully on my behalf." His expression softened. "I am grateful that she would do this for me."

It was this tenderness that gave the monk hope for the youth in whatever vocation he followed. So Thomas swore as Richard wished him to do, but his heart remained heavy. Not only was this lad he loved like a son under the harmful influence of Father Eliduc, but he was still a confessed murderer and no other had admitted to the crime or been found guilty. Before he could enter into the next trial of his young life, a war with his father, Richard must be found innocent of the crime.

Chapter Sixteen

Prioress Eleanor and Brother Thomas strolled through the walled garden outside the queen's chapel, a place designed for Queen Eleanor of Provence by her adoring husband, King Henry III.

Spring is a deceiving time, the prioress thought. The season mocks with the promise of warmth but then betrays hopes with cruel storms. Her mood was grim, and nothing she did could brighten it.

On their way here, the prioress had glimpsed the grove of one hundred pear trees near Everswell, the idyllic retreat known best for the bittersweet love of King Henry II and the Fair Rosamund. The limbs seemed lifeless now and were starkly black against the gray sky, although Eleanor thought that buds must be forming. A few apple trees, imported from France to appeal to the current Castilian queen's love of fruit, would not awaken with new life until later.

To their left, the prioress saw the fish pond planned by the father of the current king, and, beside it, the herbage enjoyed by his mother. Although some herbs had been imported from Castile and added to the garden, the plot retained the look enjoyed by the elder king and his queen. Eleanor of Castile and her mother-in-law might barely tolerate each other, but the current queen was wise enough to know that more conflicts are won by diplomacy than battle. She would make only the smallest of changes while the queen dowager lived.

Today the air felt soft. Yesterday it was sharp and bruised the skin with an icy bite. Much like life and death, the prioress concluded. She shook her head and blamed her stubbornly troubled mood on the excess of a melancholic humor.

But the earth was beginning the labor of birth that brought forth new life. "Much like our queen has done," she murmured, knowing she should look on that as a wondrous thing. When they returned, she would seek advice from Sister Anne on banishing this dark brooding.

Brother Thomas said something, and she realized she had not been listening.

"Forgive me, Brother, I have been lost to petty musing."

"You have been given too much to bear, my lady. Your father's health, your nephew's confession to murder, as well as his defiance of his father with his longing to take vows. Now you have heard the reasons he had for his false declaration of guilt, yet he cannot be released until the murderer is caught. I do not think any musing you might fall into would be trivial."

She smiled at him. When the demon that infected her with lust for this monk retreated, she enjoyed the calm Brother Thomas often brought her soul. His gentle company soothed her, and he owned a unique wisdom that opened her eyes to insights she otherwise lacked. God has looked into his heart and found grace, she thought, and silently thanked Him for the gift of this man.

"I am convinced that your brother loves his son," he said.

"As am I, but I am equally confident that he will rage over Richard's desire to become a priest."

"Is Sir Hugh so angry with God?"

"No, but he holds priests in contempt. Father Eliduc exemplifies why he does so."

"I would agree," Thomas growled.

Eleanor never told her monk that she had learned of his dual loyalties years ago, but, after Father Eliduc told her that he was releasing Brother Thomas from his obligations to ferret out Church enemies, she discovered her monk loathed the priest as much as she. Of course, she might have found out why he had fallen under Eliduc's domination and the reason he felt obliged to continue the allegiance for so long, but she chose not to seek those answers. Whatever the explanation, her monk's sins had been purged years ago, and Brother Thomas had proven his devotion to God as well as loyalty to her and her family many times over.

She stopped and studied the earth where something of a vibrant green was struggling to emerge. "My brother was a gentle youth once, Brother, full of dreams born of the legends of King Arthur and tales of the Lionheart. When he returned from Outremer, he did so with a heart so mutilated that it has lost joy. He has yet to speak of the cause that changed his faith into this hollow thing."

"King Edward returned, robed in zealous Christian faith."

She did not respond. Instead, she bent to touch the vulnerable shoot, then drew back as if fearing to damage it. "Our father suffered a similar falling out with God when our mother died. My brother will find the path again in time, but his contempt for priests who serve worldly interests rather than God may last longer. Hugh believes honest men do not try to disguise their true loyalties."

Thomas looked away.

Eleanor noted the gesture and quickly added, "He understands those who are struggling to find their true allegiance but not men, like Father Eliduc, who have found their vocation but choose to disguise it behind piety."

"Your brother owns no love of monks either." Thomas looked at his prioress with a questioning look, but saw that her expression was kind. If she knew his past with the priest, he decided, she had forgiven him.

"But you saved his life and thus became the exception. As for me, I am his sister. He is forced to tolerate me." She smiled.

"His son?"

"Let us worry first about asking my brother to help save his life. Of his love for the lad, I have no doubt. He would take Richard's place on the scaffold if he could."

"But not let him choose God's service over knighthood as his vocation." Thomas cleared his throat and told her what Father Eliduc had in mind for her nephew.

She fell silent as she thought about this news. "I see merit in the plan, both for the family and Richard, but my brother may not. If Father Eliduc did place my nephew in this excellent position with the new Archbishop of Canterbury, my brother would be in his debt. When our father dies, Hugh will become the head of our family. His debt to the priest becomes one we all own."

"I may agree with your brother, my lady." Thomas had not realized that this debt was the prize and was angry with himself for not grasping the implications.

"As do I, in part, but I am not without hope that we may pay what is owed without dishonoring our name. My brother is not a fool, nor am I."

"Father Eliduc knows you are a worthy opponent, my lady. He would not rashly go into battle against you. As for your brother, he may not know him as well, but he is aware of his reputation as a man of war."

They walked on in silence for a while, and then stopped to watch a flock of birds fly overhead.

"First, I must speak with my brother, discover if he was in the corridor outside Hawis' chambers, and if he had lain with her," Eleanor said. "Whether or not any of this is true, I shall tell him that his son confessed to save him from suspicion or rebuke from the queen. Richard did not specifically prohibit that revelation."

"If Sir Hugh was there, will he admit to it?"

"My brother sins openly with married women. Although he never brags about his many conquests, he would admit his adultery with Mistress Hawis to Sir Walter himself, if it meant Richard would be freed of all suspicion."

"Then why has he not said he visited the dead woman?"

"I doubt it was he."

"Indeed, my lady, so do I."

"Nonetheless, I must ask him, while keeping silent about Richard's secret desire for another vocation. Sadly, my brother feels no guilt about lying with these women. He will tell me without a qualm, but I think we will find that the man my nephew saw was not his father."

"If he was, he may have seen something important even if he doesn't realize it. Or else we must seek the man who was in the corridor."

"I shall speak to Hugh in private after he has spent some time by our father's side."

"What do you wish me to do, my lady?"

"Go to my father as well, Brother. Your prayers and consolation give him strength to face death. He seems more at peace after you heard his confession. I know from past remarks that he respects you as a man of God."

"I am not worthy of that honor," Thomas replied, "but he is an admirable man who should travel with a purified soul to God. I shall do all I can to help him accomplish that."

Eleanor thanked him, and the two walked back through the garden to the manor entrance.

At the door, she turned to her monk. "Later, we shall see what all must be done to bring the perpetrator of this sad crime against Mistress Hawis to face the king's law." She stiffened and stared down the long hall that led to the room where her father was dying. "No matter what earthly sorrows infect my heart, Brother, my duty to God remains supreme. Whatever is needed to render His justice, I am bound to do it."

Chapter Seventeen

Sir Walter Clayton was a lean man of ruddy complexion, a bright hue that extended from his shining bald head down his scrawny neck. In contrast to this intensity of color, his blue eyes were a watery shade reminiscent of fish ponds.

Immediately behind him stood Torold, a poor knight who served the wealthier gentleman in exchange for roof and food, although his liege lord's benevolence did not extend to the expense of a wife. He was possessed of such abundant dark hair, impressive musculature, and stone-gray eyes that an observer might be taken aback by the physical extremes the two men represented.

The High Sheriff of Berkshire ground his teeth and swallowed the curses he longed to utter. He had greeted Sir Walter with expressions of sorrow and then regret for having to bring him the news of his wife's tragic death. Now he was angry he had even bothered.

"Why would anyone think a lad, whose beard is a joke, could do a deed like this?" Sir Walter stroked his own closely shaven chin.

"He confessed."

"Then I shall rephrase my question. Why would any man of reason think a child would kill my wife?" He laughed unpleasantly. "Have you not three Jews to arrest?"

FitzRoald asked what he meant.

"The traitor's mother threatened to murder my wife. Did this child, whom you have put into a locked room, ever utter one word that suggested he had a grudge against her?"

"He con—"

"Don't be a fool! The child lied. I do not know why, nor do I care. Hang him, if you want, but he is certainly innocent of this crime. But the old Jewish woman? Now there is a wicked creature."

"As you have said, Mistress Chera is old."

"With granddaughters young and strong enough to do the deed at her command."

The sheriff grew uneasy. He had not taken that possibility seriously. Although he was disinclined to believe they had committed a crime, he also knew they would not be the first children to do violence unto others, although murder was far beyond the usual rock-throwing in the streets.

"And string her up to make it look like she had killed herself."

FitzRoald winced. Clayton argued well. Had he been a fool to dismiss the women's possible guilt? Yet the more he thought on it, the harder it became to agree with the widower. He might not be fond of Jews, but, other than their misguided beliefs, they were neither more nor less prone to human frailty than Christians, in his experience. And the girls were still children and less likely to commit great iniquity than their elders.

"My wife knew I was raiding the houses of coin-clipping traitors and came with a group of her friends to see the vile creatures arrested and their possessions confiscated for the coffers of our noble king. Did you not accompany the women, Torold, to make sure they suffered no harm?"

The man grunted assent.

"When I arrested Lumbard ben David, this Chera ran after me, hurling curses and calling down all sorts of demons on my head in revenge." He looked around with a nervous glance. "I am fortunate not to have children, for she might also have sent an imp to bleed any son of mine dry so she would have his blood for her foul Jewish rituals."

Although he had never witnessed such things himself, Fitz-Roald had often heard these malign tales about the Jews. But whether the rumors were true or not was a matter of little significance to him now with a murder to solve. He chose to nod encouragement to the widower so he might continue.

"My men quickly barred the door to the house so she could not reenter. Then the creature spewed her hatred on them, claiming they meant to sully the honor of her granddaughters who were still within." Sir Walter smirked, exposing a gap in his teeth. "I ordered my soldiers to seek out the traitor's spawn and throw them into the street as well and into the claws of their granddam."

"You said the old woman threatened your wife," FitzRoald said. "Did she swear to kill your wife or did she utter general curses?" So far in this tale, the Jewish woman had done nothing more than anyone would who lost possessions while husbands and sons were sent off to dungeons and hangings. To his knowledge, the curses had never amounted to anything. God seemed to protect those who served the king's justice against traitors.

"My wife was upset over the cursing and urged her friends to help defend me. They threw a few rocks and uttered invocations to God to protect us against the demons who serve these unholy people. Then the old woman turned on my wife and spat at her! In defense, my wife slapped her. It was then the crone swore to kill her."

"I took Mistress Hawis home to safety." Torold put a hand on Sir Walter's arm to silence him. "And urged her friends to return to their homes as well. Great Jewry Street was a place of violence that night and no place for gentlewomen to be."

"There are other tales that suggest another, besides Mistress Chera, had cause…"

Sir Walter roared with laugher. "You mean the rumors that my brother was having an affair with my wife? That is nonsense."

"I said nothing about that," FitzRoald said. "But if you…"

"You would be negligent if you did not ask me. Many have whispered the tale, and the Devil must have stopped up your ears if you had not heard about it. My wife told me the gossip, and we jested about it. Even my brother laughed. He admitted he admired my wife. She was a beautiful woman, but his adoration was a chivalrous thing, nothing more. Sadly, Maynard is not a poet or he would have written verse to her in the fine tradition of chaste longing."

The sheriff replied with a thin smile, not being a man who cared about poetry, chaste or not. Give me a juggler any day, he thought.

"But you are remiss in not arresting the women, Sheriff. Why have you let them roam free when it is clear they had motive and were here when my wife was killed? The crone did swear she would do it."

"They are not free to wander about. They are confined to the chambers of the Prioress of Tyndal. They are forbidden to leave until we discover the undoubted murderer."

"The Prioress of Tyndal? Perhaps she will convert them from their wicked faith, a not impossible accomplishment considering her holy reputation." His expression grew disgruntled. "If she does, and the creatures are guilty of my wife's murder, I suppose we must accept that God may choose not to send their souls to Hell after their bodies are hanged."

FitzRoald realized that Sir Walter was convinced the children were not only guilty but believed they should hang with their grandmother if she committed the crime. Thinking of his own brood of beloved sons and daughters, he shuddered. Some were of like age to the Jewish girls. Maybe the granddaughters could be pardoned if they converted? After any trial, he would urge it.

Sir Walter's face now faded to a dull pink. It was obvious that the knight was under great strain and no longer had either energy or patience to continue the conversation. For the first time, he rubbed a hand across his eyes as if tears had finally arrived.

"We should perhaps continue our discussion later," FitzRoald said in a sympathetic tone.

Clayton nodded, and then turned to Torold. "I cannot sleep in that place where my wife was so foully murdered!"

"I shall find you other quarters, my lord."

Sir Walter waved his hand, and the man was off. "He is like another brother to me," he said and, with no further word, walked away.

The High Sheriff of Berkshire gnawed at a knuckle in frustration. He had learned precisely nothing to help him in the investigation.

Chapter Eighteen

When Prioress Eleanor told her brother she must speak with him, he had suggested a walk along the ramparts of the manor house where they might have privacy.

The pair stopped to look out across the valley. The wind had sharpened, but their thick woolen cloaks and hoods kept them warm. Her brother leaned against the wall and stared at the landscape as if searching for an enemy army.

She ran her hand over the stonework. The notched battlements appeared decorative, but that was deceptive. After an assassination attempt against him, thwarted by one of his queen's ladies, King Henry III had increased security. Glancing at her brother, Eleanor was saddened to see that Hugh was happier pacing fortified walls than walking through a peaceful garden.

Baron Adam was resting comfortably, although his conscious moments were now few. When Eleanor told Sister Anne she must speak with her brother alone, the nun had assured her that she would send a swift messenger if her father's condition changed. No longer did she speak of the strong battle against Death. All knew the baron was ready to surrender.

"What did your sub-infirmarian mean when she said prayers were stronger when the suppliant was refreshed?" Hugh's eyes darted left and right as he surveyed the countryside.

Eleanor was certain she had seen a brief upward twitch at the corner of his mouth. "She needed to do something for our father and wanted us out of her way." Although she pretended to enjoy the view, she scrutinized her brother out of the corner of her eye.

"Your sub-infirmarian is allowed to give orders to her prioress?" This time he was grinning.

The smile was so rare that Eleanor put a hand to her heart to keep it from beating too loudly. Was it strange that he could find humor at a time when their father was dying and his son was accused of murder? But she rejoiced at the brief glimpse of the happy boy she remembered within the troubled man she now knew. In response, she laughed and found her spirits lightening.

But the laughter was blown away by the swirling wind, and Sir Hugh's expression grew dark. "I know you have something to say to me, dear sister."

They preferred frank speech with each other, although there were things that each knew must not be addressed with the other. "It is Richard," she replied and suspected her brother might welcome a chance to talk about his son to a sister who loved the lad as much as he did.

He nodded. "I was hard on the boy."

"More than hard."

Striking his hand on the stone wall, he turned to her. "I wanted to drive the truth out of him!"

"Surely you did not think he had killed the woman?"

"I didn't know what he had done. He is young and foolish but wouldn't be the first boy to lie with a woman, think he was in love, and grow wild with jealousy." His tone was brusque with frustration.

"It was the first time he had known any woman. I doubt he had time to feel anything but confusion over what had just happened to him."

"You have spoken with the lad?"

"Brother Thomas has."

Hugh scowled, and then shook his head. "He should have been the father and I the monk."

"You have no longing for celibacy, brother, and he has no wish to lie with women."

"But surely even he has done so."

Eleanor detected a hint of mockery in his tone but let it pass. Hugh had never believed that men who vowed themselves to God were as chaste as they claimed. "Any past sins have been repented and forgiven. I have no wish to learn of lusts cast aside many years ago. While in my service, he has been a virtuous man."

Hugh studied his sister for a long moment, then nodded.

Eleanor felt no condemnation in his look but was curious about the sadness she noticed in his eyes.

"Has my son at last admitted, at least to the monk, that he did not kill Mistress Hawis?"

"He did and has returned to his first story that the woman was alive when he left her bed."

"Then why beg for the hangman's noose?" His expression betrayed the war he fought between relief and puzzlement.

"He was angry when you condemned him for cowardice, incompetence, and then treated him like a common felon, but that is not the only reason." An argument that made no sense unless she betrayed what she had sworn not to reveal, she thought, then hurried on to a cause her brother might understand. "He was trying to protect you."

"Me?"

"Richard thought he had seen you outside the chambers of Mistress Hawis when he approached. Although he could not see this man clearly, he said the person fled and suspected it was either out of fear of discovery or guilt. Your son is now a man and would die rather than let any blame in this crime stain you. You should be proud of his loyalty and love."

Hugh's mouth dropped open but his face flushed with shame. "I give you my oath that the person Richard saw was not me. Of course I lie with women who please me, but Mistress Hawis was never one of them. When I heard rumors she was coupling with her brother-in-law, I laughed. That was nonsense. The woman preferred virgin boys." He looked away. "I only wish my son had not been one of them."

Eleanor raised her eyebrows. "Dare I ask how you know this about her?"

He forced a smile. "It is an oft-whispered tale at court. Our queen had spoken harshly with her about it, having no tolerance for whoring, but Mistress Hawis denied the rumor. I do not doubt that she would have been dismissed for her sins. Queen Eleanor is not a fool, but Sir Walter's wife was for thinking she had deceived our lady and assuming past favor would protect her position at court."

"Why this preference for boys?"

"According to some, virgins are more amenable to learning how to please a woman." He shook his head. "I fear there is some truth in it. Every boy's first woman is perfect and wondrous. It is the second who becomes mortal."

She gave him a questioning look.

"Do not look at me so, sister! I have suffered no betrayal by any member of your sex and my heart holds no bitterness, but I am a soldier who spends his life with other men living in a rough camp while besieging castles. The company of women is like eating at the king's table, a rare pleasure. All I wish is a woman who is capable of amusing me for a short time and being a competent bedmate after. Once sated, I forget them."

Suddenly, a question came to her mind, and Eleanor felt compelled to finally ask it. "Was Richard's mother your first woman?" No one in the family had ever asked who the boy's mother was or even if she had died of the birthing.

He shook his head, but her question had brought to mind the image of a young woman lying in the sweet grass at the castle known as Doux et Dur. For an instant his heart did ache. There had been a shared innocence in that coupling. He doubted his son had felt the same with Mistress Hawis, and he regretted that. Turning away without further reply, he walked on.

Eleanor followed and stared at the broad back of her eldest brother. Lust was a sin she suffered often enough, yet she fought against it and begged penance. But sometimes she wondered if

Hugh committed adultery, less from the pleasure it gave his body, than to carry out a sin he understood well enough to confess.

She had heard him screaming in his sleep. What unspeakable acts had he committed and seen in Outremer, perhaps later in Wales, that tortured him that much? She feared that they were so terrible he was incapable of describing them, even to God. For the first time, she noticed a streak of gray in his hair, and the sight made her tremble. How much time did he have before his own death to learn how to tell God of the sacrileges he had committed and beg forgiveness?

Hugh spun around. "I have heard that Mistress Chera and her two granddaughters are here."

"They share my chambers."

"Why? They are Jews."

"They, too, are suspects in this murder." Eleanor explained the circumstances and why she had taken them into her custody.

"I am one who believes her son was innocent of the crime for which he was hanged." Hugh rubbed his hands over his eyes. "Had I been here at the time of those raids, I would have tried to save him."

Eleanor was surprised. "Mistress Chera told me that you brought Lucas to her son before his death. What knowledge do you have of the man and his family?"

"I have nothing substantial, and absence of evidence does not argue loudly when there is assumption of guilt and no fair trial. Lumbard ben David was a physician. No one in his immediate family lent money or had access to ingots. I find suspect any evidence of coin-clipping, and fear it was deliberately hidden in the roof out of envy, revenge, or," he uttered a soft oath, "a desire to acquire as much property as possible."

Eleanor waited. Knowing the death of Lucas had left an unhealed wound in her brother's heart, she did not want to aggravate it by asking the wrong questions.

"Ben David was good to Lucas when he was dying. Although he had no cure for him, he gave my friend medicine to dull the pain. Other physicians simply told him the agony was God's will and he must suffer without hope of relief...." He turned his face away but not before tears rolled down his cheeks.

Eleanor walked a few steps away and let him fight to contain his grief by himself. She had never learned what the bond was between her brother and Lucas, but she understood that there was no way she could comfort Hugh for the man's death. Soon she felt him at her side and turned to see his face freshly stripped of emotion.

"I have said all I know of this matter regarding ben David," he said. "Rather, let us speak of my son. My heart yearns to see him released and utterly cleansed of any hint that he is guilty of this murder."

"Then you must help him."

"I will do all I can." Once again, he turned to gaze out on the land as if expecting an enemy to arrive at any moment.

The prioress noticed that a mist had gathered in the distance. The wind had drawn in the fog as if intending to disguise all hints of emerging life lest some imp destroy it with a deadly blight.

"I love my son, sister, but I cannot talk with him. I long for us to be closer, but I draw back when he reaches out. What I know how to do is train him in fighting skills, the destruction of a man's craven weaknesses, and how to stay alive. When we go into battle side by side, that will become our bond and the greatest gift I can give him."

"Are you sure his hopes and ambitions match yours?" Eleanor spoke without thinking and wished she could take the words back.

Hugh stared at her as if this prioress had uttered a blasphemy. "He will soon enter King Edward's service. Who, among the squires not so chosen, fails to envy him? Do I regret that my eldest child was born out of wedlock? Yes. But I have arranged a future for him that will bring honor to the family and wealth enough to him."

"All I meant was to suggest that you go to him with arms open and speak softly as you truly wish to do. That will gain his confidence. Of his love for you I have no doubt, and I certainly think he has proven his loyalty to you." Eleanor took a deep breath and silently asked God to forgive this evasive falsehood she had just uttered.

"I shall go to him in the morning."

"And do not bark at him like a hunting dog!" Eleanor smiled as she grasped her brother's arm. "This is the time when a father can be tender, as our own father was with each of us. There is time enough, in the future and in other circumstances, for you to be firm."

Hugh nodded, his eyes growing unfocused with a private thought. "Aye, our father could be a gentle man."

As they walked on, they shared a few memories of the past when their mother was still alive and their father played with them in that world of fragrant air, sweet bird song, and childhood innocence which now felt so distant as to be mythical.

Chapter Nineteen

Father and son looked at each other in a silence thick with tension. Neither knew how to shatter it, nor what to do once it was.

Richard might have hoped his father would declare his support, praise him for his loyalty, and embrace him with paternal love, but he knew better. To Sir Hugh, loyalty was to the power and wealth of family. Love was a word the man never uttered.

The father longed to hear his son swear an oath that he was innocent so he could praise him for honorable intentions, even though misdirected ones. Once he had, Hugh wanted to leave this cell with his son and return him to his rightful place within the circle of young squires closest to King Edward. But the latter was a dream after Richard's reckless confession. Once the real killer was found, he might see that moment.

The knight spoke first. "You are innocent. Why did you lie?"

Richard turned his back and strode to the table where a small pitcher and two masers sat. "May I serve you wine, my lord? The sheriff has been generous in the comforts he allows me."

"You would show better judgment and more respect to your father if you answered my question."

Pouring a drink for himself, the youth sipped at the wine and ignored the comment.

Hugh squeezed his eyes shut to control his temper, then walked stiffly to his son and dropped a hand on his shoulder.

The lad flinched.

"Your loyalty touches me," Hugh said, quickly removing his hand. "Your aunt told me that you had confessed because you thought you saw me in the hall that night you went to the whore's room and feared I might be a suspect in her murder."

Richard did not make eye contact and backed a few steps away.

"I give you my word that I was not there. Never once did I lie with that woman. There is no need to protect me against any accusations." He waited for a reaction suggesting relief from his son.

Slowly putting his cup down, the youth walked to the side of the room where a crucifix hung on the wall. Folding his hands, he bowed his head.

"You need not be ashamed, Richard. I was a virgin until I found a woman eager to lie with me. No matter what your fellow squires may say, they have either humiliated themselves with their ignorance or have yet to find the courage to approach a woman. You should have come to me about it. My father advised me…"

Hugh stopped as he realized he had never spent enough time with Richard for the lad to voice his fears about manhood. And surely the sodomite monk would have been of little support. Bitterness quickly filled his mouth as he was forced to admit that Brother Thomas had been more helpful in all matters than he had ever been to his own son.

Turning around, the lad smiled but the expression was fleeting. "Your words comfort me, my lord."

"Then tell the sheriff the truth. No one believes your confession. Shame over your virginity and a noble desire to protect me from suspicion are nothing to hide. I can prove I was not in the hall that night." Deciding a cup of wine might be a good thing after all, Hugh went to the pitcher and poured some into a mazer.

"But I have still confessed, and the cross I wear was found by the corpse."

The knight shrugged. "You may have to stay here until the slayer is caught." He looked at his son.

Richard had turned back to look at the crucifix.

"FitzRoald has already made the confinement comfortable, and he will do all he can to treat you almost as an honored guest. Brother Thomas, your aunt, and other friends may visit."

"I may not have killed her, but I have sinned."

"We are men, Richard. We sin. Talk to your aunt if you want consolation or to Brother Thomas if you seek absolution." Hugh instantly regretted the rough tone of his voice when he mentioned the monk. His son was fond of him and with good reason. Perhaps he would explain, one day when his son was older and wiser about Man's nature, why he was of mixed mind about Brother Thomas, but this was not the time. "Both serve God well," he added, although he knew he had not done so quickly enough.

"Dare you speak so lightly of blackened souls?" Richard spun around and glared. "Men are obliged to fight against sin. Our souls are more valuable than our bodies."

Hugh shrugged, another dismissive gesture he instantly wished he could take back. Although he did not disagree with his son, he had seen too many terrified men, screaming in a bed of their own guts, to accept simple answers so beloved by callow youths. There were holy men who understood God's inexplicable and often cruel vicissitudes, but they were rare. He had met only one—Lucas—and God let him die.

"You deny God?"

He felt a chill and closed his eyes against the sudden roaring in his ears and the smell of rotting corpses. He wanted to scream but dared not show his weakness to a mere boy who needed to learn how to be a man. Rousing himself from the violent whirlpool of his inexpressible terrors, he waved aside his son's question. "Forget the incident with Mistress Hawis. I shall soon find you a wife so that you may slake your lusts within the sanctity of marriage. The search will not take long. Since you are entering the king's service, with the promise of great influence and gifts of land and wealth, many families will be eager to offer a daughter."

The youth approached with a smirk on his face. "Shall I be allowed to see her and decide if I want her in my bed?"

His father laughed. "I would not force an ugly woman on my only son."

"You shall seed more sons in the heat of your own marriage bed, my lord. Surely your bastard is only worthy of a lesser woman when fathers have reason to hope that their more comely daughters might win your eye for your true heir."

Hugh was shocked. Never once had he valued the lad less because of his illegitimate birth. For a fleeting moment, he recalled the first time he held the babe and the eagerness with which he fled with him, joy bursting the limits of his heart, to his own father. Baron Adam had reacted to the child with a welcoming smile, swearing he would rear Richard as Hugh wished. But what had delighted Hugh most was the love he saw in the baron's own eyes for his first grandson.

"How little you know me if you think I have not done all I could to bring you to a knighthood, the companionship of our king's sons, and the promise of great honor." He glared at his boy.

Richard turned as pale as milk. "You care so little for me that you would send me into battle, as you have done, and let my soul wither as yours has?"

For an instant, Hugh grew blind as if his eyes had been drowned in blood. Only because he loved this boy so much was he able to keep from striking him with his clenched fist. "I fought for God in Outremer, whelp," he hissed. "You dare insult me? A child who has never faced a man in holy battle? One who let his seed fall on the earth like a babe unable to control his pissing?"

Richard roared with mortification. "And you, who swore I had nothing for which to be ashamed, have mocked me as if I were a slave, a cokenay, or a three-legged cur! This is the way a father treats a son he loves? Nay, my lord, you see me only as another means to gain worldly power for the Wynethorpe family, a family whose name I do not fully bear and only that little by your begrudging grace. I am not a son. I am your pawn!" He spat on the ground.

"A lie!" Hugh gasped and stretched out his hand, the closest he could come to pleading forgiveness. "You are my son. Other men have let their bastards starve. I took you on the day of your birth to my own father and demanded he treat you as if I had been married to your mother."

"Ah!" Richard put his hands on his hips and looked at his father's open hand with contempt. "Then I may choose my wife, among those of the highest rank, despite the low birth of my mother and my less-than-noble seed."

Hugh realized from his son's expression that something was eating at Richard like a canker and it was not the choice of a wife.

"And shall I have a voice when lands are offered or rents?"

"I swear it, although I expect you would be guided by me in this matter."

"Henceforth I must be directed by you in all things?"

Hugh felt his temper surge again. "That is the way of the world. I was ruled by my father as he was by his."

"If I recall, my grandfather did not want you to go to Outremer on crusade. You insisted and went. He wished you had married, as the eldest son must, and you have chosen to ignore this virtuous path and swyve whores. My grandfather showed his love for you by letting you do as you wished. Thus I conclude that you love me less since you demand I follow your commands without asking me if I concur."

"What do you want that I am not offering?" Hugh now lost control of his passions and slammed his hand down on the table. The ewer overturned, knocking the masers to the floor. The wine seeped into the rushes, leaving a large dark stain.

Richard stepped so close to his father that they could smell the sharp odor of anger in each other's breath. "I want to take vows, father. I want to become a priest."

Hugh staggered back.

"Father Eliduc has been teaching me what I must know to do so and wishes me to enter the service of the new Archbishop of Canterbury. Are you so blasphemous that you would dare deny that such a position brings great honor to the family? My aunt has done so as prioress of Tyndal and many say she has been blessed by the Virgin with a vision. Has she not brought honor to the family? Dare you deny what God's service brings to our souls?" He knelt. "Prove your love for me, as my grandfather proved his love for you. You longed to win Jerusalem back from the Infidel. Grant my plea to become a priest so that I may save souls."

The pounding in Hugh's ears grew as loud as the crash of rocks flung by trebuchets against castle walls. His eyes lost focus, and he blinked furiously, trying to clear his vision of the blood red haze. Reaching behind him, Hugh braced himself against the stone wall and tried to breathe. But the wall felt about to crumble and bury him in dust and sharp rock. He gasped as if the dust was already choking him, and he began to hear the screams of men buried in rubble around him.

"I wait for your response, my lord."

Hugh shook his head, and the visions from Hell retreated. Opening his eyes wide, he looked down at his kneeling son and saw a callow, self-righteous youth who smugly dared to condemn him like so many other ignorant men who pointed fingers at others while breaking God's commandments themselves.

"Never," he hissed.

"I would rather hang than become a man like you, drinking blood like wine and reeking of impious lusts like a goat." Richard shouted. "You are evil!"

Hugh spun around and strode to the door. As he put his hand against the wood, he turned and looked again at the son he no longer recognized.

"Then hang," he said and disappeared out the door.

Chapter Twenty

Sir Walter looked around the small room, cluttered with items that had belonged to Hawis. He rarely spent time with her so was surprised at the disarray. Had the latest maid fled like the last one over her perverse demands?

He exhaled loudly and with annoyance. If his dead wife preferred to live like a swineherd, he did not care, but he had hoped a brief search would reveal anything that ought not remain here after her death and become the subject of unwarranted questioning. At times, his life and hers had been intertwined in ways he now regretted.

Impatiently, he tore off lids to boxes, tossed aside the few pieces of jewelry, and kicked at clothing on the floor. It was all of no avail. There was nothing found except a dead mouse under the bed.

The sight of the stained bed linen he greeted with a grunt of contempt. "Whore," he muttered, but his derision was not so complete that he could not ram his fist repeatedly into the bedding to test it. There were no lumps in the mattress or pillows that warranted further investigation.

Walking over to the large chest, he swept his hand over the wooden lid to remove impediments to his search.

Pottery shattered into shards on the floor, or bounced into corners, scattering colored powders and odd-smelling liquids.

He raised the carved lid, looked inside, then drew back in revulsion. There was a strong odor of menstrual blood from unwashed cloths. He slammed the lid down and tried not to vomit.

As a man, he barely tolerated the odor of a woman's courses and expected the creatures, including his mistresses, to seclude themselves on those days when they bled like wounded sows. The Church properly forbade intercourse when they did, but he never understood why a man would want to lie with a woman at such times. The very idea disgusted him.

"My lord?"

Sir Walter looked over his shoulder.

Torold responded with a meek demeanor when he noticed the heightened color of his lord's face, a hue that meant he had either drunk too much or was angry about something. "Your brother begs to speak with you," he murmured.

"Of course, he does," Sir Walter snarled. "He is a most inconvenient man. Where is he?"

"He asks that you go to his chambers." Out of habit, Torold quickly stepped aside.

His liege lord stomped past, with little regard for the narrowness of the space, and into the hall. Torold frowned, but a clearer manifestation of complaint was imprudent. Although he sometimes dreamed of it, he was wise enough to understand that he would starve if he acted on these wild imaginings.

As he was expected to do, Torold shut the door. Following Sir Walter to the rooms of the brother, he asked himself whether he disliked the dead whore more or her bawd husband.

◇◇◇

"Where is it?" Sir Walter poured a large cup of wine and took a full mouthful. His eyes grew big, and he spat all of it onto the floor. "Surely the income I so generously grant is enough to offer me a wine that hasn't turned to vinegar."

Maynard folded his arms and tried to look defiant, but he was more accustomed to quailing. Lowering his head, he mumbled an apology.

"Speak, you idiot! I gave it to you for safekeeping. Where is it?"

"I don't know," Maynard whispered.

"You do not know. You do not…" Sir Walter spun around and hurled the rest of the undrinkable wine into his younger brother's face.

The wine stung his eyes, and Maynard cried out in pain.

Walter walked up to him and grabbed a handful of cloth around his brother's throat. "You were never clever enough to fool a newborn babe, but I did think you knew how to hide something as simple as what I put into your safekeeping."

Maynard's eyes bulged as his face turned a light shade of purple. "I beg…" he coughed out but could say nothing more.

"Cokenay! You wonder why I laughed when my wife told me you had been trying to bed her?"

The brother attempted to shake himself free.

Walter pushed him away. "Oh, don't look so wretched. I didn't care what you tried to do with her. The rumors of your inadequacies saved me from wearing any horns on your account. A squirrel would be embarrassed to own a member the size of yours."

"Brother, I…"

"Where is the document signed by ben David? Do not think you can lie. Your attempt to do so would be feeble, and I am disinclined to tolerance at the moment."

"It is missing."

Sir Walter backed him against a wall, pulled out a dagger, and held it under the younger brother's eye.

Maynard howled in terror.

"You do not need these if you could not keep a watchful eye on the agreement I gave you."

"It was in that chest near my bed when I last looked." Terrified beyond endurance, Maynard's bladder emptied.

Walter stepped away and watched the pool foaming on the rushes around his brother's feet. "Clean that up, you wretch. It smells like a latrine in here."

Maynard found a rag, sopped up what he could of the urine, and tossed the cloth into the small fireplace. "I swear on any holy relic that it was there. I looked every day. It is now gone."

"And you laid it on top of everything else in the chest. Am I right?"

Maynard nodded.

"So anyone could find it easily and steal it quickly if they wished."

Maynard wanted to vomit. At least he had nothing left in his bladder.

"Was my whorish wife ever in here?"

"Once or twice."

Walter's grin was sarcastic. "Her idea?"

Maynard knew there was no need for a reply.

"I thought so. She sent me a message about it, you see, along with tales of how you begged her to pleasure you. Shall I now describe in detail how she mocked that tiny flap of flesh you call your manhood?"

"I have never been disloyal to you!" Maynard slid to his knees and raised his hands for mercy.

"Stand up, cokenay. I do not accuse you of disloyalty because you fumbled at my wife. I condemn you for incompetence, a far greater crime."

"The document must be in her chambers."

"So even a half-wit would assume. But I have looked and found nothing hidden amongst her silly baubles and pots of whatever women use to make themselves look younger for virginal boys."

"Did I not tell you that she lay with boys?" Maynard looked hopeful.

"And do you not realize that I already knew? It suited me for awhile. Besotted youths give gifts of value, which she passed on to me for sale. But her usefulness had ended. Queen Eleanor discovered her sins and planned to dismiss her. I was arranging to exile my wife to a convent for her impious lust. That would reclaim my honor and find favor with our liege lord." He glared at his brother. "But you have failed me in a far worse manner than she did with her whoring."

"I did not know…"

"Nor did you look for the document until I asked for it." Sir Walter smiled as he slowly lowered the knife he still held in his hand until the point rested on Maynard's groin.

"Please, brother!"

"I am losing patience, Maynard. I keep you from starvation, but you do little except sin against me in return."

His brother yelped in protest.

"Dare you deny it? You expose your nakedness to my wife, hoping she will make a man out of you. You lose a document that I gave you for safekeeping. Torold serves me better than you. Tell me why I should not pay him all I waste on a useless brother? After all, he might like a wife to share his bed."

"Because you and I came from the same womb!"

"Then prove it! Find the document. If you cannot, I must conclude our mother was a whore and you are no kin to my father."

"I may not be able to do so. FitzRoald and Prioress Eleanor were in the room after your wife was found dead. Perhaps one of them found it."

Sir Walter put his knife into his belt, took his brother's head in both hands, and slowly squeezed until Maynard whimpered. "Listen carefully. You shall find it and bring it to me. I do not care what you have to do, but I hold you responsible for finding my document. Should you fail, I may find evidence that my mother committed adultery, and you are no heir to my father." He shoved him back. "Think of your belly, Maynard. It may soon make friends with your spine if you must beg on the king's highway. Indeed, no one would blame me for casting you forth, if you made me a cuckold after stealing money you had no right to beg from me. I swear I shall humiliate and abandon you."

Maynard fell to his knees on the damp rushes, squealing for mercy.

Sir Walter spat at him and strode out of the room.

Reaching back in to grab the rope handle, Torold pulled the chamber door shut behind his master.

Chapter Twenty-one

Hugh found the hour ride to Oxford on his ambling palfrey calming. He ought to have remained at his father's side in prayer, but God surely preferred the spiritual purity in his sister's pleas. If their father died before he returned, he would add this failure to the multitude of sins he was rapidly accumulating.

He glanced upward and noted that the color of the sky was neither blue nor gray. Even the world reflected his quandary. He was bitterly amused. One day he might be able to define all the reasons he raged against God, but his simpler grievances included deaths that made no sense and why men called godly acted more like Satan's imps than angels.

On the rare occasion he did pray, he spent the moments abusing God. Although priests had accused him of choosing Satan as his liege lord, he had never been so tempted. It was God he held responsible for the ills of the world. Only He had the power to create and destroy. In comparison, the Devil was a boring mountebank.

But most of the time, he did not even bother to rail, letting himself fester with enmity in silence. If he chose to speak, he put the full force of his ire into mocking those who claimed a closer connection to Heaven because they had a round spot shaved in the middle of their pink skulls.

Brother Thomas, however, was a dilemma. Hugh had hated the monk, believing he had raped the son of a friend. Sodomites were despicable, disdaining the gender with which God had blessed them. He exemplified all Hugh found loathsome in men who took vows, then lied about honoring them.

But the monk had saved his life at the risk of his own, served his sister and the Wynethorpe family with devotion and honor, and stood by his son when he needed a father and Hugh was nowhere near. Often he resented the bond between monk and Richard, but he loved his boy too much to deny what Brother Thomas had done for him. With a feeling oddly akin to regret, Hugh finally cast aside his contempt and, in a figurative sense, decided to embrace the monk.

And now he was at war with Richard and did not know how to parley with him. How could his son rebel against him? His sister had urged tenderness, but this gesture was impossible for him. The lad had chosen a vocation filled with liars and frauds, despite Hugh's long expressed objections. He might be skilled in dialogue with the enemy while besieging their castles, but this was one treaty he did not know how to negotiate.

To his surprise and discomfort, Hugh was tempted to confide in Brother Thomas. As different as the two men were, he sensed the man would understand his confusion and certainly shared his love for his boy. Perhaps he could also understand why Baron Adam had wanted this monk to hear his final confession. When it came time for him to die, Hugh realized he might well call on Brother Thomas himself. Only a great sinner like the monk could comprehend the depths to which Hugh was falling.

The horse snorted and pulled the knight out of the reverie. Looking down the road, he realized he was approaching the walls of Oxford and his intended destination, the Jewish Quarter.

Was there a connection linking ben David's hanging to the arrival of the women at Woodstock Manor and then to the murder? It was in the Quarter he hoped to learn something that would shed light on what had happened to ben David, a mockery of justice about which he felt deeply and one that might also shed light on the murder of Mistress Hawis. This was also a journey only he could undertake.

He wrinkled his nose. The distinctive odor of the town's tanneries was growing stronger.

When he had left his son, he fled to his own chambers and smashed every breakable object he could find until his palms bled. He did not even realize what he had done until his choler cooled and his humors regained balance. In that exhausted calm he knew he had to return to the Oxford Jewish Quarter and seek answers.

He was able to use the word *love* when he thought of Richard, but it was not a word he could utter. The last time he had spoken the word was to Lucas, a man who converted from Islam to Christianity so he could return with Hugh to England. While he lived, Lucas was the only one who knew how to calm Hugh's rages and soothe him when he awoke, screaming from nightmares. They had been like brothers, and then Lucas began to feel pains in his belly. By the time he had sought Lumbard ben David, the cancer had eaten through him. Now Hugh was alone. Only the servants heard his howls and saw his furies. The wise ones soon learned when to run from his feral violence.

The throng of merchants and travelers grew larger. He set aside his sorrow over the death of a good man and guided his horse with care.

Hugh had left Woodstock Manor to find those who might talk to him, despite the raids and hangings. He would not be welcome in the Quarter, but, for the sake of Lucas, a man well known in this community for his healing skills, he hoped he would be tolerated enough to get answers. The High Sheriff, Brother Thomas, and Prioress Eleanor most certainly would not.

He entered the town gate and eased his palfrey through the crowd of marketing wives, bickering students, pleading beggars, and rattling carts. His heart ached with sorrow. The route to Great Jewry Street was one he swore never to take again, and he made himself concentrate on why he had been forced to break that oath.

Hugh thought it odd that Mistress Hawis' murder occurred at the time ben David's mother and daughters arrived to see the queen. He doubted the trio had done it. Mistress Chera was too old and the girls too young for such a crime, although they had every reason for anger. Ben David should not have been one of the eight from Oxford arrested and hanged for money clipping.

Why had he been? Was the king growing so lax about justice, so desperate for money, that he arrested an entire community, held mock trials, and confiscated property without caring who was guilty or not? King Edward always needed coin, Hugh reminded himself, but he also believed in the rule of law.

When it came to imagining what harm would be done to the Jewish community as a consequence of his decisions, Hugh had learned that the king was oblivious. And, as it did four years ago when he proclaimed the Statute of the Jewry, it took Edward a long time to understand that his orders were being used to hide acts of revenge and greed. Hugh suspected that many had taken advantage of the coin-clipping arrests for their own gain.

His sister told him that evidence of the treason had been found. Based on what he and Lucas had known about ben David, Hugh suspected that the proof must have been placed in the roof by someone with a grudge against the physician. The unwarranted arrest surely hid a sinister motive.

Hugh reined in his horse and sat for a moment looking up the hill from the poorer neighborhood to the more affluent one. Although this area surrounding Great Jewry Street was predominantly Jewish, many Christians lived here as their neighbors. How sad that this harmony of trust, which had lasted for years longer than most men lived, should have suffered these wounding blows.

Compared to the bustle of the central town, Hugh noted that this street was quiet. The Jews remained inside their mostly stone houses, fearing arrests and even greater violence. The Christians did the same, not knowing how to respond to the recent accusations against many they called friends or how to deal with the fear on the faces of those who had not been imprisoned.

Hugh urged his horse forward. It did not matter to him that guilty men, and perhaps one woman, had been hanged for a crime deemed treasonable. He cared only that one innocent man had also been executed and his own son might face the hangman because that death sentence had taken place.

Chapter Twenty-two

Hugh dismounted in front of a row of shops. Most were closed, although he was quite aware it was not the Jewish Sabbath. If memory did not fail him, there was a tavern in the basement of one of these places. An inn might be for travelers and townsmen alike, but a tavern was where neighbors gathered without the uneasiness strangers always brought. If he was fortunate, he might be welcomed there as a friend of Lucas and learn something that an ordinary stranger could not.

A small group of men emerged from a dark alley but were so engaged in what appeared to be a friendly but heated discussion that they failed to see him a few yards behind.

One man did hear Hugh's footstep, spun around, and uttered an alarm.

Like a flock of threatened birds, the men dispersed in several different directions.

"Wait! I bear you no malice," Hugh shouted after them. "I seek the home of Lumbard ben David, the physician. He gave ease to my brother before he died, and I have come to pay the good doctor what he is still owed."

Although the others chose to ignore his pleas and disappeared into the shadows of overhanging buildings and narrow walkways, an older man turned back.

"How long is your arm?" he asked as he approached the knight. His cap, riding atop his lead-gray hair, was soft. The peak curled over on itself in the style often worn by Jewish men outside their houses.

"I do not understand," Hugh replied.

"You will have to reach beyond the grave. The man you seek is dead."

The sorrow Hugh expressed was honest, even if his surprise at the news was feigned. "Then I shall give what is owed to his family," he said. "Tell me where they live. I believe he was a widower, but his mother, Mistress Chera, lived with him and his two daughters."

The man raised an eyebrow, a bitter smile showing through his thick gray beard. "Where have you been, my lord, that you have heard nothing about our people's recent trials?"

Hugh forced himself to blink with mild confusion, and then confessed he had just returned from the north.

The man carefully looked him up and down. "Engaged in service to our king, I would guess."

Before he could reply, Hugh saw several younger men step out of the shadows between the stores. Although they bore no weapons, their grim expressions declared their intent not to permit any harm to come to this older man who had chosen to speak with the knight.

One young man stepped forward. "Rav, this man accompanied Lucas the Wise to consult with Lumbard ben David. I saw them together. Our physician declared that he found no malice in this man who now stands before you."

The older man studied the knight's face but showed no sign of recognition. "Your name?"

"Hugh of Wynethorpe. Lucas was my brother in all ways except birth. He saved my life in Outremer and was rightly called the Wise for his skill in rebalancing the ravaged humors after the body's war wounds had healed. He and a good physician in London often consulted. When Lucas fell gravely ill, Master Gamel referred him to Lumbard ben David, a man the physician called a friend and whom he respected for his knowledge and compassion. Because my brother has died, I have finally come to pay what more is owed, for ben David showed mercy, did all he could to save Lucas' life, and then helped to make his death a less painful one."

"I have heard of Master Gamel of London," the older man replied as he glanced at the young man who now stood beside him.

"This man is not one of the soldiers who ravaged our homes," the young man added in a softer voice.

With a slight smile, the older man watched Hugh's reaction to the scrutiny, and then said, "Lucas was not of your faith while he lived in Acre."

How did this man know that? "He converted, but I met him before then. As I have said, we were brothers for a very long time." Hugh carefully laid emphasis on that last sentence.

The older man nodded his understanding. "Then come and share a cup of wine, Hugh of Wynethorpe. I shall tell you the news of what happened while you were in the north, and you will see why the purpose of your journey must remain unfulfilled."

"You cannot go to our tavern, Rev," one of the men behind him said, extending a cautionary hand. "The owner may no longer sell food and drink to a Christian, lest both he and the customer be fined."

The old man sighed. "In Oxford, we and our Christian neighbors have always lived together in harmony," he said to Hugh. "This old prohibition of social separation has long been honored best by disobedience. But, when our king returned to England, he looked around his land and concluded that many had lost respect for the law. Now, he insists on rigorous enforcement, even when it causes sorrow amongst those innocent of any ill intent."

"Yet there is merit in rectifying the laxity we suffered under his dead father," Hugh replied. "A country without the rule of law is no place for good men."

"Indeed, my lord, yet is it not a sad time when friends discover they may no longer greet each other with affection but must now react with fear?"

Hugh chose not to reply or, as he truly suspected, he remained silent because he had no answer.

"But, if you are willing to accompany me, I offer a meager hospitality within the walls of my home, where no money shall be exchanged and the courtesies may be accepted or rejected as you wish."

Hugh followed him up the hill.

◇◇◇

Hugh sat on a bench and bit into a portion of bread that was still warm from the oven. "I have told you my name, but I am ignorant of yours. The men called you *rev*?"

His host poured wine and set the cup within reach of his guest should he wish it. "I am a teacher of the Torah, my lord, and thus men honor me with the word which means that in our community. You have met some of my former pupils. Like most who teach, I am both loved and not so loved."

Hugh laughed.

"Joshua of Oxford is my name. I am a baker by trade but offer lessons in the yeshiva without payment, as my faith requires."

"Can any price ever be placed on wisdom?" Hugh replied.

"I hear the voice of a man called *Lucas* in that question. Members of my family knew his in the land you call Outremer," Joshua of Oxford replied. Then he sat down, took a sip of wine, and grew solemn. "You did not come here to debate the glory of knowledge or the meaning of truth, my lord." He studied the outside of his cup for a moment. "Nor did you come here to repay a debt. You did not need directions to the house of Lumbard ben David. You knew it well."

Hugh nodded and finished his wine. "I do not understand why ben David was arrested."

"Nor do we. He was innocent, although Sir Walter found evidence of treason, but we all knew it was hidden by someone with malign intent. There was no trial worthy of the name, and ben David was one of hundreds hanged across the land." He sighed. "We have sent word to our king that his representatives have cruelly abused his good name and without his knowledge in this sad matter. Blameless ones have been executed. The pace of executions has slowed, and we hope to save those still imprisoned but not yet hanged."

"Why hide false evidence? Did the physician have enemies amongst Jews or Christians?"

"Within our community, he was beloved, a generous man to the unfortunate and a skilled healer. Although in times past I would have doubted that anyone of your faith in Oxford would have disliked him, let alone despised him enough to call him a traitor worthy of the scaffold, we have been forced now to wonder if we are not all loathed by our neighbors."

Hugh took another chunk of bread and chewed it, waiting for the man to continue.

"I must beg your forgiveness. If one man condemns everyone for the sins of some, does that mean I should do the same? It is wrong, yet I have just committed that error. You are a rare man, here to seek truth and not convenient conclusions." He paused and took a deep breath. "Despite the raids and hangings, I know of no one in Oxford, Jew or Christian, who wanted to send this innocent man to his death."

"Those words show a generous spirit, but I am not convinced he had no enemies."

"Then I shall swear it again. Lumbard ben David had no foes. We honored him. Many Christians sought out his skills, praised him, and paid his honest fees."

Hugh shook his head, clearly unhappy.

Joshua frowned and sat back. "But there was one strange incident."

Hugh grew eager with anticipation. "Explain what you mean," he said and asked for more wine.

"There were many raids that night. Sir Walter and his men took nothing from the houses where arrests took place until the next day. At ben David's home, the king's man sealed the doors and left one guard until he could return. Even Mistress Chera and the girls were thrown into the street so no one remained inside. Yet a man slipped into the house that night. I saw him."

"And why were you there?" Hugh asked. He regretted his chill tone, but it took all his strength to still his pounding heart. If this detail were confirmed, it could lead to something more that might save his son. He was desperate.

"My cousin had been arrested, and I was seeking a place for his large family to find refuge." He gestured around the room. "As you see, these lodgings over my bakery are small. Otherwise, I would not have chanced any meeting with soldiers that night. It was a dangerous time for anyone of my faith to be on the streets."

"A man entered?" Hugh betrayed his impatience. "Was he kin to ben David? A friend?"

"Neither, as far as I could tell. I did not recognize him, but he was not in the house long. He soon left with a large bag and disappeared. Needless to say, I did not follow him, but he fled away from Great Jewry Street toward the center of town."

Hugh was not sure what he should make of this news. "What more can you tell me of this?"

"The next day, I saw Sir Walter when he retuned to the house. He was outraged to discover the theft. There were items missing, objects he considered valuable and would fatten the king's purse. The first thing he did was threaten to beat the guard, but the man swore he was innocent and claimed he could not be everywhere at once."

"Did you mention what you had witnessed?"

"At first, I did not. Sir Walter was in a rage, now claiming one of us had committed the crime. He even accused Mistress Chera and her granddaughters of slipping inside, despite the guard, and taking the treasures."

Hugh frowned. "That part I find perplexing. The house is not hard to watch. I wonder that Sir Walter so easily accepted the guard's argument that he could not be everywhere at once."

Joshua smiled. "These were my thoughts as well. The guard did not appear on his rounds until after the thief had left." He shrugged. "To be fair to the man, he may have needed to unburden himself of a tainted meat pie."

Under different circumstances, Hugh might have laughed, but he was too worried. "Did you ever find the right time to tell all this to Sir Walter?"

"Yes, but he accused me first of being blind and next of lying. With adequate courtesy and a meek enough demeanor, I persuaded him that I knew the difference between a woman and a man, a child and a grown woman, so the culprit could not have been either ben David's mother or his daughters. He remained convinced the thief was a Jew, and I could give him no adequate description. Soon he left us in peace. Indeed, we were grateful that he did not send his soldiers on a new search of all our houses in retaliation for the theft at ben David's."

"Did he do anything more to find the items that had been taken? Question others? Suggest any known thieves in Oxford who might have done this? Students are often good suspects."

"He did not confide what his plans were, but he still has not instigated any further night raids, nor has he questioned any of the Jewish families who lived near ben David."

Further discussion produced nothing more of worth, but Hugh was thankful for the information he had gained. Joshua of Oxford promised to send word if he learned more. The tale of the thief did not solve the murder of Mistress Hawis, but Hugh decided that his sister and her wily monk might see meaning in such things that was lost to him.

He thanked his host and rose to leave.

"If you think of any way in which I can be of further help in finding the answer to this tragedy, please send word," Joshua said. "You know where I live."

"I shall," the knight replied.

As they walked out into the street, Hugh realized that this older man's company had been congenial and believed the teacher might feel the same about his. Perhaps he could come back, after peace returned to Oxford, and find some of that comfort he had lost after the death of Lucas?

Then he chided himself for the thought. Hope, in Hugh's opinion, was the most deceitful and cruel imp of all.

As they stood by the knight's horse, Joshua suddenly said: "Forgive me, my lord, if I cause offense by this observation, but it is kindly meant. I fear you suffer a torment so profound that a man might die from it." He paused, and then added, "I shall pray that you find solace."

Hugh said nothing. For a long moment, he looked at the silent street that had once bustled with carts and merchants. In a space between buildings, a whirl of dust rose and spun like a tortured ghost. He winced as he fought back the image of yet another horror from Outremer. Men might deserve suffering for the deeds they committed, he thought, but why did God curse the innocent?

As if reading his thoughts, the baker's expression softened with compassion.

With a swift gesture, Hugh reached into his cloak and drew forth a fat purse. "This is for the children who have now been made orphans," he said in a whisper to Joshua of Oxford and tossed the purse to him.

Then Hugh mounted his palfrey and rode off before the teacher could either protest or thank him.

Had the knight turned around, he might have seen the older man, no longer forced to hide his profound grief, weeping.

Chapter Twenty-three

Brother Thomas sat near Prioress Eleanor in the dining hall. Quickly glancing at her face, he realized that her eyes had sunk even deeper into bruised sockets since this murder had occurred. She was so weary with fatigue and grief, he thought, but she never complained.

When Sister Anne had sent them away on some vague pretext, he knew she wanted him to force their prioress to get some rest, no matter how brief. Not only was he glad the nun had come to care for the dying, he was grateful she was here to watch over the living. Even Sir Hugh listened to her with a hint of meekness, something he did not do with others.

"Where is my brother?" The prioress looked around, ignoring the food he had brought from the kitchen and placed in front of her on the table.

"Someone might have called him away." He edged a mazer of ale closer to her hand.

She looked up at him with affection. "That was a kind hint," she said and took a courteous sip. "But I have no interest in eating, despite our sub-infirmarian's orders to the contrary." Looking down at the offering, she grimaced. Although he had brought no meat, honoring her commitment to the Benedictine Rule on diet, he had chosen bread not long from the oven and a fine piece of cheese. The fragrance may have tempted him, but it did not tempt her.

"Sister Anne's commands should never be ignored," he replied with calculated gravity.

Eleanor nodded and took a morsel of cheese. Her expression betrayed her realization that the taste held greater appeal than expected. After another bite, she looked up. "Have you met Sir Walter?"

He shook his head. "I have seen him with his brother and servant but held no conversation with any of them."

"From all reports, he is a man of the world and a successful one at that. Surely he was not ignorant of the tales about his wife coupling with squires since the queen knew. She was so angry, she told Mistress Hawis that she would dismiss her from court, a decision and rationale she would have shared with our king once she was recovered enough to travel to his side."

"And we mustn't forget the rumors of an affair between Maynard and Mistress Hawis. Sir Walter did not look pleased with his sibling."

"Even if that tale was untrue, the brother must have known about the squires. He spends more time near the court than Sir Walter. Perhaps the source of his displeasure was Maynard's failure to tell him about it."

"I agree that he must have heard. Few husbands are blind when men point to the horns on their heads. Even if the tale did not come from Maynard, Torold is a loyal and sharp-eyed servant. Little would escape his knowledge. Although there was no cause for him to do so when I walked past, the man kept his eyes lowered but watched me nonetheless. I believe he would have told his master of rumors."

"Torold is not exactly a servant but holds a lesser status than a friend. He is a poor knight whom Sir Walter supports. Neither fish nor fowl, I fear. That must be hard to bear."

"So is starvation," Thomas replied, but he agreed with his prioress. "Torold looked like a man who holds his survival dearer than virtue."

"Then he would have told Sir Walter that his wife invited boys into her bed."

The odor of horse sweat announced the arrival of the man who joined them on the bench.

"From the expressions on your faces, I must assume you are having a profound discussion. If it is not theological, may I join you?" Sir Hugh looked grim. "How fares our father?" he asked his sister, ignoring the monk.

"He is alive but not for long, I fear." She chose not to ask where he had been.

But he read her expression well enough and held up a hand to suggest he had a tale to tell. First, he swung around to face the monk. "I spoke to my son. We argued. He is innocent but refuses to recant his confession. He also told me of his mad desire to become a priest and has been driven to such fervor that he prefers death if he is forbidden to take vows." With fury burning in his eyes, he leaned closer to Thomas. "I thought he was becoming a man, but he remains an ignorant child who knows nothing of the world and has had his wits blunted by a wicked man."

Eleanor remained silent.

"I had naught to do with his desire for the priesthood, my lord. You are his father," Thomas replied with care. "I would expect him to share any hopes and the reasons behind them most fully with you." This news that Richard had refused all compromise on vocation frightened him, and he grew angry again with Father Eliduc. He must speak with the lad. This once, he agreed with Sir Hugh. Men might choose martyrdom, knowing full well what the decision means, but a child who has never had his hand burned does not understand flames.

Hugh's smile was thin, but he nodded acceptance of Thomas' remark. Leaning on the table, he now bent forward to speak more privately with his sister. "I shall not leave our father again, but the conversation I had with my son drove me to seek some fact, a detail, anything that would prove his innocence. I rode to the Jewish Quarter of Oxford and have just returned." He explained why he had decided to find out more information about Lumbard ben David's arrest and repeated the baker's tale of the thief.

Eleanor looked hopeful "Might this man identify the thief if he saw him again?"

Hugh shrugged. "I failed to ask, but he did say that the man was not of the community and most certainly was not a woman."

"You know ben David's family to be honorable," the prioress said, "which was my impression of Mistress Chera when we spoke after she was confined to my quarters. But her appearance here just before the murder of a woman, who had cruelly mocked her, is an unfortunate coincidence. That still troubles me. This new detail does not clear Mistress Chera of suspicion, but it might help to weaken any accusation against her. Do you know if other houses were robbed?"

"Again, I confess I did not think to ask, but Joshua of Oxford suggested that Sir Walter was furious over this theft, as if it were an unusual lapse. That makes me believe the crime only occurred at ben David's house."

"The sheriff does not believe ben David's mother is guilty of murder either, but he cannot ignore the threats she made against Sir Walter's wife, any more than he can ignore your son's confession and his proximity to Hawis on the night of her death." Thomas watched Hugh turn ghostly pale.

"Let us summarize thus." Eleanor began to touch each finger. "We have the raid on ben David's house by Sir Walter, the threats by Mistress Chera against Mistress Hawis after the latter's abuse, the mysterious thief, and the murder of Sir Walter's wife on the night Richard commits adultery with her and the Jewish women arrive at Woodstock." She looked over at her brother. "And we have the man in the hall outside the dead woman's chambers who your son thought was you. This unknown man may or may not be guilty of the murder, but he might be a witness to one and we have yet to identify him."

"The robbery might not be related to the murder, but it did occur in ben David's house and perhaps was the only incident of plundering." Thomas shook his head as if to clear it.

"And because of that, we must not set it aside," Eleanor replied. "Shall we all agree that we have two factors here which no one has investigated: the theft and the man outside the chambers?"

The men nodded agreement.

"The lurker in the hall may have been a servant," Hugh said. "It was most certainly not me."

Eleanor raised an eyebrow. "Where were you?"

He glared at her. "I was with another one of our queen's ladies."

"Will she vouch for your presence?" Her expression suggested she was both relieved and displeased in equal measure.

His grin was brief. "One of the queen's dogs will. He is a spaniel named El Acebo and seems to have grown fond of me. He followed me to the lady's chamber. To keep him from raising any alarm, I gave him a bit of meat. He was so grateful he did not betray me, and I am sure he will remember the bribe."

In spite of herself, Eleanor laughed. Hugh may be a sinful man, she thought with less conviction than she knew she should feel, but she was touched by the gift of food to the dog. The gesture suggested that her brother had not lost all gentleness.

Hugh looked around to see if anyone was within hearing distance. "I should not be a suspect, although I pray that the woman shall remain nameless. She fears the queen's wrath."

"No one has accused you, my lord," Thomas said. "There should be no reason for her to be shamed." He glanced at his prioress.

Eleanor nodded, then grew solemn. "I think it best if you tell us all that my nephew imparted in your conversation, including the reason you quarreled further."

Hugh's cheeks burned with fury. "Did you know of this abomination?"

"What do you mean, brother?" Her tone was icy.

Hugh bent over as if he had been stabbed in the belly. "That he wants to be a priest," he hissed in agony, "a follower of that imp in black, Father Eliduc." He reached out to his sister. "Swear that this is none of your doing!"

"I did not urge my nephew to find a vocation with God instead of King Edward. And I most certainly would not have encouraged his attachment to Father Eliduc. Shall I swear it on the altar?"

"You are my sister. Your word is enough." Hugh turned to Brother Thomas. "And you? Did you know of this folly, even if you did not cause the cancer to take hold?"

The monk was angry and slammed his palm on the table. "The first I have heard of this vocation is here at Woodstock Manor." He feared that was saying too much but hoped the knight would not consider his phrasing too carefully.

"When he told me he would rather hang than follow the ways of knights," Hugh said, his voice cracking, "I told him he could hang."

"Hugh!" Eleanor leapt to her feet. "I do not care how much you hate men who serve God. Some are godly, even though others, like Father Eliduc, are not. If your son has a wish to serve God, let him do so. He is a good lad and will bring the family honor."

"Aye, sister, there are good men who chose to serve Him. In you, I have before me a saintly woman of the same vocation, a virtuous servant of God who brings renown to the family name. Nonetheless, I shall refuse his wish. He shall do as I, his lord and father, command, and he will do so with respectful obedience!"

Thomas cleared his throat. "May I make a suggestion?"

The knight half-stood, his features distorted with fury.

"Silence, Hugh," Eleanor said to her scarlet-faced brother. "Let him speak. If you disagree, do so with courtesy. He is a monk of my priory and deserves to be heard." Seeing him sit back like a chastised boy, she let out the breath she had been holding.

"Should we not set aside the issue of Richard's vocation until he is freed of all guilt in this murder? He spoke as a child might of martyrdom, not as a man. I cannot believe he would actually choose to hang as he told you, but, once proven innocent, he will not have the option of martyrdom. As we all love the lad, we must set aside any differences and use all our wits and energy in proving him innocent, whether or not he wishes that. Then he can be approached with reason."

Hugh dug his fists into his eyes, then looked at the pair of religious before him and laughed. The sound held no merriment and was rough to the ear. "I cannot argue," he replied with a gesture of surrender. "I want my son to live."

"The news you got from the Jewish Quarter is valuable, Hugh," Eleanor said. "Since Mistress Chera is in my chamber, I shall question her further about anything she might know. Perhaps she saw or even recognized the robber."

"And I shall question others, my lady. I feel there is much more to know." Thomas gave her a significant look.

Eleanor knew exactly whom he wished to question further. It was a man whose name should not be mentioned in front of her brother. And if Father Eliduc had infected her nephew with this deadly zeal, she would hate him more even though she feared it would be a long time before she could repent the sin.

"I shall seek out the lady with whom I spent a pleasant night," Hugh said as he rose. "I need wine and comfort after the ride to Oxford." He turned away.

"Hugh." Eleanor's tone suggested a rare plea.

He looked back and smiled sadly. "Not all trysts lead to sin, dearest sister, and my weariness precludes more than a few chaste kisses. Fear not. I shall seek confession before I leave here and perform whatever penance I am given." He looked at Thomas and raised his eyebrows with a question. "Will you hear it, Brother?"

The monk, bewildered, nodded agreement to hear the confession. His first thought was to wonder if this man was able to feel profound contrition or even understand the depth of his sins. His second was to remind himself that he also had quarrels with God over acts deemed by the Church to be monstrous.

"I may be a wicked man, sister, but I am not unaware of the consequences." With that, he bowed and left them in the hall.

Eleanor watched her brother walk away and grieved. With a father dying, a beloved nephew accused of murder, and a brother teetering on the edge of Hell, she had more sorrow than she could keep locked within her heart.

Chapter Twenty-four

Thomas did not like the company of courtiers.

When word came that Baron Adam was dying, Brother Thomas was honored that his prioress asked him to stay by her side through the expected anguish of bidding a father that earthly farewell. Nonetheless, he would have preferred not to go to Woodstock Manor.

Looking around as he hurried down the corridor, he was grateful that the people here were mostly the queen's attendants. There was less likelihood that he would be recognized as his dead father's illegitimate son.

"How arrogant you are," he muttered aloud and slowed his pace.

After almost ten years, the tale of the bastard son who had been caught in bed with another man, imprisoned, and then sent off to an obscure priory in East Anglia had surely been forgotten or else never heard. King Edward might recall, or others in his company, but those men had left the manor before Thomas arrived.

Hearing the sharp barking of many dogs, he stopped at a window and glanced down at the courtyard. The queen's hunting pack was being taken out for exercise by the young man whom he remembered as Richard's friend.

The monk smiled. Might a young priest in service to a great bishop be allowed the gift of a pup, he wondered. A hunting pack was inappropriate for a sincere man of God, but one dog does not make a pack. Even if Sir Hugh refused to relent and forced his son into a military vocation, Thomas decided Richard should have a dog to bring him comfort when this terrible time was over. Men might claim that animals had no souls, but he knew that some men's hearts glowed with love for these creatures deemed inferior. He would mention the gift to his prioress at a more peaceful time.

Looking beyond the leaping hounds, he noticed Maynard and Torold standing together near the stable. What a mismatched twosome they made, the monk thought. Even standing, Sir Walter's brother was awkward and pale, quite unlike his rubicund brother. Torold had the bulk of a rock and was brown from the sun. Was Maynard capable of killing a woman out of jealousy and making it look like self-murder? Rage gave even a weak man unnatural strength, he thought.

"What an odd pairing."

The priest's voice was both unwelcome and too close. Thomas felt the man's hot breath and winced as if touched by fire.

"I wonder at it." Father Eliduc smiled like an imp eager to begin the torment of a new soul in Hell.

Thomas edged away from Father Eliduc as politely as possible. The priest's frightening ability to utter what he himself was thinking put him on edge. But as much as he might hate the man, the monk needed him in this matter of Richard's involvement in murder.

"You seem quite taken by them as if they brought back some memory, yet neither looks like Master Durant." The priest glanced up at the monk with an expression devoid of meaning

Thomas felt his face blaze with heat. "Why do you mention that name?" He instantly wished he had not asked.

Eliduc shrugged. "I thought you were good friends. Before the wine merchant left to follow the king, I noticed you sought him out and spent time in his company. Indeed, the night before he departed, I saw you both in the shadows, standing very close and engaged in what I can only assume was—a fervent conversation."

"I resent the implications in your words! We did nothing that God would find offensive," Thomas hissed. "I do not deny that we have found many reasons for friendship between us. There is no sin in that." He knew he had again said more than was wise and fell silent. No observer would have seen any evil in two men exchanging a brotherly embrace of farewell, although he secretly feared there was more warmth than God might find chaste in the one he and Durant had exchanged that night.

"Are you not also friends with Crowner Ralf in Tyndal village?" Eliduc steepled his hands prayerfully. "Have I ever suggested that relationship was less than virtuous? Why is your spirit so tender, Brother?"

Thomas turned back to the window and gestured at the two men still speaking below. "You came to discuss them, did you not?" He could not blunt the sharp edge in his voice.

Smiling, Eliduc once more moved close to the monk so he could see through the window.

Thomas inched away.

"Torold is loyal to the man who feeds him. Maynard wishes he had leapt first from their mother's womb." The priest had lost interest in taunting the monk and now shifted his interest to the death of Mistress Hawis.

"Does that longing mean he has committed adultery with his elder brother's wife?"

"Have you spoken with Sir Hugh about his son?"

Never a man to forget that he is due payment before handing over the item desired, the monk thought. "As I feared, he is utterly opposed to the idea of Richard becoming a priest and your charge, even if this means his son would gain a fine position in the Church."

"Sir Hugh is a fool."

"But a man who loves his son." Thomas hesitated, watching for some hint that Eliduc understood paternal feelings. Realizing the hope was unreasonable, he continued. "Sir Hugh and his sister have agreed to set this argument to the side until the murderer is found and Richard freed. When that time comes, Prioress Eleanor will do all she can to persuade her brother of the merit in your plan."

"That your prioress stands with God in this matter does not surprise me." The priest reverently bowed his head.

"And thus your wish may be fulfilled if you choose to wait for an answer to your proposal and continue to assist in freeing an innocent man."

"Well presented, Brother Thomas, although you need not have asked for my cooperation. Of course, I shall be happy to do all I can for young Richard. It is my belief that God's will demands he be found innocent so the lad may render the life of service he longs to offer Him."

Thomas decided not to ask the priest if he knew that Richard had sworn to offer his neck to the noose if his father did not allow him to take vows. As soon as this crime was solved, he would destroy that misdirected zeal. Remembering the young Simon, who went off with Father Eliduc years ago with flames of obsessive ardor flashing from his eyes, the monk was not going to let Richard fall victim to the same passion that forgot or banished reason.

"Come with me," Thomas murmured, as he saw a group of jesting men gathering nearby, and he led the priest to a quieter place. There the monk told Eliduc what Sir Hugh had discovered in Oxford.

At the news of the thief, Eliduc's eyes grew round.

"Prioress Eleanor will talk with ben David's mother about this," Thomas said, not a little delighted that he had news the priest did not already know.

"Perhaps I should join her."

Had Thomas liked the man, he might have described the light in the priest's eyes as the joy of angels dancing. He did not.

"If you will forgive me, Father, I think it best that my prioress speak with her alone. The woman has seen her son dragged away for hanging by Christian soldiers, all her possessions taken by Christian men for a Christian king's coffers, and she has been spat upon and cursed by others of our faith. If she is willing to talk to anyone in her current condition, it is not likely to be a priest."

"I am a man of God, not a soldier of the king. Tell me why this Jewess should fear me more than your prioress?"

"Prioress Eleanor is a woman, Father. Her gentleness with the family may be our best hope for getting details that could lead to Richard's freedom and even to the salvation of the women's souls." He shrugged. "As a man, you are not possessed of that softness possessed by frail women. In this instance, the weakness can be useful."

Father Eliduc considered the merits in this, then nodded. "The ways of God are often a mystery, Brother. He used Sir Hugh, a man well-known for blasphemy and weak faith, to learn about the robber from the impious Jew. Perhaps your idea will work. I shall expect a full account of what your prioress learns."

The monk bowed his head with, he hoped, the appropriate gratitude for the priest's concurrence. "You are knowledgeable about the courtiers, Father. Do you think Sir Walter was ignorant of his wife's wanton adultery?"

"The marriage between them was agreed upon solely to please Queen Eleanor," the priest muttered in a hoarse whisper. "Each found the other repugnant in the marital bed, as I have heard, and their brief couplings provided no heir. But they found another common interest that made their union fertile. Yes, Sir Walter most certainly knew of the line of virginal squires who sought fruit from the Tree of Knowledge offered by Mistress Hawis' hand. She found that many of the youths were eager to offer her baubles of some worth, all of which she gave to her husband to sell."

"He was willing to do this even though men would mock him for the horns she placed on his head?"

"Sin often blinds men in peculiar ways, and avarice glitters most brilliantly." Disgust was evident in Eliduc's expression. "He has his own consolations in London. With the news that the queen was displeased, however, I would not be surprised if he found a way to regain his honor by banishing his wife to a convent. It is commonly done."

"But was he bawd enough to tolerate his own brother swyving his wife?"

Eliduc frowned. "That was a recent rumor, one I doubted was true. There was something about their relationship I found odd.

Master Maynard was as besotted with her as a lap dog is with his mistress. That much was clear." He looked up at the monk. "Sir Walter's younger brother was never known for fondling women in dark corners. Why would he change his behavior? Lust may be man's basest sin, and few are immune from its temptations, but I have long suspected that this man was incapable of acting on his desires."

"Do you think either brother might kill her out of jealousy?"

"She whored for her husband. Why would he kill the one who brings in gold? There are other ways to punish her." He laughed. "Banishing Mistress Hawis to a convent, away from her finery and young men, might be best for her soul but would be akin to torture for her until she learned repentance. As for the other brother…" The priest snorted in contempt.

Thomas continued to wonder about Maynard. Lusts may be hidden and rarely acted upon, a practice he understood well. He was not as willing as Eliduc to dismiss the brother as a murderer.

"You are musing over the sins of Maynard, Brother?" The priest smirked.

"I was thinking about what must be done next." Thomas returned the look with a showing of teeth, a gesture he hoped might be interpreted as a smile. "Perhaps you should speak with Sir Walter and see if he will reveal some interesting detail. Although his wife was ill-loved, she still brought him gold as you so astutely noted. The abrupt loss of that must bring him honest grief, for surely he had hoped for a little more profit before the queen banished her."

The priest laughed with a rare and honest merriment. "Then I shall. Meanwhile continue to assure your prioress that I am eager to help her nephew keep out of the hangman's hands. Whatever I discover will be shared with you both."

Knowing that Eliduc would still find a way to exact his price for this cooperation, Thomas turned to leave.

"And what are your plans, Brother?"

The monk looked back and noticed the priest was looking especially sanctimonious. It was not a comforting sight. "Perhaps I shall approach Maynard and question him."

"I will pray, Brother."

As the monk walked away, he wondered whether the priest's prayers would be for the success of his encounter with Sir Walter's brother or for the triumph of one of the many other devious schemes the man was always plotting.

Chapter Twenty-five

Father Eliduc found Sir Walter in the stable.

Torold was rubbing down a favored brown horse. Outside the stall, a pile of reeking straw lay, ready for a stable boy to remove. Sir Walter, sitting on a wooden box, drank from a large goblet of wine.

The priest's nose twitched. Stables housed grunting beasts, and their stench was a pungent reminder of earthly decay and filth. He rarely went near them and was grateful that Heaven would be a place without bodily fluids where the only scent was that of holy purity.

"Father Eliduc! What a pleasure to see you. I thought you would have traveled to the king's side by now." Sir Walter took a long drink of his wine, and then stared deeply into the goblet before setting it down beside him with evident regret.

The priest modestly bowed his head. Sir Walter might be successful in his pursuit of worldly gain, but he was no worthy adversary in the finer points of cunning and manipulation. A knight of little education and less cleverness, Father Eliduc found him boring.

"I beg a blessing," the man said.

The priest noted that he did not kneel in the dirt but remained seated on his rough box. Nevertheless, in view of the recent tragedy, he gave the man what he wished where he sat. "I grieve over the death of your beloved wife," Eliduc said in a voice properly pitched to convey the right note of sympathy.

The knight looked away, but his eyes expressed sorrow only when they fell upon the empty wine goblet.

Father Eliduc was surprised. Sir Walter had no cause to lament the wife who not only put horns on his head but polished them frequently, yet even relief was not evident on the man's face. Did the adultery trouble him so little?

How foolish, the priest thought. He should not equate the feelings of a virtuous or even typically sinful husband with one of Sir Walter's ilk. The man swindled others out of their coin, stole the gifts of the boys who swyved his wife, and gave none of that profit to the Church in penance. If avarice had so thoroughly conquered him, being a known cuckold might not have shamed him at all. The priest quivered in disgust. Bawds and their whores were not people with whom he had gained much acquaintance in the court of kings and the palaces of bishops.

A horse snorted.

Startled, Eliduc jumped back. Fortunately, the knight and his man did not see his fear, but he decided he could not bear to stay in this place much longer.

"I have heard that she was murdered." He stopped to watch Sir Walter's face for any interesting reaction.

The knight simply nodded

"I have also learned that the mother of Lumbard ben David came to Woodstock shortly before the crime took place and is suspected of Mistress Hawis' death. Did she not curse your wife when you arrested her son?"

Sir Walter's thick eyebrows rose to form two equal peaks. "She cursed me first! Never have I heard such venom from a woman, nor have I ever heard such curses from Christians. You heard her, Torold."

The man did not slow the rhythm of his work. "I did. And when your wife and her friends rebuked the traitorous Jews, the beldam refused to bow her head and then spoke to Mistress Hawis with a cruel tongue. Yes, she threatened great harm against your wife, so I swiftly led Mistress Hawis and her friends to safety, far away from the Jewish Quarter."

The horse's coat was beginning to gleam.

"You had much to do that night, Sir Walter," Eliduc said. "There were so many houses to search and traitors to arrest. I am surprised you did not have to take an army with you. It is a brave man of pure faith who faces the enemies of God with so few. I think it a wonder there was not much plundering for I gather you did not have time or men to remove all the valuables the same night as the arrests."

Sir Walter looked at the priest with a questioning look.

"I did hear that some minor theft occurred," the priest replied sympathetically. "Nothing that suggests you failed in your responsibilities and duty to the king, of course."

"I secured the houses and left one man to guard each. The Jews were too busy wailing over the arrests. There was little danger of them thieving from the king."

Eliduc molded his expression into one of awe. "No robbing at all?"

"I was diligent," the knight huffed.

"I meant to suggest nothing other than to remark on the favor God showed you if such was the case."

Sir Walter narrowed his eyes. "Yet you have heard criticism, Father. Rumors of theft? If so, I must hear the details. Either the tales must be proven false or the felon who took anything from those houses must be caught. He is as guilty of treason for stealing from King Edward as the arrested Jews were for clipping coins."

Eliduc's heart rejoiced over his success. "Oh, there was only one tale I overheard." He waited with humble expression for the knight to beg for details.

"One? Only one?"

"Only one. May God be praised!" He drew in a shallow breath to give just the right pause. "What is one minor robbery compared to everything you have gathered for King Edward's coffers?" He could smell the rank fear wafting from the knight.

"Tell me the details, Father." Sir Walter's voice was rough with emotion. "I would not let the king be robbed and now swear to seek out this man for hanging. Was it a Jew?"

"The same night you arrested ben David and sealed the house against his spawn and dam, a man was seen entering the physician's house. He soon left with a large bag and disappeared toward the center of Oxford."

The knight turned pale. "I had not heard that!" He turned to Torold. "Have you?"

"No, my lord." The man ran his hand over the horse's coat.

"Who told you this?"

"I did not recognize those who spoke together, for it was very dark, and assumed the men were soldiers. But I thought little of it, thinking it might be rumor, and you did set a guard as you have now confirmed."

Hissing, Sir Walter slammed his hand into his fist. "He must have fallen asleep! I shall have the lax creature whipped until he screams for his mother."

"Then the house was robbed?"

The man flushed, realizing he might have betrayed knowledge of the theft, and stared at the pile of dirty straw. "I did not notice anything of worth missing."

"Perhaps he did not steal plate or coin but only records of debts, deeds, or other financial documents?"

"He was a physician, not a money-lender, Father, or at least to my knowledge. I found only a few accounts of medical fees owed which I burned. There were Christians on that list, despite the king prohibiting us from seeking treatment from Jewish doctors, and I did not want their names known." He thought for a moment. "As for deeds or other documents that might suggest he took land or houses in payment for any loans he might have done informally, I found nothing, not even proof he owned the house we confiscated. Perhaps his mother burned that evidence, but the house now belongs to the king. It matters not what the beldam did."

"But you did find proof that he clipped coins." The priest was not pleased with this news, but the man had tried to lie once already. Eliduc suspected he was telling more falsehoods. Sir Hugh's source gained nothing by telling the story of the theft, and thus he believed him. Sir Walter had good reason to deny it.

"Hiding it all in the roof thatch was a witless choice by ben David. A child could have found that."

Eliduc watched the knight's face for any hint that he was lying.

Sir Walter did not even blink. "Was there a reason you were interested in this matter, Father?"

Now the priest saw a darkening in the man's eyes. "The curiosity of one who loves a godly story, Sir Walter. Is it not a miracle and a credit to your faith that so much was retrieved for the king's coffers after the treasonous acts of those under his benign protection?" He smiled back, but made sure his expression suggested he was not a man to threaten either. "I feared you might not have heard this tale of plundering and wanted you to know of it, should anyone try to dishonor your good name."

"It would be a fool who tried to do so, but I am most grateful for what you have said. I will certainly question the soldier I left to guard the house. If there was a man who stole from the house, I shall find and hang him." He turned to Torold. "You will look into this matter."

"Aye, my lord," the man said, and continued to make the horse's coat gleam.

Satisfied that Sir Walter had been caught in two lies, one about the thievery and the other about not berating the guard at the time the theft was discovered, the priest decided he had remained too long in the fetid stable. Someone else could pursue why the man had lied. Eliduc longed to cleanse his nostrils of horse sweat and manure, preferably with the sacred smoke from altar candles.

Chapter Twenty-six

Thomas stood in the back of one of the many small chapels and watched Maynard Clayton squirm and moan in prayer. The only words the monk could hear were: "Mercy! Mercy!"

The cry brought back memories of his time in prison where men screamed for death to escape the agony of flesh rotting from putrefied wounds. The images grew too vivid for Thomas to bear. He loudly cleared his throat to announce his presence.

Maynard leapt to his feet and stared at the monk in terror.

"Forgive me," Thomas said, walking up to him. "I did not mean to startle you."

"I thought you were someone else." The man was as pale as moonlight.

"May I speak with you?" The chapel light was dim. Perhaps, Thomas thought, I have misjudged the cause of his pallor.

Maynard nodded with evident reluctance. His quick look around was not lost on the monk.

"Richard FitzHugh has been accused of the murder of Mistress Hawis, a charge I wish to disprove. Since his aunt, Prioress Eleanor, must stay with her dying father, I have sworn to do all I can to bring her peace in this matter and safely return her nephew to his family."

"I know of nothing to help you, Brother." Maynard glanced longingly at the open chapel door just behind the tall, broad-shouldered monk.

Thomas grasped the man's arm, although he kept his grip gentle. "I give you my word that my questions are not intended to cast blame, but I have heard some things for which I need clarification. Will you help the Prioress of Tyndal in her time of sorrow to free her beloved nephew of this false charge? It would be an act of Christian compassion, something upon which God always smiles."

Maynard looked heavenward with an expression that suggested he needed all the help he could get. "Of course," he murmured. "Will you also beg her to pray for me?"

Thomas agreed with a show of gratitude, then led the man into the hall where no one could approach without being seen. He gestured to a window seat so they could speak in peace.

Maynard crumpled more than sat, as if an invisible but heavy burden rested on his narrow shoulders.

"I know Mistress Hawis was your sister-in-law, but not everyone in a family has a loving bond. In this case, I have heard that you and she were on very good terms."

"I do not like your tone, Brother. It suggests rebuke." Maynard stood as if intending to leave.

"Please sit," the monk replied. "If you fear the consequences of sin, find your priest and beg God for forgiveness. I only seek answers to free an innocent. The rest is between you and God."

Maynard's eyes narrowed with suspicion.

"Surely you are aware that men claim you were her lover. For my cause, it matters little whether you were or not, but you spent much time in her company and thus might name enemies she had. On my prioress' behalf, I seek foes, not lovers."

Maynard blinked, but sat back down. "Brother, I sinned less with her than many think. It was not virtue that held me back…" He flushed, then slammed his fist against the stone wall. "I am impotent. Does that satisfy you?"

Thomas decided that the dead woman's brother-in-law spoke with sincerity. Not many men would so quickly admit to the loss of their manhood even to a monk. But he was also wary of the ease with which Maynard did this. Had it been intended to distract him from asking certain questions? "I am grateful for your honesty, but you knew her and her habits well in other ways. Did she have particular enemies, and, if so, who were they?"

Maynard blushed again, then turned away and began to sniffle.

"As I have also heard, she shared her bed with many young squires. Is this true?"

Covering his face, the man whimpered. "She did, although she found time to…" He looked at the monk, his eyes overflowing and his lips trembling. "She forbade me her chambers, coming to mine when she was willing to…"

Thomas struggled to hide his annoyance. Was the man so obsessed with his inadequacies that he could now speak of nothing else? Perhaps he was dwelling on them to avoid mentioning something worse about which he dared not speak? Murder came to mind.

"Were you jealous?"

"No!" Maynard stared at the monk in horror.

"You would not be a man if you weren't," Thomas said.

"Then, yes, but what could I do about it? Only rarely could I…and then I could not…"

"Sustain it?" The monk heard the sharpness in his voice.

The man gulped and nodded.

Thomas took a deep breath and berated himself for an impatience with this man when his own manhood had been lost years ago. But he had taken vows of chastity. Maynard had not. A little kindness was in order. "Forgive me," he said softly. "I meant no cruelty."

Surprised, the man sat back and rubbed his hand under his nose. "If you want to know if I killed her, Brother, I did not. Whether or not I was jealous of the virile young men in her bed, I loved her deeply, took what she was willing to give, and now suffer grief beyond endurance." He began to shiver. "But she was my sister-in-law. I have still sinned! Oh, how I have sinned!"

"Confession and penance," Thomas replied. "God forgives the repentant."

Maynard threw up his hands in despair and surrender. "Ask me what you will. I shall answer. I long for justice in her death as much as you want Richard FitzHugh found innocent of it."

"Did any of the squires grow possessive or threaten her?"

After a moment's thought, he shook his head. "She never mentioned that. A few lads were obsessed with her, but she never pretended that any had won her heart."

"Out of jealousy, did you ever wait outside her chamber to see who entered it? I ask in case you overheard something of note or were there the night of her death."

He shook his head. "Only once, in the beginning, and she saw me. After that, she forbade it. I obeyed. In truth, it hurt too much to know how many arrived or whom."

"You may have obeyed most of the time, but all mortals are weak-willed creatures. Were you outside her room the night of her death?"

"No! I swear it! She came to my chambers. We had supper together. She left." He turned purple with profound humiliation.

Thomas nodded understanding as a kindness and gestured for him to continue.

"When she went back to her chamber, I found consolation in a jug of wine."

"Did any of the youths ever hover by her door?"

Tears began rolling down Maynard's cheeks. "She told the few that, if they continued, she would deny them her bed."

"Men? Did she have adult lovers?"

Once again, the man shook his head. "It was my one consolation."

This time Thomas felt some sorrow for the man. He might not like him, but this procession of young lovers would have been hard to bear. "Did your brother know of this?"

Maynard looked up at the ceiling. "We never spoke of it. If he heard rumors, he asked no questions."

The man is lying, Thomas thought. Of course, Sir Walter knew. He was not a stupid man.

"My brother spent little time with his wife. Soon after their marriage, he told me she was barren. There was never any affection between them, although they were companionable enough when required to please the king and queen, especially Queen Eleanor. He spends much of his time in London, caring for his investments and acquiring wealth. That is a practice in which he shows much talent." Maynard's eyes had come to rest on the monk's face.

If he had owned any remaining doubt that the knight knew of his wife's whoring, Thomas now lost it. Sir Walter was not so blinded by love for his wife that he saw only what he wished. Still, what price was worth accepting a cuckold's horns? Thomas smiled, his expression full of sympathetic understanding. "You are a beneficiary of his increasing affluence?"

"As are others."

"Please explain."

"My brother asked family loyalty from me, a small enough payment for his largess. You have seen Torold? He is another recipient of Sir Walter's goodness. A knight, who could afford neither horse nor armor, he would have starved had my brother not called upon him to serve as needed."

Thomas mulled this over. He thought any man who would have bedded his brother's wife, had he been capable, was patently lax in family loyalty. Yet Thomas knew this was neither the time nor place to debate this issue with the younger brother. He opted for another approach. "What do you know of the events during the raids to arrest coin-clippers?"

Maynard looked puzzled by the inexplicable change of subject. "Almost nothing, Brother. I was not with Sir Walter that night."

"His wife was, or so I have heard."

"She went with a group of her friends to mock the traitors."

"What did she tell you about what she saw?"

"Little enough, only that she had some sport with the mother and daughters of Lumbard ben David when her husband's soldiers pushed them into the street after the man's arrest."

"Did the physician's mother threaten her?"

"Oh, that! Yes, the old woman did, but Hawis cared little about the ranting of a beldam." He frowned in thought. "My brother did worry because he had too few soldiers to quell a riot should the Jews decide to attack his men in the course of their lawful duties. Torold escorted Hawis and her friends back to safety. She was most displeased, believing that her soul benefited from her actions against the Jewish woman, but she properly obeyed the commands of her lord husband."

Thomas tried not to smile over her decision to obey this one command while breaking her marriage vows to Sir Walter by whoring. Maynard, however, seemed oblivious to the incongruity. "I have also heard that the house of ben David was robbed that night, after your brother went on to arrest other men."

"That I had not heard, Brother, although Sir Walter told me he was displeased that he found little of value in that particular house. When he returned the next morning with soldiers to confiscate all valuables, he expected fine plate and a cache of hidden silver buried in the gardens there. He said he feared the king would not be pleased that there was little wealth when far more was expected." He sat back and wiped his nose on his sleeve.

Thomas bowed his head to subtly observe the man next to him. Maynard had seemed eager to tell the truth, yet he seemed to be lying a second time. But why?

As he looked at the lank and now pale man, Thomas doubted he was capable of killing a healthy woman before she could scream for help. To be honest, this brother's professed love for Hawis sounded more like the mewling of a child denied a whim than a man rejected. It was Hawis who possessed the lusty ardor. Had Maynard been the hanged corpse, Thomas would have been more likely to suspect that she was the killer.

"Thank you," the monk said, standing up. "You have clarified issues that needed resolution." There was nothing more he could glean from this man, a sallow creature with an equally colorless soul. Like all men, Maynard did sin but surely God must look upon him as far less capable of evil than many others.

Sir Walter's brother said nothing. Only his widened eyes suggested fear, but the cause was buried too deep in his soul to be easily read.

As the monk began to walk away, Maynard called to him.

Thomas turned around.

"Will you hear my confession soon, Brother? My soul reeks of sin, and I long for God's mercy."

"Come to me tomorrow morning after the early Office, and I shall hear it," Thomas replied, his heart softening a bit. "I would do so now, but I cannot stay any longer. Prioress Eleanor may wish God's comfort in her earthly grief and her father needs my prayers."

Maynard thanked him, but his eyes now looked like those of a dying fish, flopping without hope of salvation in the bottom of a boat.

Chapter Twenty-seven

Baron Adam felt a fatigue so deep that he longed for sleep, but he knew the weariness resided in his soul, not in his body.

Sleep was not what he truly prayed for. He wanted to die. At one time he believed that he would fear this moment and be filled with regret over his leaving of the world, but now he felt neither.

He had confessed, repented, and said his goodbyes. Of course he was anxious about God's judgment. He had killed, connived, and left the field to evil men when he should have stood for justice, but he sincerely grieved over his sins. Some he had lamented at the time he committed them. Now he regretted all.

There were a few good acts in his life. He had let his beloved daughter take vows, even though the man he hoped she would marry was wealthy and influential. When his eldest son begged leave to take the cross and follow the present king to Outremer, he had granted the plea, although he suffered from worry every day the boy was gone. He did not want Hugh to die or fall victim to lingering battle wounds as he had himself.

The gaunt face of the son who returned, however, was a shock to him. He wanted to weep, although it was a change he recognized. He had also struggled with scars to his own soul, but Hugh had been more sorely afflicted from those furies of war. Since he had let his son go to fight for God, Adam decided that God must heal him. A father could not.

As for his middle son, Robert, he had resisted the temptation to force either a prayer book or sword into his hands. Instead, he watched the lad grow into a fine manager of rents and farms. Regarding his own stewardship of family interests, Adam had succeeded without being greedy, as others often were.

And he had been loyal to a king whom many called weak and unworthy of the crown. In fact, Adam had found common ground with Henry who was a good husband, a loving father, a benefactor to the poor, and finally his friend, despite the faults for which so many condemned the man.

As he lay musing on all of this, he suddenly smelled the scent of flowers. A soft breeze wafted over his face, and he opened his eyes. What was this meadow bursting with spring blossoms?

Although he knew he was in a bed in a room in Woodstock Manor, he saw only the vague shadows of those mortals he knew to be at his bedside.

What he was not prepared to see was his wife, Margaret, sitting beside him. He gasped.

She smiled.

His heart leapt in joy.

"It is time, beloved husband," she said. "I have wearied of waiting for you." Then she laughed.

Her laugh had always been one of the things he loved best about her, the sound so beautiful that it reminded him of a choir of nuns singing hymns. In the years since she had died in childbed, he tried not to dwell on the void she had left, but the music of her laughter remained buried in his heart. Hearing her now, he wanted to weep, not from sorrow but out of happiness.

"Oh, Adam, do you think I haven't missed you as much as you have missed me?" She reached out and brushed her gentle fingers across his cheek. "How many husbands have found the beds of other women, both before and after a wife's death? Do you not know that I was aware of your fidelity to our vows and love?"

"I could never…" he gasped.

"Nor would I, had you died before me."

He blinked back his tears and looked around. What a wonder! He was no longer in Woodstock Manor. He was actually in a meadow filled with flowers, humming bees, and singing birds. What place was this?

"Are you surprised that Heaven is filled with so many earthly delights?" His wife slid closer to him.

He nodded.

"As your sister, Beatrice, might say, God didn't make all those miracles of creation to simply throw them away. There is no sin in finding awe in what He has done. Now you can enjoy an eternity of perfect beauty."

Adam smiled, then grew uneasy. "I have never forgiven myself for your death. Have you been able to forgive me?"

"Sweet husband, we are both to blame in equal measure for what happened. My agony was intense but short. Death came swiftly, although not fast enough at the time. You have endured the torment for over twenty years. Which of us has suffered more?"

"You," he said.

She bent closer, her hair brushing his cheek. "And I would say that you had." Then she sat back and studied his face. "There is something more that troubles you."

"I think I shall miss our children."

"The passage of time is different after death," she said. "They will eventually find their ways here, each on a different path. In the meantime, be content. They own good souls." She waited for a moment. "Even Hugh."

Suddenly, he realized that he no longer felt the heaviness of his body that he had suffered since his attack of apoplexy, and he sat up. The shadows of the living had grown so faint he could hardly see them, but the forms of the dead now took on shapes he recognized. Over by a nearby tree, his father and mother waved to him. And was that his old friend and liege lord, Henry? Had God forgiven his sins as well?

"Come, beloved," his wife said, standing up and offering her hand. "You have had enough of mortal things. Let us enjoy peace together in the company of those we love."

And with a cry of delight, Adam of Wynethorpe leapt to his feet, took his wife's hand, and ran beside her into the light.

On his bed, he had left behind all his earthly responsibilities to Baron Hugh of Wynethorpe, Robert of Wynethorpe, and Prioress Eleanor of Tyndal.

Chapter Twenty-eight

This chapel was close to the one where her father's corpse lay, but Prioress Eleanor needed that small distance from the inescapable evidence of death. As she knelt before the altar, however, she found she could not pray for her father's soul. Perhaps I am too worldly and selfish, she thought, but she was certain that God understood the frailties of His creatures and would guide her back to His path soon enough.

So she turned her pleas from mercy for her father's spirit to her longing for comfort. Looking down at her hands, she frowned. "They are not a child's," she acknowledged to God. "My age, vocation, and rank give me the status of a woman, but tonight I am a babe."

Death was a familiar visitor to all and stopped near Eleanor neither more nor less than anyone else. When she was six, her mother had died in childbirth, her body torn by a child too big for her to bear and one who fled the earth with her. The prioress also had friends who fell victim to fevers and accidents. But she had been a child then and could seek the comforting arms of the aunt who raised her in Amesbury Priory.

Tonight, her aunt was far away, frail and edging toward Heaven herself, and her father was dead. Soon she would have no one older than she to hold and counsel her. Although she had a strong faith, she was struggling to accept that loss and learn to look only to God.

When she left Amesbury to lead Tyndal Priory, God had chosen to add violence against others to her especial burdens and demanded that she render His justice in these crimes that so angered Him. The reason He had done so was one of His many mysteries, but her faith led her to obey without question—or at least to argue only briefly.

This was a rare time when she drew back from the obligation and begged for mercy. The struggle to obey God in this matter of Mistress Hawis' death while watching her own father die had been more than she could endure. Covering her face with her hands, she moaned with agony but soon understood that the bitter draught would not be removed from her lips. She must find a way to obey despite her grievous sorrow.

"Let me seek comfort now for my personal grief," she murmured to God. "Then I shall have the strength to seek justice for the dead woman." She hesitated as the image of ben David's young daughters passed before her eyes. "And do whatever else You wish done on Your behalf."

Within the silence of the chapel, Prioress Eleanor heard no reply, but a soft breath of air brushed her cheek. That, she decided, must be her answer.

"I am not ready for the duties passed on to me with my lord father's death and the loss of his guidance," she whispered. "I could have faced my own death better than his." Sighing, she sat back on her heels. There were so many set prayers that gave others comfort in these times of sorrow, but they offered nothing to ease her heart and little to address her fear. "I mean no ill, Lord, but I need wisdom and must ask for it more directly than may be meet." She stared at the altar, and then bowed her head. "Forgive me, for I do not mean to offend."

In that chapel filled with guttering candles and twisting shadows, Eleanor stretched herself out on the cold stone floor and wept, pleading and arguing with God like any child unable to understand why a parent would desert her even if it was for Heaven.

◇◇◇

Eleanor opened her eyes. Where was she? Her body was chilled, and her cheek bore the uneven imprint of the stones against which she had lain. Then she remembered that she had come to this chapel to pray.

Rising to her feet, she felt drained. Had she fallen asleep or had God sent her soul on a journey to gain greater wisdom than her mind could comprehend? Whatever had occurred here, she found her spirit at peace, although her body ached. She turned to the altar and offered wordless gratitude.

Now I am ready to seek a murderer, she thought.

The death of Mistress Hawis gnawed at her. She might be thankful that Brother Thomas said he would take on the task of freeing her nephew from all charges, but she had taken into her care those deemed by many to be the most likely suspects in murder. That trio, she realized, were her particular responsibility.

Mistress Chera and her granddaughters had behaved with great courtesy while sharing her rooms, asking nothing and honoring her sorrow as well as her need for quiet reflection and prayer. At the beginning of their confinement, ben David's mother told Eleanor that she would pray on her behalf as well. Eleanor thanked her, but then her heart froze. Was it a sin to accept the prayers of a Jewish woman?

Eleanor shook her head. She might have asked Brother Thomas for his opinion, but she knew him well enough to believe he would say that all prayers to their mutual God were no sin.

The Church often taught contradictory things in this matter of the Jews. From one source, she was told that they were a stiff-necked people who had killed the Messiah. From another, she was taught that they must be treated mercifully and protected because the end of the world could not occur without them.

And now the current king, whose ancestors had promised protection for these families, was turning his back on a people who had been loyal subjects from the day King William had invited them to his conquered England. Usury was a sin, yet Christians from merchants to kings found it necessary and thus allowed the practice. Why persuade a people to sin, offer them protection to do so, and then cast them aside as King Edward was doing?

"I am only a frail woman," she whispered to the silence of the chapel. "I do not understand."

Who were the sinners and who were the innocents when men could not agree on whether usury should be encouraged, whether it might even be wicked to borrow when interest must be paid, and how to treat those who had not accepted the Christian Messiah?

"Instruct me," she asked.

In the meantime, her heart believed that the answer must lie in the teaching that all must love one another. It should not be completely wrong to obey the wisdom preached by one far greater than mortal priests and bishops. Until otherwise enlightened, Eleanor decided to follow that precept when dealing with the women who shared her rooms.

The prioress walked quietly toward the chapel entrance. The candles had gone out, but a weak moon cast enough light through one of the high windows to guide her footsteps. She longed for her bed and hoped sleep would bring her strength. In the morning, she would pray beside her father before his corpse was prepared for the final journey to the family sepulcher.

A figure passed the doorway.

She took in a breath and grew still. Most mortals were asleep at this hour. Even those waiting upon the recovering queen had found a place to rest. Of course this could be someone, a servant perhaps, with an honest reason to be hurrying down the hall during Satan's hour, but something made her suspect this was not the case.

She stepped closer to the doorway and carefully peered into the hall. Although she could not identify the person, and had no logical reason to do this, she chose to follow at a distance.

It is the curse of Eve, she thought, to pursue a path because curiosity tempts. The lesson of the apple should have stopped her but failed. If this was a man racing to the bed of his lover, she would continue on and offer a prayer for their souls. If not...

The man stopped and looked over his shoulder.

Eleanor pushed herself against the wall. As a small, thin woman, she hoped she might remain invisible.

Apparently seeing nothing, he scurried on and disappeared around a corner.

She pursued but hesitated when she reached the place he had vanished.

Were those voices?

Her heart pounded too loudly to hear anything for certain, and she was afraid to reveal her presence. Not daring to look around the corner, she tried to listen and prayed no one would come back this way and find her here.

"Eliduc," someone clearly said and then muttered a few more words.

"The document," was the only reply.

Suddenly, she heard a cry. Something heavy fell. After that, the only sounds she heard were those of departing footsteps.

Now Eleanor did look around the corner and saw a body on the ground. Down the hall, a figure rapidly became another shadow.

She ran to the fallen man and dropped to her knees beside him. Turning his head to the moonlight, she gasped. She may have only seen him briefly, but she knew it was Maynard.

He groaned. A knife hilt protruded from one side of his spine. Blood flowed rapidly from the wound and pooled on the floor.

"I shall bring help," she said, bending to speak in his ear. He was surely dying, but she wanted to give comfort. "Who did this to you?"

He mumbled.

She put her ear close to his mouth.

"The Jews," he whispered before blood burst out of his mouth.

Eleanor knew he was dead.

Her robe and face stained with blood, she ran to get Fitz-Roald, Brother Thomas, and Sister Anne.

Chapter Twenty-nine

Sheriff FitzRoald knelt a short distance away as Sister Anne finished her examination of Maynard's body.

Brother Thomas glanced at his prioress, worried that she was not unscathed despite her assurances. In the bright light from the torches carried by two soldiers, the dead man's blood still glistened where it had stained her robe. She had cleansed her face and hands.

The nun rose. "He was stabbed in the back. There were other wounds but not fresh enough to have been inflicted with this attack." She looked at the monk. "I suspect he scourged himself." She bent to pick up a bag and handed it to the monk. "I make no conclusions about this."

Thomas opened it up and shook out some of the contents. A scattering of bright coin-clippings covered his palm. They were of various sizes and shapes, but he recognized the design from edges of the new coinage and bits of the king's image. He showed them first to Prioress Eleanor and then to the sheriff.

FitzRoald muttered a mild curse.

"It lay near his hand," Sister Anne said.

"I did not see it when I found him, but I did not take the time to search before alerting you, Sheriff," Eleanor added. "The light was also very dim." Her voice shook.

"My lady, I grieve that you should suffer this so soon after your father's death." FitzRoald bowed his head to honor her grief. "You have told me the tale of Maynard's death. You need not remain here…."

"I was there when he was killed," she replied. "You may have more questions to ask as you think more on what you see. God is caring for my father's soul. My brother tends to his body."

The sheriff started to protest but quickly fell silent out of respect for her vocation and rank.

Sister Anne stepped closer to her prioress and gently touched her arm.

Eleanor looked up at her with gratitude.

Thomas sifted through the bits again, and then shook his head. "I find nothing else that would help us find the killer."

"Why did he have coin-clippings?" FitzRoald stared at the ceiling as if seeking an incontrovertible answer, preferably from God.

"Why was he murdered? Who was he talking to? How is this related to the killing of Sir Walter's wife? It surely must be." Thomas poured the coin fragments back into the bag.

"And my own inquiries have led nowhere. I can only keep the news of her attendant's violent death from the queen a little while longer. Now that I have a second death to solve and few favors left to offer those who should keep silent…"

"Be patient," Eleanor said softly, although her glance at the monk suggested she was failing to take her own counsel. "Please tell the sheriff what you have learned," she said to Thomas. "It may mean more to him than to us."

The condensed version of the monk's discussion with Maynard and Eliduc's talk with Sir Walter did nothing to improve FitzRoald's mood. The one bit of information that temporarily brightened his expression was the story about the robber that Hugh, now Baron of Wynethorpe, had been told.

"We also have Maynard's last words in which he accused the Jews of his death," the sheriff said at the end of the tale.

"An ambiguous remark," Eleanor replied.

He raised an eyebrow. "Ben David's mother cursed Mistress Hawis when the physician was arrested. Soon after the old woman comes to the manor, Sir Walter's wife is strangled and hanged to look like self-murder. With his dying breath, Maynard names the Jews as his killers. He has a bag of coin-clippings in his hand. The evidence against the women accumulates."

"Near his hand," Sister Anne said. "The bag was not in it."

"I do not see any difference between holding the bag and dropping it as he died." FitzRoald's tone was sharp with frustration.

Eleanor smiled at him. "Indeed, but that evidence might have been placed there to mislead. Mistress Chera and her granddaughters are the favored suspects. The killer must know this so why not add another detail that suggests ben David's family is guilty?"

"My lady, surely you cannot ignore the motivation they had for committing the crime?"

"Mistress Chera is unlikely to have the strength to strangle a younger and more agile woman who was capable not only of protecting herself but killing the elderly mother instead. Even if Mistress Chera did kill her, how could she lift a dead body to make the death look like self-murder?"

"A point in her favor, perhaps, despite her strong motivation."

"She has also given her word not to leave my chambers. It is unlikely she did this current deed."

"You do not know if she slipped out while you were elsewhere. Who would be the witness? Her granddaughters, both of whom would surely lie?"

"There are guards."

"They might have fallen asleep or been otherwise distracted. I know the men feel uncomfortable standing too near your door."

"Very well," the prioress said, "but is she likely to have the strength to stab a man through his clothes with enough speed and force to stop him before he can strike her? Note that the weapon was driven into the body up to the hilt."

FitzRoald shrugged, but he still looked doubtful.

"Might the attempt to disguise the cause of the first murder have a counterpart in the dropped bag of coin bits? If Sister Anne had not discovered that Mistress Hawis did not hang herself, we all would have concluded that the woman committed self-murder. The killer would have carried out the perfect crime. The bag of coin-clippings points to the Jewish family, perhaps as another means of hiding the real murderer."

"With respect, my lady, I may agree that the old woman is an unlikely person to strangle Mistress Hawis, perhaps even stab Sir Walter's brother, but the bag as a means to disguise motive is speculation."

"So is the assumption that the bag points to a Jewish killer."

FitzRoald conceded with evident reluctance. "While you were hiding, could you hear the voices?"

Eleanor remembered that the priest's name had been mentioned. Looking at her monk, she decided to speak with him first about this. As much as she disliked Father Eliduc, she did not believe him capable of murder, but, as a servant of the Church, he would face religious, not secular, authority if he had any involvement in the crime.

"Forgive me," she said. "I did hear Maynard and his assailant speak, although their conversation was unclear. The only thing of note was the mention of a document. As to gender, I am uncertain. The one speaking to Maynard had a low voice, but that would not be uncommon with muted speech no matter which gender was involved. That is all I could swear to now."

"The bag may suggest something other than an attempt to confuse or guilt," Thomas said. "It might be payment to Maynard for some service or item." Then he frowned. "But why pay the man and then kill him?"

The prioress thought for a moment. "We also have the unknown thief. If Maynard knew more about the robber than he admitted, perhaps his identity, he might have demanded payment to remain silent. Perhaps the robber is at Woodstock and had paid Maynard just before he met his killer. Maybe this man is not the same as the thief."

"That does not explain his dying words, my lady."

"The reason for his murder may be found in the plundering of the ben Davids' house," she replied. "If that theft is tied to his death, Maynard may have tried, with his last breath, to point to the incident of the physician's arrest, hence he said 'the Jews,' even though his killer was Christian."

"An interesting deduction in light of the treason committed by the coin-clippers. I have little confidence in the honesty of the families of people condemned for treachery." It was clear that FitzRoald thought Eleanor was being illogical, as women were wont to be. But choosing to honor her vocation with courtesy, he said nothing more.

Thomas bent close to his prioress and whispered, "If you can bear it, should we search Mistress Hawis' chamber?"

Eleanor nodded. "I can and we must, yet I fear it may be too late to find anything of value."

The sudden noise of arriving solders startled them all.

Sir Walter rushed forward, then came to an abrupt halt before the corpse. He slid to his knees. "Now the foul killer had murdered my brother! Why do you stand here doing nothing?" he raged at the sheriff. "I shall send a complaint with the news of these events to the king." He shook a fist at FitzRoald. "Violence against members of the queen's court is rampant. Are you so witless that you do not see that the queen herself may be in danger?"

Chapter Thirty

Sir Walter paced around the space now empty of his brother's corpse which mercifully had been removed to the nearby chapel.

"Fools! Of course it had to be the Jews," he shouted. "My brother may have been guilty of many things, as we all are, but he would never have accused unjustly as he died." He glared at Brother Thomas. "His soul! He cared about his soul!"

"An old woman?" The sheriff glanced at the prioress. "Is it likely she could have stabbed your brother or hanged your wife?"

"Does she not have in her care the young spawn of Satan's imp, ben David? I saw them the night of the raid. One tried to give me the evil eye, but I sketched the sign of the cross under her nose and she backed away, spitting like a cat. Tell me why I should not conclude that Satan would give these minions the strength of ten demons?"

Eleanor bit back a response, knowing the knight had no more interest in listening to her than he did in accurate recollection. She doubted either girl would have spat at Sir Walter, even the one who had shown some spirit. The grandmother would have stopped them, and the prioress had noticed how well they obeyed her. The Devil's imps were never that meek.

Sir Walter spun around and strode toward Eleanor. "Are they still in your chambers?"

"They agreed to the confinement. The sheriff has posted a guard outside to make sure they do not leave."

"You were in the chapel and saw my brother walk by to his death. Were they in your chamber at that time?"

She glared at him. Not only was his tone rude, he was standing too close to her. "Step back," she said, her outrage barely controlled. "You insult God as well as my vocation when you fail to acknowledge that courtesy."

FitzRoald walked up to the man and laid a hand on his shoulder. "And the Prioress of Tyndal is grieving. Her father, Baron Adam, has just died."

Sir Walter glowered at the sheriff, before stepping away and turning his head to gaze at the prioress. "Then you understand my sorrow over my brother's murder, a killing that should not have happened if my counsel had been taken," he said, his tone softened only slightly. "My question? If you will, please answer it."

"How could they leave if the door was guarded?" With no hesitation, Eleanor had accepted Mistress Chera's word as she would that of any honorable woman. Had she erred? Yet the sheriff had also suggested they might have escaped. She looked at him and silently prayed he was wrong.

FitzRoald cleared his throat. "When Sir Walter arrived, I sent a man to confirm that the Jewish women were safe in your chambers."

Eleanor shivered.

"The guard had left the door to seek the garderobe. Something had caused his bowels to suffer."

"Might an imp have been summoned to jab at the guts of good Christians?" Sir Walter grinned with evident satisfaction. "As I suspected, there was no one to keep the creatures in their comfortable quarters."

"And were the women in my chambers?"

"I knocked but there was no answer."

"That means nothing!" She looked around at the company. Only Sister Anne looked sympathetic. The expression on her monk's face was unreadable. "If you were a frail woman, confined under the suspicion of murder, would you open the door when a man pounded on it?"

"An innocent woman would have no fear when the king's justice demanded entry and had a righteous cause," Sir Walter replied.

"I told Mistress Chera that she should not open the door unless she heard my voice. I promised her safety."

Sir Walter turned scarlet and pointed at the prioress. "You should spend more time on your knees in prayer and in consultation with your priest if you take the side of perfidious Jews!"

Thomas leapt forward and placed a restraining hand on the knight's chest. "This is the second time you have insulted a woman vowed to God's service. If anyone needs to beg God for mercy, it is you."

Sir Walter looked up at the monk's eyes and believed he saw God's own wrath blazing there. He paled and threw himself onto his knees in front of the prioress. "I meant no ill, my lady. My grief for my brother's death, so soon after the murder of my wife, has…"

"Stand, Sir Walter. I take no offense." Eleanor gave her monk a brief smile as the knight struggled to his feet. She had been insulted but, as hard as it was with this offensive man, her faith demanded she forgive him just as it demanded she practice compassion. Nonetheless, her tongue hurt as she bit back her rage.

Any humility the knight might have felt was short-lived. Sir Walter stood, turned his back on the prioress, and faced Fitz-Roald. "The coin bits are evidence that clearly point to the Jews. Who else would have such things? As for the murders, the imps in the beldam's company could have done the deeds. They are strong enough to strangle my wife, hang her as a mockery, and kill my brother. Think carefully about this. Think! Ben David was hanged for treason so they hanged my wife as vengeance!"

"But why should the women come here to do this? Surely they knew they would be caught." FitzRoald refused to look at the prioress.

Eleanor feared he was growing more inclined to believe Sir Walter. She could not imagine the girls committing the crime, but she used a woman's logic to arrive at the conclusion. To the sheriff and the knight, it was logical that one death would be matched by another.

"Women do not reason! It was an act of revenge. I arrested ben David for treason after finding the evidence in his house. I confiscated all the valuables I could find, arranged to sell the house, and sent all the profit to the king's coffers. Under law, I acted properly, but what felon thinks the law is fair?" The knight spread his hands as if pleading for understanding. "The only thing they cannot blame me for is putting the actual noose around the man's neck, yet they did not care. They still hanged my wife." Repeating his conclusion made his face glow with the satisfaction of being irrefutably right.

"Why leave the bag of coin fragments by your brother's hand?" Thomas' voice was pitched low in an attempt to keep his temper under control. "That is an obvious indication of guilt. Either it was gross stupidity or suggests another deliberately dropped the evidence to wrongly condemn the women."

Sir Walter ignored what he did not wish to address and continued with his argument. "The three must have hidden some wealth from us at the time of the raid and were not as poor as they claimed when they came to Woodstock. Since they have been in possession of these coin bits, they have committed treason as well and ought to be hanged." He pounded a fist into his palm. "But, even if that cannot be proved, they shall swing from the scaffold for two murders!"

FitzRoald turned to the prioress. "At least I can confirm that your nephew is safe in his cell. He is not a suspect in this killing."

Eleanor might have been grateful, but she was going over what she had seen after Maynard was killed. The escaping figure was vague, only a shadow. Might it have been one of the girls? She doubted it but could not prove otherwise and chose to keep her observations to herself.

"I insist you chain those miscreants and lock them into a proper prison!" Sir Walter was wringing his hands like a cook might wring a chicken's neck. "Or must another innocent fall victim to their wickedness before you act?"

Again the sheriff turned to the prioress. "There is cause, my lady."

"Indeed, I concur," she replied quickly. "But they shall remain in my quarters, unchained and with their modesty safeguarded. Until the evidence against them is stronger, they are still women, deemed to be innocent, who require protection in a world that has proven violent to them."

"They were under your protection, and they still escaped to kill my brother!"

"Unproven. The sheriff can surely provide more soldiers to sit outside my door." She turned to FitzRoald. "My sub-infirmarian and I will be the only ones to leave and enter without permission. If you need to speak with the women, they may be brought forth for questions." She smiled and bowed her head. "I am sure you will give your word that Mistress Chera and her granddaughters will be treated honorably, but I insist that Brother Thomas be present before you speak with them."

FitzRoald quickly swore to add men to the guard and to summon the monk should interrogation be required. Then he took the knight by the arm and led him away before Sir Walter could utter any more protests.

After they left, Sister Anne shook her head. "I cannot believe the women are guilty of murder. Mistress Chera would grieve as any mother does over her son's death, and the daughters must weep for their father as you do for yours. But did you hear even a hint of guile when Mistress Chera said she came only to beg the means to send her granddaughters to family on the continent? The queen is known to be merciful, when approached directly, and might have granted the boon had she not been in childbed."

"My own heart agrees," Eleanor replied, "but the heart is weak in logic and is often deceived. Still, only fools would leave such obvious evidence as a bag of coin-clippings by the side of the murdered man, and Mistress Chera is no fool."

Anne looked toward the chapel. "Perhaps the corpse has more to tell us," she murmured, and then shook her head in despair.

"I fear that is a misguided hope. I tried to be thorough before they took him away."

"Return to our chambers and sleep," Eleanor said. "I shall seek my own bed soon."

Sister Anne drew her prioress into an embrace and whispered words of comfort into her ear.

After the sub-infirmarian left, Eleanor rubbed her cheeks dry of tears and then turned to Thomas. "Now we must go to Mistress Hawis' quarters while others are otherwise occupied. Let us pray there is something in the room that will lead us to a killer."

"And also beg God that we find an answer soon to these crimes, my lady. The sheriff is right that the news cannot be kept from the queen. It is a miracle she has not heard already."

"And if we cannot catch the killer, the king's anger may scorch us all," Eleanor replied, her tone grim. "Future gifts to Tyndal Priory will vanish if King Edward believes we put his wife in danger by protecting a killer. We may not think ben David's family is guilty, but we are alone in that conclusion."

Chapter Thirty-one

Eleanor and Thomas stood motionless in the room where Hawis had died.

The quarters felt abandoned, but an odd musty smell remained. Although they saw no tortured spirit or any malevolent shadow, something lingered here. It was a sorrowful presence.

Whether merely sinful or profoundly wicked, the woman had died without any chance to atone. Many on their deathbeds were allowed to beg forgiveness from those they had injured and to ask clemency from God. Mistress Hawis' soul had plunged into Hell where mercy was banished and hope was unknown. That was cause for lamentation.

Eleanor broke the silence first and pointed out where she had found Richard's cross. The stained sheets had not been changed. Even the rope from which the body had swung still dangled from the beam. She looked around. "I remember nothing else of significance," she said.

Thomas nodded and started searching one side of the room. The prioress began at the other. Little conversation was needed to perform a task both did well.

Outside the chambers, a young servant woman, summoned from her early morning duties, stood quietly by the open door and provided the religious with proper attendance to avoid scandal. She watched dust mites dance in the struggling light of dawn.

The room was in disarray. Strewn across the floor was clothing of various kinds, items deemed suitable for a woman attending a queen at leisure as well as during more formal occasions. Although Sir Walter was not a poor knight and could afford some luxuries, there were few jewels or other finely crafted adornments.

The two monastics assumed that the items of greater value and beauty were gifts from Queen Eleanor. The prioress found it odd that this husband spent only the minimum required to maintain his wife's status and avoid shaming her in the company of her equals. Considering she whored for him, Thomas remarked, even a miserly man knew that prey is best lured to the trap with tempting bait.

At last, the pair met in front of a large wooden chest bound with iron bands. Thomas lifted the heavy carved lid, then wrinkled his nose at the stink. "Did Mistress Hawis not have a maid to care for her possessions and provide her with clean linen?"

"She must have, and I find it strange that this has been left so foul," Eleanor said.

"Perhaps the sheriff has forbidden anyone to touch it," Thomas said.

"We should question her servant even if FitzRoald has done so."

The monk gestured at the floor where scattered and broken bits of pottery lay. "Does this mean someone has been here before us?"

"Nothing broken was on the floor when I saw the corpse. Sister Anne examined the body where those pieces are," the prioress replied. "As I feared, we have come too late to find anything of value. The room has not been guarded, and, if there was anything the killer wished to retrieve, he has had ample opportunity to do so."

"Shall I seek the maid now?" Thomas noted that his prioress had assumed the murderer was a man and was ignoring the women in her chambers. Although he rarely disagreed with her, he wondered if she had erred in so quickly absolving them of the crime. Her arguments on their behalf were strong, but the sheriff had also expressed reasonable doubts.

She looked at the chest. "You must. We have gone through everything but this. While you find her maid, I shall look through the chest, but I suspect there will be nothing in it besides filthy linen."

He bowed and left.

Eleanor bent over and began to search the contents. "How could a woman allow her servant to leave her chambers in so much disarray?" The cloths stained with menstrual blood lay on top and in such number that Hawis must have suffered courses of long duration to have accumulated so many. "Very peculiar indeed," the prioress said.

Then an idea struck her, and she knelt to study the chest with more care. There was no lock on the front.

What better place to hide something of value than an unlocked chest? Wouldn't most conclude there was nothing of importance within? She sat back on her heels. And how many men would shift through a woman's bloody linen to search in case there was?

As she and Brother Thomas had done, when they first glanced into the chest, most would assume that the woman had been cursed with a lax servant. Others would conclude she did not care if she reused cloths turned rough with dried blood. No matter how poor, women did not do that, Eleanor thought, but how many men would think of it? And a woman of Mistress Hawis' rank would not have saved this much dirty linen for that purpose. She would have demanded clean cloths and tossed the soiled, if she had no one to wash them for her. Sir Walter's wife had a reason for doing this, Eleanor decided. The woman may have been very clever.

Slowly sliding one hand down the side of the chest, Eleanor discovered that the stained linen formed a thick layer on top of a folded sheet. Carefully, she pulled the sheet up and dropped the pile onto the floor. Underneath, there were a few pieces of simple jewelry along with bundles of cloth that could be embroidered and sewn into items suitable for court. Scattered over the top of this were pouches of lavender to keep insects away. Bending closer to sniff, the prioress realized that they also drove away the stench of the bloody linen. She smiled, even more impressed with the knight's dead wife.

Yet Eleanor recognized the signs that another hand had delved deep within the chest before she had.

Although the prioress owned little, she had a finely wrought robe for those times when such was obligatory, as well as items for travel or inclement weather. All these were carefully stored in a cedar chest, folded, protected, and ordered according to need or weather by her maid. What she saw in the dead woman's chest was not well organized, although an inexperienced eye might think it was. The pouches lay mostly to one side. The pieces of cloth were wrinkled from being badly folded and unevenly stacked. Mistress Hawis would not have allowed this.

The previous searcher did not understand that more care in replacing disturbed items would have been wise. That suggested that the individual was not a servant of either gender who would have known better, and, the prioress decided, the person was likely to be a man.

She continued to run her hand on top and through items and carefully turned them over to minimize evidence of her own exploration. But she found nothing. Neither was there any proof that the previous searcher had been more successful. Each layer proved that the seeker had continued to probe further.

So did Prioress Eleanor.

Finally, near the bottom, her hand brushed against something hard in the middle of the chest. She lifted up the piles of cloth.

Underneath was a carved casket. As she pulled it free, the top slipped askew. This box had a lock, but it had been pried open and the lid twisted off. One hinge had been ripped out of the wood. As she smelled the freshly exposed wood, the prioress knew the damage had been recently done.

Looking inside, Eleanor's hopes died. The box was empty.

As she bent over to see if anything had fallen out, she saw a ring and a gold cross with a broken chain. Considering the size of this casket, she knew it must have held more, but whatever else had been in it was gone.

What had been so important to Mistress Hawis that she concocted this vile but elaborate method of concealing it from discovery?

Eleanor placed the casket back in the spot she had found it, and then carefully replaced everything on top of it, including the sheet with the soiled linen. "This was not a casual theft," she murmured. "The jewels may be few but worth enough to a thief. Someone was looking for a specific item."

As she stood up, Thomas returned.

"There has been no maid serving Mistress Hawis since early in Lent, my lady," he said. "I spoke with one of the servants. Few stayed with her long."

"And no one else had taken her place?"

"Some of the other women here shared their maids with her from time to time, but Mistress Hawis was not well-liked. From the man I spoke to, I learned his wife was one but did not like cleaning up after the boys had left the mistress' bed. She also found the recent orders that the bloody linen be saved especially distasteful." He shook his head.

Eleanor laughed. "I have found the reason for that," she said, "which I shall explain in a moment. One question before I do. Were there any tales amongst the servants about Maynard Clayton and Mistress Hawis?"

"None of the servants believes he was her lover. If Maynard thinks his impotence was a secret, he was foolish. It was widely known."

"An affliction that you reported to me after he told you, but do you believe him?"

"The man may have played the adoring puppy with his sister-in-law, but I am convinced he told me the truth and never did couple with her."

"Was he known to be a violent man?"

"Too meek, or so the servant I spoke to had heard. 'Neither man nor maid' was what he said. That was all I learned, my lady."

"My own search has been both interesting and unrewarding, Brother." Eleanor explained how she had discovered the clever method of keeping the curious out of the large chest, and then told him about the evidence of the prior search and casket with the broken lock. "There was little within it, but I suspect it once held what we need to discover the purpose of these killings."

"If the woman was killed for what she had, perhaps Maynard was murdered because he found it?"

"A possibility," Eleanor said. "But what was it?" She thought for a moment. "There was that one word I overheard, Brother, before Maynard was killed. *Document*. Even thinking back on that moment, I could not say which person uttered the word, the speech was whispered, and I am not familiar with Maynard's voice."

"Would a document have fit inside the broken casket?" Thomas gestured at the large chest.

"It depends on the size, of course, but a roll could have fit inside."

"So did Maynard kill Hawis for this? Did he see something he should not have? Was he even killed by the same person who killed her?"

"In truth, apart from the need to ponder all conclusions, I rarely believe in two separate killers," she said, "and thus feel certain that Maynard was murdered by the same man. He must have been involved in whatever matter this is, or he would not have been killed."

"So we have found new evidence, but that only leads to another mystery," Thomas said with frustration.

"At least we are getting closer to proving that Richard did not kill anyone." The prioress gave him a weak smile. "Since he could not have killed Maynard, he did not murder Hawis. His confession that he killed her out of humiliation is shown for the falsity it is."

Thomas nodded as he watched her gray eyes grow dark.

"We cannot let this additional puzzle deter us. It is my fault for having sheltered the three most popular suspects, but

I also know the consequences of my decision if they prove to be the killers. I have forced us into an indefensible position if I am wrong, and I cannot rest until we solve these cruel deeds, something we must do at once." With those words, she spun around and left the room.

Thomas followed. It did not matter whether she was right or wrong about ben David's family; she would discover the truth and reveal it, even if it reflected badly on her. If she was proven wrong, however, he swore not to let her be humiliated. He would find a way to take the blame.

Chapter Thirty-two

The following night, Sir Walter stood in the damp shadows by an open window and waited in the darkness.

An owl hooted softly in the distance.

His heart began to pound so loudly he feared it might awaken the sleeping nearby, but, above all, he was impatient.

He had heard that Queen Eleanor now knew that his wife had died by violence. Self-murder might be a matter for God's judgment, but murder was like a virulent plague. Each man wondered if he would be the next to be struck down.

Everything connected to his wife's death and that of his brother must be settled without delay, he thought. He wanted the right felon caught and sent off for hanging. If this was not done, he might be brought before an angry King Edward and questioned. Could he be certain that no flaw would be found in his work for the king? Every man had his enemies. He was confident that he knew those most likely to turn on him, but what if he were wrong this one time?

The owl hooted again. This time the sound was closer.

Sir Walter cursed the bird for its death screech and trembled. How long was this going to take?

Finally, he heard quiet footsteps and began to breathe more easily.

This nightmare would soon be over, he thought, and closed his eyes.

The blow landed sharply on the back of his head.

Chapter Thirty-three

Sir Walter groaned.

"You were struck on the back of your head," Sister Anne said. "You bled, but the wound will not kill you unless it festers."

FitzRoald bent over the blinking man. "What do you remember?"

Sir Walter winced. Despite his wound, he still glared at the sheriff. "Have you arrested them?"

"Who?" Prioress Eleanor stepped closer to the side of the bed. Brother Thomas was immediately behind her.

"What are you doing here?" The knight turned his head to look at her, then yelped with pain.

"Since my brother is planning the transportation of my father's body, Sister Anne, Brother Thomas, and I were with my nephew in his cell to console him on the death of his grandfather. We left to pray in the chapel," she replied, "and found you lying in the hall." She longed to show sympathy for this latest victim of the one who had already murdered two, but she was finding it difficult. "Did you see who struck you down?"

"The Jewess with the help of her young devil spawn!"

Eleanor bit back her dismay. When they found the knight, she sent her monk to bring the sheriff, but as soon as they returned, FitzRoald's first question to her was the whereabouts of the ben David family. When he courteously but firmly insisted her word be confirmed, she reluctantly chose to agree.

Even though Mistress Chera and her granddaughters were in the prioress' chambers, they were dressed as if ready to flee. Finding this suspicious, he questioned the grandmother who said she had heard a loud commotion, feared that soldiers might be coming to break down the doors, and made sure they were clad to endure the night chill.

"They are in custody," FitzRoald replied to Sir Walter.

Despite her objections on the family's behalf, the sheriff maintained he must put the women into stronger confinement until this attack could be solved. Eleanor had hoped that it would be a brief stay in quarters she knew were damp, cold, and without light. Now that Sir Walter was insisting that the blow had been struck by one of the family members, she knew there was no likelihood the women could return to more comfortable quarters.

"I hope you will hang them," the knight muttered. "Soon."

FitzRoald stiffened. "We live in a land ruled by law," he said.

"Then execute it!" The knight tried to laugh at his own wit. No one else was amused.

"I think Richard FitzHugh should be released," Brother Thomas said. "He could not have killed Maynard nor struck this blow against Sir Walter. It follows that he did not kill Mistress Hawis."

Although his expression suggested sympathy, FitzRoald shook his head. "He confessed to one killing, Brother. Until we are sure we have the killer and know why the crimes were done, he must remain in custody."

The monk began to argue.

"I agree that the case against him has faltered because he could not have attacked these brothers. As long as the lad is locked away, however, he cannot be accused of any further crimes. Surely, it is best if he be cleared of any involvement so none may ever cast doubt on his innocence in the future."

Eleanor nodded agreement, although her lack of enthusiasm for the decision matched Thomas' unhappiness. Her nephew longed to pray by his grandfather's body. His grief was profound.

"There shall not be any more murders, as long as you have locked away the Devil's own trio." The knight gingerly touched his bandage. "I am fortunate to have escaped with this painful wound."

"Leave that alone, Sir Walter," Sister Anne said. "A paste of woundwort heals well if allowed to do so."

"I am not ruled by women," he replied.

"Then do as you will and seek the advice of another," she snapped, then turned to her prioress. "One of the queen's ladies had asked for my opinion on a troubling condition. May I attend her?"

Eleanor granted leave. Rarely did her sub-infirmarian show impatience, but the prioress could not blame her for replying sharply to Sir Walter.

How could he blame the Jewish family? He was struck from behind and could not have seen the attacker. As far as she was concerned, he was simply eager to blame the women for no reason other than hate. She longed to shake some sense into the man, but he was wounded.

Eleanor felt weariness weighing ever more heavily on her but was determined to solve these crimes. Willing herself to find the strength, she stiffened her back and asked the sheriff to follow her a short distance away. Briefly, she spoke to him and received his assent to her request.

"Come, Brother," she said to Thomas, "we must speak with Mistress Chera."

FitzRoald gestured to a man standing further off.

The soldier dutifully followed the monastics at a respectful distance.

◇◇◇

The cell was a hole dug into the earth beneath the manor. Although empty, it looked as if it had once been intended as a storage place for food stuffs should the manor be attacked. It was also unfinished. Stones lined the walls, but damp had streaked them black with mold. The floor remained earthen, moist, and fetid.

The three women huddled together for warmth.

With a candle in hand, Eleanor knelt beside Mistress Chera. The one girl drew her grandmother closer and further away from the prioress.

"Fear not," she said. "I have no wish to hurt any of you and long only for justice."

"My son did too, my lady, but he was hanged nonetheless." Chera's voice was rough, either from tears or the damp.

"I cannot bring him back to you," the prioress replied, "but you are alive. Help me keep you so."

"My granddaughters cannot be guilty of any crime. They should be released."

"Please answer my questions so I may persuade others of that."

The one girl whispered into her grandmother's ear. Chera shook her head. "If I have discovered nothing else in my long life," she said to her granddaughter, "I have learned that there are always good people hidden amongst those who hate us." Then she turned back to the prioress. "Ask what you must, and I shall be truthful." In the wavering candlelight, her face matched the sickly yellow of the badge she wore on her robe.

Eleanor shuddered. "Did you kill Mistress Hawis, Master Maynard, or Sir Walter?"

"Sir Walter, too?" She shook her head. "I did not, nor did my girls. Why would I be so...?" She took a deep breath, then finished her sentence. "Why would I be so unwise?" Her words were heavy with resignation.

But Eleanor noted that she was surprised when told Sir Walter had been killed. The sheriff might not take it as an indication that she was ignorant of what had happened before her arrest, but the prioress did. "Were you planning to flee after you had given me your word that you would remain in my chambers? The sheriff is convinced you were."

"He is a man who has never been damned solely on assumptions, my lady. We are Jews. We are condemned for all evil, including wickedness that we abhor as much as Christians do." She uttered a soft cry, and then reached out to the prioress. "My words were born of hopelessness. Forgive me! You are suffering great sorrow after the death of your father, yet you have been kind to us. I have added to your burdens and did not mean to offend."

"Nor have I been," Eleanor replied softly. "Please continue with your tale."

"After being awakened by the noise of soldiers entering our house, when we were all abed, and seeing men drag my son away to die, I cannot hear the sound of armed men pounding on our door and conclude they mean no harm." She bent her head toward the girls. "For myself, I care nothing. I am an old woman. If the king chooses to have me hanged, the loss of a few years of life means little. But my granddaughters? Even if they were not hanged, I know what soldiers do to young girls when they are children of those they hate. Yes, my lady, I confess I would have urged them to flee to save themselves, if it had been possible to do so, but I would have honored my word to you and stayed behind."

"But you all remained in the chambers."

"Only because I was too slow to sense the danger."

"Is there a witness to confirm that you remained in my quarters all night?"

"The soldiers outside the door should, but I cannot swear that they did not fall asleep or slip away. I never opened the door to see if they were there or what they were doing." She shrugged, but tears glistened in her eyes. "Even if they were watching outside for the entire night, they might lie because…" She looked away.

Mistress Chera did not need to finish her sentence. Eleanor knew what she would have said. The prioress might find it impossible to understand why the Jews refused to convert, a rejection that put them in danger of Satan's claws, but she had never believed the absurd tales told of them and the presumption of dishonor.

"Did you know about the thief who entered your house the night of the raid?"

"There was a robber?"

The prioress nodded. How she regretted not asking the woman about this before, but she had failed to do so because of her need to be by her father's side and to pray for his soul. Had she asked, might she have prevented this last attack?

"I saw nothing. We had been taken in by a family who lived a few houses down from my poor son, my lady. After that, many of us who lost everything, moved from one household to another. We never entered our house again. I could not bear to walk past it, nor could my doves."

The sheriff might be an honest man, Eleanor thought, but he shared the common suspicions against those in the Jewish community. The more she spoke with the grandmother, the stronger her belief in the virtue and innocence of these three. And when the heart remained good, there is always hope for salvation. FitzRoald might be inclined to find them guilty. She was resolved to fight on their behalf.

"May I ask if anyone else is truly suspect in this violence, my lady? Please tell me the truth."

"My nephew confessed to killing Mistress Hawis, but he could not have committed the subsequent crimes. As for his confession, he has admitted he lied and explained why he confessed in the first place. His guilt is no longer believed."

"For your sake, I am glad."

Eleanor felt a stab of sympathetic grief and reached out to grasp Chera's hand. Neither had to say that Lumbard ben David had not been as lucky to escape the gallows as the prioress' nephew.

"With no other suspect, I have a proposal for you and the sheriff." Chera stood. "Will you swear to let my girls go and make sure they return safely to the Jewish Quarter in Oxford to one whose name I shall give you?"

The girls cried out in protest. She hushed them.

"And what is the price for this?" Eleanor knew the answer and felt tears smart in her eyes.

"I shall confess to the crimes and swear I did it by myself. My girls remain innocent of all violence."

"That is not true!" the more spirited girl cried out. "You did nothing!"

"You are as innocent as they," Eleanor said. "I join them in urging you not to do this."

"As innocent as my son? His death stripped everything from us except our lives and the clothes we wore. We are already condemned, my lady. The only boon I ask is that my granddaughters be allowed to live. On the gallows, I shall find comfort that they have escaped this persecution, will find husbands in a safe haven, and that one of their babes might bear my name."

Eleanor embraced this woman who was far braver than most mortals. "I shall fight to save your granddaughters, but I will not let you give a false confession. The real killer will be found. I have not given up hope."

The old woman smiled with gratitude, but her look betrayed her certainty that they would never be found blameless.

The prioress read that in her eyes and bent to murmur in her ear, "I think we both can agree that there has been enough killing of innocents. You shall not be another in that number."

With that, Eleanor left the women, climbed out of the dank hole and into the light.

When she emerged, Brother Thomas saw that she was weeping.

Chapter Thirty-four

Thomas walked down the hall to the small room where Richard was confined.

In front of the door, two soldiers sat playing with dice. One was grinning; the other looked grim.

Father Eliduc emerged from the youth's cell and turned to shut the door. Before he had a chance to react to the wickedness of gambling taking place at his feet, he saw the monk and hurried toward him.

"He is in better spirits, Brother!" Unlike his usual contrived looks, his smile appeared to be genuinely happy. "The sheriff allowed the lad to pray by his grandfather's corpse, albeit under heavy guard."

Thomas said nothing. The sheriff had permitted this at the request of Baron Hugh, but the priest's demeanor suggested he had been the source of the kindness instead. The monk was outraged but knew it was best not to speak until his temper had cooled.

No matter what the circumstances, he loathed being in the priest's company, but Thomas had to use this convenient meeting to find out why the word *document* and the name *Eliduc* were mentioned together just before Maynard was killed. This is for Richard, he reminded himself, and he would do anything to prove him innocent.

Eliduc was looking up at the monk with an expression of such freshly hewn innocence that even his breath smelled like newly chopped wood. "I have been thinking about details learned in this tragic series of violent acts, and I have decided that something I know, which I otherwise considered of no interest in this matter, might be mentioned."

Thomas replied to this with a look of well-chiseled curiosity. Was the priest about to tell him what Prioress Eleanor had wanted him to ask? If so, he still suspected the motive. Father Eliduc was deceitful, yet not without his occasional virtue. It was harder to deal with those of mixed integrity. When someone was focused solely on evil, it was easier to know what to do. With others, one never knew whether to rejoice or flee.

"Let us step away from ears that flap like the wings of young birds." The priest gestured to a private spot near a window.

While Thomas looked down at the courtyard filled with tradesmen, beasts, and a few hopeful beggars, Eliduc lowered his head as if praying for guidance.

The monk waited.

"In the months leading up to the raids on homes of coin-clippers, Lumbard ben David sent for me. After the Statute of the Jewry was enacted, he had suffered a growing fear that hatred for those of his faith might lead to violence. As he noted, King Edward had found another source of income with Italian bankers, the Riccardi. The reasons for protecting the Jews had therefore diminished, and the increasing taxation, as well as restrictions on money-lending, had begun to impoverish many."

"He might have left England if he feared for his safety."

"Indeed. Many have since the Statute, but ben David was reluctant to do so. He was a physician, not a money-lender, and Oxford had been home to his family since they arrived from Rouen at King William's behest."

What must it be like, Thomas wondered, never to feel secure in a place and be forced to leave a land where the family had lived for so many generations? He had lost his dwelling and family when he was thrown into prison, but he had found another home at Tyndal Priory and had no fear he might be displaced from it.

"His reason for calling on me was to pay for protection."

"Pay you for protection?" This was intriguing, the monk thought.

"Not me. He wanted to pay the Church to protect him and his family."

"Then he wished to convert?"

"Sadly, he was stubborn in his misguided faith, but, as I assume you know, the Church can sometimes be more patient in these matters than kings."

That depended on the pope, Thomas thought, but King Edward was not known for his patience in matters he cared about. Like his father, he was a deeply pious man and looked upon conversion of the Jews as one of his fervent goals. He had continued to maintain a house where converts to Christianity might live, albeit in simple monastic style, and which was paid for, in part, by a tax on the Jewish community.

"I shall make this story a short one. Ben David offered to give his house and other material goods to the Church in exchange for protection should he be in danger from a riot against the Jews. In my presence, he signed a document stating that all his property, other than an agreed amount required to support his family, would revert to the Church after his death."

"But the Church did not save his life."

"He was accused of treason and hanged, Brother. The Church would not wish to argue against the evidence found within his house that proved he was a traitor to the king. That is quite different from threats due to a riot."

"As I have heard, everything went to the king."

"It did, although the document, had it been presented, might have caused our king to bow to the Church's interest." His smile dripped like sweet honey on hot bread. "Our king is devout. Ben David's property would have gone into his coffers, as the possessions of all traitors do, but I am confident he would not have denied the Church generous recompense had he seen the agreement."

"What happened to this item?"

"Ben David had it in his possession. Out of fear, he hesitated to give it to me, lest he need proof that he was under Church protection if violence occurred. I saw him put it into a box and place it with his other important records."

"Why did he not show it to the soldiers the night he was arrested?"

"The men had the damning evidence of treason when they entered the house. Ben David was arrested and hauled away in chains. I doubt he had time to present the document. Even if he had, he was condemned under the king's law."

"Then they knew where to look for the coin-clipping items," Thomas murmured. "Perhaps someone did hide the proof so ben David would be arrested even though he was innocent."

Eliduc looked impatient.

The monk suddenly realized what the priest was more interested in. "Of course, the physician did not produce the agreement, did he? Had he done so, Sir Walter would have brought it to the king's attention before any action was taken to sell the house and dispose of the valuables."

Eliduc smiled with relief that the monk was no longer distracted by conclusions of little concern to him.

"And the document has disappeared?"

Father Eliduc brightened as if faced with a clever student. "I think it was stolen, along with other valuable items, when the house was plundered that night after ben David's arrest."

Thomas felt like stars were exploding in his head as reasons for the recent events began to link. "Prioress Eleanor found a casket very well-hidden in a chest in Mistress Hawis' chambers. The lock had been broken, and casket was inexplicably empty. An unnamed document was mentioned between Maynard and his slayer. Might she have had this item?" He did not mention that Eliduc's name had been spoken as well. The link was now clear.

"If she did, I cannot imagine where she got it." Eliduc scowled. "I am sure she was incapable of reading anything, most certainly Latin, but, if she knew the content, she might have seen a use for it. Had Mistress Hawis confronted the queen with the agreement, the woman could have hoped the queen would change her mind about dismissing her. After all, if the Church was supposed to get ben David's property, the king could be accused of stealing from the Church when he put the profits into his own coffers." He thought for a moment, and then shook his head. "I doubt she was that clever. She probably did not know what was in it, but, if not, why keep it?"

A loud burst of laughter from one of the soldiers caused Eliduc to spin around and glare. He ignored the triumphant look on the one, who had previously been so sad, and reprimanded them both for their sins.

Although the men tried to look contrite, they failed.

The priest lost interest, turned back to Thomas, and shook his head.

The soldiers went back to their game of dice.

"I doubt she had the document," Eliduc said. "I see no reason why she should."

"Maybe she knew the robber, and he gave it to her?"

"Why would he have done so? As I said, unless the thief was a cleric, a most doubtful conclusion, he wouldn't have known what the document meant. I think he stole it, but wanted the well-crafted box it was in. Surely, the thief would not have cared about ben David's papers. They were of no worth to anyone except those who owed money to the physician, and, as I have heard, Sir Walter burned the debt records. If we find the robber, we may find the document if he has not destroyed it before selling the casket it was in."

Thomas tried again. "This kind of theft leads to the scaffold. If Mistress Hawis knew who that person was, she might have been killed to keep her silent."

"And Maynard? And Sir Walter? Why were they attacked?"

Thomas was frustrated. There was something crucial missing here, but he could not see it. Finally, he gave up and asked the one question which he was certain would result in a useful answer. "Why are you telling me about this missing agreement between ben David and the Church?"

"To help save Richard's life."

"That is not the reason. Richard is innocent, a conclusion that the sheriff has come to see. He waits only for the killer to be found before he releases the lad. If nothing is resolved, he will eventually let him go anyway. What do you really want to achieve?"

"I want the thief found. Whether or not he is guilty of killing the woman, as you suggest, there is no reason why we cannot decide he is the culprit. As one who robbed the possessions of traitors, he is a traitor for he stole from the king. Why not a murderer? He will hang anyway, and Richard will be freed of all blame."

"And let the real killer go free? Are we to ignore justice?"

Eliduc's expression was grim. "I also want what is due the Church returned to it. If the king is presented with the agreement between ben David and the Church, the king may not be able to give the house and possessions back, but he can honor his duty to God and gift the Church appropriately."

"And ben David's mother and his daughters? What do they regain?"

"I fear they have lost all, Brother. No one can say what they may be owed, if anything. Ben David's innocence cannot be proven so we must assume he was guilty of treason, as he was originally found. This whole matter is between the king and the Church." He smiled. "Perhaps the women will convert and live under the benevolence of King Edward's charity."

Thomas felt his anger ready to explode. No matter what their faith, this old woman and her granddaughters deserved better. Forced conversion was no conversion at all. Not only was that his judgment, but it was also the stated opinion of several Churchmen who were far wiser than he.

But his fury would solve nothing, and he pushed it back. The one who had killed two and attacked another must be found or the grandmother might still be hanged and the girls as well. If it was the thief, and the priest's precious document was found, all would be content. But he wanted the murderer caught, not appointed as a convenient solution.

"You must tell Prioress Eleanor about this, then the sheriff," he said with an exhausting effort to appear calm. "The information about the missing agreement may lead us to the killer, a result for which we all pray. Surely you would agree that there must be no doubt about Richard's innocence, once he is freed. None of us would want suspicion to linger because the actual killer remained free." He hesitated for emphasis.

Eliduc's expression suggested he was suffering more conflict than he ought to be. A man of secrets, he was disinclined to such cooperation with others, but the struggle was quite short. In a tone that was uncharacteristically sincere and obliging, he agreed.

For a brief moment, the monk pondered this rare show of graciousness. Might the priest have actually grown fond of the lad, apart from any use he might have for Richard in the future? As Thomas and the priest walked away, he decided against that conclusion. When had he ever seen evidence that Father Eliduc possessed a heart?

Behind them, the soldiers continued their game in which Fortune was once again smiling on the man who had won first.

Chapter Thirty-five

Prioress Eleanor had dark circles under her eyes, and her complexion was almost as gray as her eyes, but determination flashed in them.

The men, who stood with her outside the chapel where her dead father lay, gazed with awe at the force of her authority.

Her brother looked at her with both esteem and sympathy.

Father Eliduc lowered his gaze to avoid giving away any opinion of this daughter of Eve. He had tried to argue against including her in this meeting but failed. Baron Hugh had insisted her opinion be heard, and no one in this company dared to thwart the grim-faced friend of the king.

"Who profits most from Mistress Hawis' death?" Eleanor's tone was icy. "She was the first killed, and thus I assume she was most important to the killer."

"What does the bag of coin-clippings found by Maynard mean?" Thomas spoke since no one else seemed so inclined. "He was the second killed, but the bag surely had significance worth contemplating."

"Sir Walter was attacked but not killed, nor was anything left by his side." Eleanor looked around at the assembled men. "What does that suggest?"

"I am convinced that the killer must be in this manor, my lady," FitzRoald said. "And if it is not the Jewish women, it must be someone attached to the queen's retinue. King Edward took his men with him before this all began."

Thomas raised his eyebrows. "One of the ladies who waits upon our queen?"

The sheriff shrugged with evident discomfort at that conclusion.

"The coin-clippings point to a connection with the hanging of the Jews," Father Eliduc said. "Leaving them by Maynard's corpse may suggest that he was connected to that event as well."

Hugh sneered. "And isn't it convenient that ben David's surviving family just happened to be here when these deaths occurred and the bag of coin bits was left? Perhaps we are meant to think they are involved when, in fact, they are not."

Surprised at his words, Eleanor looked up at her brother with a brief smile.

The room fell silent.

Sister Anne appeared at the chapel entryway.

"I shall join you soon for prayer," Eleanor said, her words softened with melancholy.

The infirmarian gazed at her prioress with concern, then disappeared inside.

Taking a deep breath, the prioress continued. "We currently have two suspects in custody: my nephew and ben David's family. Please set courtesy aside in this matter for a moment. Do any of you think either guilty and why?"

"In my opinion, neither is a likely killer," FitzRoald said. "Your nephew claimed to have killed Mistress Hawis because she mocked him, but he could not have murdered Maynard Clayton or attacked Sir Walter. These three are members of the same family. Your nephew had no reason to attack all. As I thought about past violent deaths I have investigated, I realized that multiple murders are usually done by the same person. I believe Richard FitzHugh is innocent of murder."

"You are less certain than you have been about the guilt of ben David's mother and daughters?" Thomas might have been pleased, but he carefully hid any hint of his opinion.

FitzRoald bowed his head, then looked at the somber prioress. "I have gone over the evidence once again and considered the wisdom of your logic. Mistress Chera is too old and weak to have strangled, and then hanged Mistress Hawis. The knife that killed Maynard was driven into his back up to the hilt. That requires more strength than an old woman has." He raised a hand. "Even if she managed to escape from your chambers, my lady, she could not have struck Sir Walter so hard that he was rendered unconscious."

"Her granddaughters? Might they have committed the crimes alone or with her?" Father Eliduc avoided looking at the prioress. "I ask, not because I am convinced of their guilt, but to hear your opinion."

FitzRoald shook his head. "The girls are on the verge of womanhood. Is it reasonable to think either could have killed Mistress Hawis, a grown woman, or stabbed Maynard with the strength it took to drive the blade that deep? And how could they have struck Sir Walter with enough force?"

"One might have held Sir Walter's wife down while the other strangled her, although Mistress Hawis was a strong woman." Father Eliduc waited for a response, then continued. "Maynard may not have been robust, but it would have taken strength to drive the knife into him that deeply. I agree that the two children were not strong enough." There was a hint of regret in his voice. "As for the attack on Sir Walter, neither girl has the power of a lad their age, and I doubt a boy could have done the deed either."

"Lumbard ben David's family is innocent." Baron Hugh's voice trembled with evident anger. "Find your killer amongst those who kill for greed."

Father Eliduc replied to the baron's fury with a thin smile.

"I shall add my support of your logic, Father," Thomas said, "I doubt the girls could have done it between them. Mistress Hawis would have screamed and lashed out while they fumbled about her neck. This strangling indicates swift action, which suggests knowledge of how to kill efficiently and the strength to do so, as does the stabbing death of her brother-in-law. If they could not have committed the first two crimes, they could not have done the third."

Eleanor looked at each one of the men.

None had further comment.

"Shall we all agree to this summary? Richard and ben David's family had some reason to kill Mistress Hawis," Eleanor said. "They were also able to do so because all were free. What motive, however, did any have to attack Maynard and Sir Walter? Richard might have been physically able to commit the crimes, but we believe it unlikely that Mistress Chera and the girls could. He was locked in a cell for the last two attacks. The ben David family was under guard, although the reliability of the watch is suspect. Finally, it seems probable the murders were done by the same person. If the suspects are innocent of one crime, they are probably innocent of all."

The men muttered agreement, even Hugh who clenched his fist at the mention of his son having motive.

The prioress briefly touched her brother's arm. "The High Sheriff of Berkshire has just concluded, as do we all, that your son must be found innocent of those crimes."

Again, the men nodded.

Hugh's dour expression did not change.

Nor would it, Eleanor decided, until Richard was freed. "Even if we assume that Mistress Chera and the girls could have killed Sir Walter's wife," she said, "we have no proof they were outside my chambers when Maynard was stabbed or Sir Walter attacked. They might have slipped out, because the guard was lax, but to assume they left my custody is as erroneous as it might be to say they had not."

No one spoke.

"I ask you all this. Can any build a logical argument that Mistress Chera and the girls are capable of these crimes, let alone be the perpetrators?"

Each man looked at the others and waited for someone to speak.

"I do not think they did it, my lady," Thomas finally said.

All but Father Eliduc agreed.

"What is your opinion?" Eleanor asked the priest.

"I do not necessarily disagree," he replied, "but I believe this violence was born when Sir Walter and his men raided the homes in the Jewish Quarter and arrested the traitors."

"I am inclined to concur, Father. My wish is to approach this problem by eliminating aspects that have distracted us from the truth and thus hidden it from us." Eleanor briefly looked behind her at the chapel where she longed to retreat to mourn for her father.

"We must carefully debate further," Eliduc replied.

Brother Thomas felt his face flush with anger. Had this callous priest forgotten that Baron Adam had just died, his daughter was in mourning, and she was speaking to them only because God had called on her to serve justice?

"Having agreed that my nephew is innocent," Eleanor said, "why should we not also conclude that Mistress Chera and her granddaughters, although convenient suspects, lack the physical strength to commit the crimes? We have no evidence that they were unconfined for the last two attacks. The case for their guilt is very weak indeed." She noted the hesitant expressions on the faces of two men. "Concentrating on them may have served only to deflect us from discovering the truth."

Hugh and Thomas nodded. There was a short, grumbling conversation between Eliduc and the sheriff before the latter said, "We see no reason to disagree, my lady."

"That leaves us with a suspect who committed an interesting and uncharacteristic crime the night of the raids." She looked around. "The robber of ben David's house. The High Sheriff has suggested the murderer is in residence at Woodstock Manor. I agree. Ben David's house was the only one plundered, which points to a prior knowledge of the raids and locations of targeted houses by the thief."

"And suggests that there might be a reason that particular house was chosen to rob," Thomas added.

"Were that person to be discovered, he would be hanged for stealing from the king. That provides a motive for trying to distract us with other feasible suspects," the prioress replied.

"Or she?" FitzRoald looked uncomfortable.

"Women are small and may slip into places that men cannot. That noted," she said, "the description given to my brother suggests a man."

Hugh nodded.

The priest rubbed his hands together, eager to start the task. "If we decide that the robber is a murder suspect and agree with the sheriff that the killer is in Woodstock Manor, shall we now begin to consider the likelihood of guilt for each man in residence here?"

"Including servants?" The sheriff looked around with dismay.

"Forgive me," Eleanor said, "but we must act swiftly and do not have the time to carefully examine the details of individual circumstances. As I have learned, the queen knows that Death walks the halls here. I am sure you all agree that her safety is our first concern, and others may suffer if this elusive criminal is not captured immediately."

FitzRoald gasped. "I could not face her or our king if a murderer continued to remain free in Woodstock Manor while she is still weak from childbirth!"

Looking at their expressions after those words from the High Sheriff, the prioress knew that nothing further need be said about the retribution each would suffer if the killer were not caught. "The swiftest way to catch the killer is to set a trap," Eleanor said, then looked at her monk." Remember what we did when Father Etienne Davoir was at Tyndal Priory?"

He nodded. It had not been a pleasant experience, but the plan had worked.

"Spread the tale that a witness to the plundering has been discovered and summoned here to identify the perpetrator," she said to the men. "Make sure that all hear that the witness is expected tonight." She gestured to FitzRoald. "You shall meet with the man in public and tell him that you have arranged particular rooms so he can rest before you question him further in the morning."

The sheriff agreed.

Baron Hugh began to beg for his son's release.

Thomas put a restraining hand on the baron's arm. "If this is to satisfy any question about his innocence, my lord, then your son, Mistress Chera, and her granddaughters must remain under a vigilant guard until we have a confession from the murderer. To make sure there is no doubt whatsoever, I urge that all four be chained to stone walls until the killer is arrested. I fear that Richard must be moved to the cell with the ben David family since it will be easier to watch one place. The cell under the manor, foul though it is, is a far stronger prison."

The prioress' brother looked as if he might strike the monk. Then he shook off Thomas' hand. "You are right," he growled, and strode to a window to stare up at the sky.

Eleanor followed after him and spoke quietly with her brother. After a moment, he nodded with enthusiasm and swiftly left the gathering.

"Baron Hugh has gone to bring our witness back to the Manor," she said with a slight smile. "I did assume we were all agreed to the setting of a trap."

They all murmured consent.

Prioress Eleanor drew them closer together and explained how she hoped to tempt the prey to the snare.

Chapter Thirty-six

Torchlight is a fickle thing, promising clarity but offering shadows instead.

Were anyone to ask who the man was that the High Sheriff of Berkshire greeted in the hall near the queen's lying in chamber, most would be hard-pressed to describe him in useful detail.

He was of modest height and dressed in a dark cloak of middling quality, if one could judge without fingering the cloth. A hood, worn to fend off the chill drizzle from the night's damp-laden air, hid his face, but a thick, iron-gray beard was visible, sparkling with flecks of moisture.

There was no mistaking the pleasure with which FitzRoald spoke with him. It was clear that the man's arrival had lightened the sheriff's previously burdened spirit.

Gesturing to a servant, FitzRoald ordered him to take the man to quarters far from the queen but ones he swore would be comfortable. The distance from mingling courtiers guaranteed quiet needed for a good night's rest, the sheriff promised him, and he would question him tomorrow on this matter of the thievery.

Then FitzRoald turned to speak with Brother Thomas, and the stranger accompanied the servant to the chambers.

Although no one seemed to notice, the pair was followed by another to whom torchlight offered no more illumination than it had to the new arrival.

When the pair arrived at a modest room near the smallest chapel in Woodstock Manor, the servant opened the door and pointed out the chest on which stood a jug of wine and a mazer. The guest muttered words with the tone of satisfaction. Then the servant gave him the brightly burning candle he held, closed the door after the guest, and hurried back down the hall to attend to his many other duties.

The one who had followed remained, lounging nearby and apparently enjoying the view. There was a break in the mist, and weak moonlight played with the vague forms of scudding dark clouds.

Time passed.

The manor house residents found their beds, with or without the comfort of a companion. Hush, if not silence, fell over Woodstock. Not even the dying are truly quiet. Even in Satan's hour the earth is never still.

At last, the flickering light under the chamber door vanished. The one in shadows waited, then left the window and crept toward the chamber where the guest must now be asleep.

Opening the door with care, he slipped inside but left the door slightly ajar to allow moonlight to enter with him. He approached the bed where the guest lay.

The dagger glinted briefly as he raised his hand. With swift strength, he plunged the knife into the body.

The impact was too soft. He pushed down on the mound in the bed with his hand. This was no body.

Alarmed, the man staggered back toward the door to escape. But someone barred the entrance. The would-be assassin tried to move to the side, but the man grabbed his arms and twisted them back with an iron grip. The knife fell to the floor, and the captive shrieked in pain.

Through the door, a small company of men, led by Baron Hugh, filled the room. Two bore torches.

Hugh went over to the bed and flipped back the cover to reveal several rolled up blankets. Bending down, he said, "You can come out now."

Joshua of Oxford dragged himself from under the bed.

FitzRoald gestured to one of the soldiers to hold a torch close to the prisoner's face.

"Torold," the sheriff said with a sour grin.

"Shall we put him in the fine accommodations now occupied by my son and ben David's family?" Hugh smiled with mocking pleasure.

"As the proven killer in these crimes, he deserves it," the sheriff said. "The women will have to share less prestigious quarters with your sister, and your son shall be released into your custody."

Torold was bound and led away, screaming with terror and pain.

Chapter Thirty-seven

"I shall not go to Hell alone," Torold said and spat on the slimy earth.

Arms folded, FitzRoald stood over him and waited.

Baron Hugh remained by the entry to the cell. His grim countenance and black robes made him resemble Death in the flickering light of the torch he held.

"Why should we believe anything you say?" The sheriff looked around as if seeking a less foul smelling place to stand.

"Because I gained nothing from my deeds and hear no cries protesting my innocence after my arrest. Have you?" His eyes expressed hope as dim as the light.

"None."

A shiver went through Torold. "I want a priest."

"You shall have one after you confess to the murders you carried out and accept the king's sentence on your crimes."

"And the man who compelled me to commit the crimes? Shall he hang beside me? That is only just. My last sight on earth must be the terror in his eyes."

"Who is this man?"

"Sir Walter Clayton."

Baron Hugh drifted closer to the man. "Whom did you kill?"

Although his bowels must have been trembling at the thought of his hanging, Torold made an effort to shrug. "Mistress Hawis and Maynard Clayton."

"And yet Sir Walter was attacked?" Hugh bent down, moved his torch to a hand's breadth of the man's face, and stared into his eyes.

Torold slid back against the wall. "Do not hurt me, my lord! I swear that I tell the truth."

Hugh straightened and walked back to the spot near the entry hole in the ceiling. "I think he shall," he said over his shoulder to the sheriff.

"I did hit him, at his command, so he might escape suspicion. He wanted all the blame for the crimes placed on the Jews."

"Tell your tale," FitzRoald said. "All of it."

Torold shifted again, but the chains that bound him allowed only a foot to change position. "When Sir Walter was directed by the king to raid the homes of the coin-clipping traitors in the Jewish Quarter, he saw the chance to gain profit for himself. Lumbard ben David was not involved in money-lending, or any activity that would put him into a suspicious category, but Sir Walter knew he had valuables in his possession. I was ordered to hide evidence of coin-clipping in the thatch of the physician's roof near the front where it could be easily found."

"Sir Walter did not fear that our king would find this plot criminal?" Hugh's words were sharp as if he had snapped off the ends in anger.

"Please, my lord, do not take this question as impertinence." Torold hesitated. "Has King Edward ordered any investigation into the validity of the arrests? I wish only to suggest that Sir Walter had a reason to assume that his deeds would not be questioned."

The question lingered too long without an answer.

Hugh broke the silence. "Our liege lord shall hear of this," he muttered.

"If your master planned to steal valuables from the physician, it was a dangerous plan. If our king discovered such a theft from his coffers, he would order the knight hanged." FitzRoald's tone suggested skepticism that Clayton would be so imprudent.

"Sir Walter loves to increase his wealth, but he is not a fool. If he got the valuables, but made sure the king got the Jew's house,

he doubted King Edward would miss the comparative pittance."
Torold looked at each man as if to judge whether they believed
him. "Sir Walter took nothing from any other house." His grin
was crooked. "He may be a thief, but he is not a greedy one."

"Were you the robber who stole the valuables and the document proving the house should go to the Church?" Baron Hugh's
voice resembled the growl of an angry wolf.

Torold nodded.

"I do not understand how your master even knew about the
document or why he found value in it," FitzRoald said.

"He pays for useful information. On whatever hope my soul
may have to escape Hell, I swear I do not know the name of the
one who told Sir Walter about it. I do recall when he announced
to me that Father Eliduc and ben David had signed an agreement
in which the Jew would give the Church his house and much
of his wealth in exchange for protection of his family against
violence. Then he said that ben David had kept the document
in his house, and my master rubbed his hands with relief."

"And the merit of stealing this?" The sheriff pinched his nose
as if the stench of the place had suddenly grown especially foul.

"If stolen, the king would never know of the agreement or
ask why Sir Walter did not honor it when he raided the house.
Our king is a man of faith and, had he known, would have
insisted that recompense be given to the Church, even though
ben David was given a traitor's death. The king might have even
insisted the compensation come from my master."

"So you stole it with the plate and jewels," the sheriff said.
"Where did it go afterward?"

"I gave it to his brother to hide until Sir Walter was certain
there was no other copy or evidence of its existence."

"Did he not fear the word of Father Eliduc, swearing to the
signing of the agreement?"

"That would take time. The house would have been sold,
and the profit transferred to the king's coffers. The assumption
would be made that any other treasure would have been included
in the sale. By then, my master would have known if there was

another record. If not, all he need say was that he found no such document and suggest the beldam had destroyed it."

"And what did happen to the valuables?" FitzRoald asked.

"Sir Walter took them to London to sell. He did so piecemeal so no one would wonder how he had so much to dispose of at one time."

"Why give the agreement to the brother?" Baron Hugh called out.

"Sir Walter told me to do so." He laughed although there was no merriment in it. "He thought he could trust him. His brother owed his food and roof to the man as much as I did. If either of us had stood up to him and refused, Sir Walter would have kicked us into the gutter to starve."

FitzRoald looked perplexed. "Why did you kill your lord's wife?"

"Because she learned of its importance and stole the document for her own purposes. With it, she could avoid being sent to a convent and demand more of her husband's wealth." He shook his head. "Knowing how much Maynard wanted to possess her, I suspect he may have drunk too much and lied about the night after the raid. Maybe he bragged that he was the one to brave the guard and steal from the house. She couldn't read, so she had to have learned the tale from him, probably as she was fondling him and urging him to tell her more of his great deeds."

"No man would betray his brother like that," the sheriff replied.

Torold snorted. "The brother is no man, but I know she found out because she sent a message to her husband that he owed her far more than usual from his new wealth. She threatened to expose him for the theft to the king and also said she had the document to prove he had plundered the house." He began to cough. "Father Eliduc would have supported her tale because he wanted the Church to benefit, as had been promised."

"So Sir Walter ordered her killed to keep himself from the scaffold?"

"My liege lord is rather fond of living. While he was in London, he sent me back to Woodstock. I arrived late at night, slipped into her room after some youth had left it, and strangled her. Then I hanged her to make it look like she had taken her own life. It was a good plan to draw all suspicion away from the idea of murder. After all, was she not a notorious harlot? Satan might have demanded her soul and sent one of his imps to get it. I erred in not realizing the skill of Prioress Eleanor and her sub-infirmarian."

"Richard," Hugh muttered.

FitzRoald looked at him.

"That youth mentioned must have been my son. When Richard came to her chamber, he saw a man in the hall outside who fled."

"I saw someone, my lord, and did slip away. I waited until he left." Torold looked hopeful. "If my testimony frees your son, will that gain me mercy?"

The sheriff gestured at Baron Hugh to silence him. "God has been known to perform miracles," FitzRoald said and then quickly continued his questioning. "After you killed Mistress Hawis, did you find the document she had taken from Maynard?"

"I had little time to do so for I had to return to London lest I be discovered and suspicion fall on Sir Walter. Although I searched, I did not find anything."

"And Maynard's death? Why?" the sheriff asked.

"After Sir Walter returned and was told the tragedy of his wife's death," Torold said, "he went through her rooms but also found nothing. Then he forced Maynard to tell him how easily the document was stolen. I overheard his anger and he ordered his brother to find it and get it for him." His coughing grew harsher, and he fell silent.

"Did Maynard threaten his brother?" FitzRoald asked impatiently. "Is that why he was killed? Or did he fail to find what Sir Walter wanted?"

"Oh, he found it and sent word of his success, but Sir Walter no longer trusted him. He ordered me to get the document from him and then kill him to guarantee his silence. My master believes he is never wrong. When proven otherwise, his anger is implacable."

The torch light was fading. Hugh shouted up to the soldiers, and a man passed a freshly lit one down to him. The yellow flame fluttered and cast uneasy shadows on the damp stone walls.

"The bag of coin-clippings? What was the point of that?" FitzRoald shivered. The damp was seeping through his robe, and he was growing weary of the need to question a murderer in this unhealthy place.

"That was my idea! Sir Walter wanted the Jews to hang for these crimes since the old shrew had threatened his dead wife. I had a few silver bits left from what I had planted in ben David's house so I dropped the remainder in that bag by Maynard's body."

"What happened when you returned the document to your master?"

"He burned it, convinced after all this time that no copy had been given to the Church or Father Eliduc. The king could keep the money from the sale of the property, and Sir Walter had the profits from the sale of the valuables taken from the house. His wife was dead, and his brother had paid the price for his treachery. Sir Walter was well satisfied."

Hugh muttered something and turned his back on the two men.

"Then you attacked Sir Walter?"

"He ordered me to strike him, just enough to render him unconscious, so no suspicion could taint him." Torold sounded bitter. "As was my custom, I did everything for him as perfectly as possible. So why am I left here in this place where even the rats grow putrid before they die? Why has he done nothing to ease my confinement, even if he refuses to admit he ordered the murders I committed? This is my reward for my years of service to him?"

FitzRoald had no answer for that question and turned instead to Hugh. "Have you any further questions, my lord?"

The baron declined the offer.

"Your son is free of all blame, although he may be a witness to the presence of this man outside Mistress Hawis' chambers," FitzRoald said. "There is also no further need to detain ben David's mother and daughters. I will tell my soldiers that they may let the three leave your sister's chambers."

"And Joshua of Oxford can find some solace in knowing he has helped bring to justice those who wrongly sent Lumbard ben David to his death," Hugh replied. "I shall tell the king how his desire for justice and the rule of law was perverted by the man he trusted to arrest only the guilty."

"If it would give you satisfaction, my lord," FitzRoald said, "do you wish to take some of my men and arrest Sir Walter before he tries to escape?"

And indeed it did gratify Baron Hugh of Wynethorpe to witness Sir Walter being seized and taken away to a cell where he might scream until his voice died and watch himself rot until he was hanged.

Chapter Thirty-eight

Prioress Eleanor and her brother walked in silence along the ramparts of the manor. Flying overhead, a flock of black birds screeched. Thick cloaks might keep away the chill that the earth brings the flesh, and death brings the heart, but nothing could banish all reminders of mortality.

Although she would have chosen a warmer place to talk, her brother was now head of the family. If he was happier on a fortified wall with an attacking north wind, so be it. This was not a battle she chose to fight.

Baron Hugh stopped when they reached a protected place where the wind sighed rather than bit. He leaned against the wall and clenched his hands. "Do you share my anger over the injustice committed against the ben David family, sister?"

"You have read my thoughts," she said. Her resentment over the cold faded in the light of this rare moment of intimacy with a brother she loved but often felt she no longer understood.

With a twisted smile, he looked at her. "That pleases me, although it should be no surprise. Apart from the love I bear you as my sister, I also hold you in high regard." He closed his eyes tightly. "I do not respect most who share your vocation."

She said nothing, waiting to hear how he wished to pursue this subject.

"You love Richard as much as I. What would you advise I do with his plea to become a priest?"

Gently smiling, she replied. "When I was your son's age, our father wanted me to marry. I wished to take vows, and our aunt supported me in this. They agreed that I should leave Amesbury Priory and live at Wynethorpe Castle for a year, during which time I was encouraged to frolic like most young women of that age." She laughed. "Young men, especially the one my father planned for me to wed, were in frequent attendance to remind me of the joys of conjugal life. But our father and aunt also agreed that, if I still longed to be a nun after that year, my father would honor my choice of a religious vocation."

"You were raised in a priory and knew little enough of the world. Richard knows only a king's court. Of a priest's life, he knows nothing."

"He knows Brother Thomas and has spent time in Tyndal Priory. Like our brother, Robert, he is inclined to reflection and far more than he, Richard enjoys a reasoned argument. In his childhood, he loved to ask questions, some of which were more perceptive than is common in a boy so young. Later, he begged to borrow books from our library and has questioned Brother Thomas on the writings of men like Saint Augustine and Aquinas."

Hugh snorted.

"You do not like Brother Thomas or you do not like Aquinas?"

He laughed "I did not like your monk. But he saved my life, and, reluctant as I am to admit this, I have learned to trust him. He has unquestionably served you and our family well." He lowered his head and flexed his hands as if he missed the feel of a sword. "How much does he know about Father Eliduc and his plots regarding my son?"

"We have spoken. He does not like or trust him any more than you and I do."

Hugh expressed surprise.

"I know more than I have ever said about my monk's past and his dealings with the priest, but all that became irrelevant long ago. Brother Thomas is suspicious of anything suggested by Father Eliduc. I can assure you that we all share the same opinion of the man. The priest has some personal gain intended with his seemingly generous proposal. That noted, Brother Thomas wonders if the plans he has for Richard might not benefit our family. A clever youth who serves the Archbishop of Canterbury would rise in the Church and might gain influence that would be of value to us. Brother Thomas' observation has merit."

"At a price, sister, at a price. And what is that cost? We shall pay in some fashion and at some time when it may not be in our best interests."

Eleanor smiled. "Have you ever met a Wynethorpe who bent to another's will when he did not wish to do so? Richard is young, but he shows the determination I remember in you when you were still dreaming of King Arthur's court. Who went on crusade when our father did not wish it?"

Hugh grinned. "And who entered the priory at Amesbury when our father had other plans?"

"No one has ever won an argument with our aunt, Sister Beatrice."

"Very well, sweet sister. I cannot swear I shall agree to it, but I will to listen to my son's wish without losing my temper. Nonetheless, he is bound first to our family's interests."

"Nay, brother, he is bound first to God, as we all are, but then he owes allegiance to family." She hesitated. "May I suggest a compromise?"

"Since you mentioned our aunt, I can guess what it is."

"Only in part," she replied. "Send Richard to study at a college in Oxford. He is the right age to go. Let him enjoy the opportunity to study with others of similar interest and rank. It might be training for the priesthood, but it would also allow him to study law. After seeing how justice was ignored so cruelly in the coin-clipping arrests, our king would surely find your son, once well-trained in legal matters, of great use to him."

Hugh gestured for her to continue.

"I cannot swear that Richard will not still choose the priesthood, and a position with the new Archbishop would be a worthy one, but the life of a student leaves him in the world for a while longer where he may discover he has no taste for taking vows. Chastity suits few of either sex, and obedience is hardest for men." She grasped his arm affectionately. "The latter is hardest for a Wynethorpe."

"You are telling me that I must permit him to make the choice himself in the end?"

"Shall we agree that we will let him discover what he wants without either of us attempting to coerce him? The path to honor may take several twists, brother. He cannot be your heir, but he can serve the family and gain prestige by vowing himself to God or to the king, by becoming a priest, a knight, or a counselor."

"As always, you are the wiser of the two of us, sister. I shall tell him that his immediate future must be study in Oxford. The decision to enter the priesthood, follow the path to knighthood, or find another vocation will be set aside until a later time. I will also swear not to speak of his future while he is a student, nor express my relief that he will be away from the malign influence of that pocky Father Eliduc."

Hugh looked away, his eyes growing dark with profound fury.

"What quarrel do you have with God, Hugh? You have one, and I fear for your soul."

He threw up his hands. "Priests lie, popes scheme, and anointed kings hang the innocent. I have known impious Christians and godly unbelievers. It is not that I deny God, sister, but I often wonder what He wants when the world turns upside down and we are told to honor the wicked."

She waited.

He looked at her, his eyes narrowed with pain. "Father Eliduc grieves only that the document proving ben David's house belongs to the Church has been destroyed. He cares nothing for the lot of the family of a man wrongly hanged. Mistress Chera was willing to surrender her own life to save her granddaughters. Which one is the ungodly one, sister? The priest or the Jewess?"

Eleanor bit her lip as tears burned her eyes. "Hugh, God does not ignore the sins of those who claim to follow His teachings but twist them into a wicked purpose. Would you not fear to send your soul to His judgment if you were such a man? As Saint Paul said, the greatest virtue is charity, even over faith. Without kindliness, we are blind to our sins, but God is not."

He nodded, but the gesture was one of courtesy, not concurrence.

She knew better than to speak of priests, although she longed for her brother to find one to heal his soul. Instead, she honored his silence. He was not the first to struggle with these things, and God did not seem to mind that. She only hoped he could make peace with Him before he died.

Hugh straightened and walked slowly on.

His sister followed.

He suddenly turned to look down at his tiny but extraordinary sister. "Mistress Chera and her granddaughters will soon return to Oxford with Joshua the baker. I have promised them that I shall arrange transportation so they can travel to France where they have family. Joshua and some of my men will accompany them to guarantee their safe passage." Hugh's eyes softened with love as he gazed at her. "And I know you shall pray for their well-being as well as their conversion. Which should come first?"

Eleanor knew from his tone that he was not mocking her, and she was glad of this change in his mood. "Both, brother. Unlike mortals, God is not limited to *either/or*."

"Meanwhile, the king will repay the Church to make up for the loss of a house. Somehow Father Eliduc will gain favor as well, winning King Edward's heart with tales of his spiritual attendance upon the queen during her travail. I suspect the priest longs to be the favored spiritual advisor in this court."

"He would have to compete with the queen's beloved Dominicans for the honor. I think he knows that and will have another prize in mind," Eleanor replied. "But, in confidence, I must ask you this. Shall our lord king admit that he hanged an innocent man? His reputation may have suffered for it."

"Although he would deny it, our liege lord is much like his father, especially in his ardent faith. Lumbard ben David was a Jew who did not convert. Although the man was innocent of treason, King Edward still sees him as an enemy of God. In that opinion he is joined by a great fellowship amongst the barons. There will be no grief or repentance over the execution. That is why I chose to take care of ben David's family. No one else will."

It was Eleanor's turn to look at her brother with shock.

He tilted his head and gazed at her sadly. "There is no disloyalty in my remark. I see our king's flaws but love him for his virtues. He is not only my liege lord but my friend. It is hard to be a man's comrade-in-arms, stare down Death together, and not form a bond that is like no other."

Briefly, she pondered his words, and then nodded. It had not been his critical tone in speaking of the king that had surprised her but his care for the mother and children of ben David. It was a gesture she would have wanted to make but could not. Perhaps it was one he made out of gratitude for the care the dead physician had given Lucas?

"Soon I shall travel on to tell King Edward that his desire for justice and the rule of law has been perverted by evil men. He will not be pleased, and will take some action, but I am not blind to his pleasure that his coffers have been replenished. The Church's debt will be honored, the Jew's forgotten."

She knew there was no need for comment, and they walked on, side by side. As they passed the openings in the stone wall, they stopped to look down on the land below, chilled with the icy mist brought by the wind from the north. She heard her brother sigh.

"Robert must marry soon," he said.

She stared at him.

He saw her confusion and replied, "Our brother must sire children."

Although she wanted to ask Hugh why he did not speak of his own need to marry and produce heirs, she knew he would ignore her query. In truth, she was grateful he had spoken of his quarrels with God in that unique moment of confidence and taken her advice about his son. Thus she counseled herself not to demand more than he could give and did not push her brother further. She would let him speak when he wished and spend many hours praying that he find peace with God and himself.

"Have you spoken to him of marriage?"

"Not yet, but I have a woman in mind."

"Be kind to him, Hugh. Let her be sweet-natured and one able to appreciate the good man she is getting. A bit like your son, he is inclined to a quiet life, loves the earth, and…"

"Fear not. She is one of the queen's attendants, a young widow with a child to prove her fertility. Of course, she comes with land, although she owns no great beauty. I have met her and know the queen would be pleased by the match. By reputation, the lady is inclined to quiet study, rather than the latest fashion in trimmings or fur, and enjoys the careful planning needed for a well-run household. Yet she made me laugh with her wit when we spoke together. She and Robert should suit each other well in time."

As they each fell into their own thoughts and turned back to reenter the company of others, Eleanor suddenly realized that her eldest brother might have asked for her opinion in the past but had never spoken to her as if she were second only to him and not just his youngest, female sibling who happened to be a prioress.

She shivered, but the cause was not the wind. The world had changed so quickly on the death of their father. Her brother was now Baron Hugh, friend and counselor to the king, and she was the Prioress of Tyndal, leader of a respected religious house, in a time when such titles and kinship spoke of power and influence.

It was a realization that brought even greater weariness to her soul and body, already battered by the pain of death and violence. Although she longed for quiet prayer and rest, she knew she had one more trial to endure here before she could find that peace, one from which she must emerge with honor.

Queen Eleanor had summoned her for an audience.

Chapter Thirty-nine

The Queen of England glanced over her shoulder at Brother Thomas who had not been invited to join the women in this garden stroll.

His head bowed, he seemed content to remain at the entrance gate.

"He is your especial monk?" she asked, the words softened by her Castilian birth.

If anyone else had asked that question, the prioress would have bristled at the suggestion of impropriety, but there was no such implication in the tone. "He advises me on Church law and counsels me in matters beyond my understanding."

The queen looked back at the monk for another long moment, then briefly studied the prioress as if seeking something in her face that she did not find. "You are most fortunate that God sent you so wise a guide."

Then they began a slow walk through the garden, the queen pointing out some of her favorite things. "A bed of red and white hollyhock will go there," she said. "I asked that the seeds be sent to me from Castile. We shall plant after all danger of frost is gone." Raising a hand over her head, she laughed with an almost musical sound. "The flowers will bloom far above the heads of mortals, even my lord husband."

As the prioress watched her, she was amazed by the queen's energy. Although Queen Eleanor had recently given birth to the couple's thirteenth child, she was out of bed and walking in this garden, despite her still-swollen belly. One attendant had whispered to the prioress that this lying-in might end before the month was done. Few took as little time to heal after giving birth, the woman had added, and it was also known that the queen's stewards had been warned to prepare for a detailed discussion of future land purchases, exchanges, or sales with her soon.

The two reached a stone bench along the path, one that looked out on a small fountain, and the queen sat, then gave permission for the prioress to do so as well.

"Your father's death grieves us all," she said. "He was loyal to the crown and stood with my husband and his father when we found ourselves so abandoned."

Eleanor modestly bowed her head. Many had forgotten that this queen had had good reason to fear for her life and that of her husband during the baronial wars under de Montfort. It was a time when the decision to remain allied to King Henry was not considered wise by many. The prioress was pleased this queen had not forgotten those who had chosen to stand by the anointed king.

"I have arranged for prayers to be said in perpetuity for his soul."

"I am grateful for your kindness, my lady."

A shadow swiftly passed over the queen's face. "Your brother also serves us well."

Eleanor noticed the brief hesitation before that remark. Hugh might be the king's loyal friend, a soldier who had been by his side in Outremer, but her brother had declined to obey some of the queen's discreetly urged wishes. Such refusals had displeased her and even caused a rare quarrel with the king.

The queen folded her hands. "In this tragedy of Mistress Hawis and her traitorous husband, you acted with courage and wit."

"The High Sheriff of Berkshire, Father Eliduc, and my brother did far more than I…"

The queen laughed. "Your modesty is a compliment to your vocation, Prioress Eleanor, but I know your reputation. I also remember that you were injured trying to save my husband from an assassin in Walsingham nearly two years ago."

Eleanor humbly lowered her gaze.

The queen tilted her head and looked at the prioress with a fond expression. "The women who attend me are not of your high birth, but, had you not chosen to serve God, you might have spent much time in my company. All the women in your family have waited upon the English queens, have they not, from the days of King Henry II?"

"My mother's family came from the Aquitaine with his queen," the prioress replied. "Had God not called on me to take vows, I would have found service to you a great honor."

The queen straightened her back.

Although she had betrayed only this one hint of weakness, the queen must be growing weary, Eleanor decided, and was grateful that the audience would not last much longer.

"Do you remember the time I almost visited Tyndal Priory?"

"I do, my lady."

"I heard of your prowess then in solving a murder and have followed your feats ever since. You have also lifted your priory from a state of near-poverty to one of affluence. Your abbess in Anjou speaks highly of your skills in service to God."

Her compliments were gracious, Eleanor thought, and she had the skill to make them sound sincere. Although she felt drawn to the queen, as many were, the prioress was not so charmed that she did not retain caution.

"If you should hear of any land or rents that do not suit the needs of your priory, I would be pleased if you sent me word."

Eleanor swiftly agreed with appropriate courtesy and was relieved she managed not to smile when the queen asked her help in increasing the royal holdings.

"I have heard of the healing powers of those who work in your priory hospital. Even the ale you brew has received high praise from those who return to court from Tyndal." Her eyes sparkled with humor.

This time Eleanor did allow herself to laugh. "Sister Matilda will be upset if no one here has praised her fruit pies."

"Then tell her that I must know her secret recipes!" And the queen smiled in return. Many jested that the queen could be bribed with any gift of fruit, but Edward's wife was willing enough to join the teasing over her weakness.

As the queen spoke further of her plans for gardens with cascading fountains and verdant paths to remind her of Castile, the prioress understood why she had kept the devotion of a husband for almost twenty-five years as well as the allegiance of many at court. Had she been of common birth, some might have whispered about witchcraft, but this woman was a queen and her lineage, from a man many called a saint, translated that gift into regal charm.

Not long after, however, the queen stood and indicated that the audience was over.

"I shall have my scribes, Roger and Philip, copy a book for you. You are a true servant of God, Prioress Eleanor, but I have also learned that you share my passion for the stories of King Arthur. I have the tales of Tristan, which gave the king and me great pleasure in Outremer. When the copy is done, I shall send it to you."

With sincere gratitude and proper respect, the prioress left the presence of the queen and joined Brother Thomas at the gate.

He noted her relief that this audience had ended and smiled with understanding.

As they hurried to bid farewell to Mistress Chera and her granddaughters, and prepare for their own return to Tyndal Priory, Eleanor felt unease over this successful audience. She was practical enough to know that her brother would be pleased at how his sister had been honored. Nonetheless, as he had said about Father Eliduc's beneficence to Richard, she wondered what price she might have to pay in the future for this very pleasant meeting with the queen.

Author's Notes

By now, some might suspect that I don't like King Edward I, a conclusion that is not quite true. He was a fascinating, complex man, and I view him with respect and interest but hardly undiluted admiration. Historical heroes and villains are best understood and more fully appreciated when their flaws and virtues are on full display.

The generally accepted conclusion is that Edward was a sea change from his father, Henry III, and became one of England's greatest monarchs. In fact, he was very similar to his father in both good and not so commendable ways. He was a faithful and adoring husband, a mercurial ally, a man of intelligence but subject to lapses in judgment, a monarch who liked to escape the demands of kingship, one of zealous faith, and a king who would do almost anything to fill his coffers and shut his barons up. What set him apart from King Henry III was less their differences than his passionate desire to be perceived as a man utterly unlike his father. To his credit, he recognized the weaknesses in his father's reign, but, in becoming the anti-Henry, he made his own mistakes.

In this book, I deal with the broadly painted image of Edward as the "English Justinian" and "the lawyer king," specifically as it relates to the coin-clipping pogrom and his ongoing dealings with the Jewish community from the Statute of the Jewry to the eventual expulsion.

By the late 1270s, English coinage had become debased. The old coins were worn, clipped to the point of significantly diminished worth, and did not even bear the image of a king who had reigned for seven years. Wisely, Edward decided to upgrade the stock, a decision that would benefit trade and vastly improve English reputation for value. Unwisely, he also decided to come down on coin-clippers with a singularly brutal vengeance but little concern for individual criminal activity or even-handed justice. As the easiest approach, and following a time-honored political practice, he gathered up and imprisoned the usual suspects, mostly a group that happened to be Jewish.

There was cause to suspect coin-clipping in the Jewish community. The allowed professions involved the handling of money, and the tax assessments against the community were increasingly harsh. What was not reasonable was the failure to investigate allegations of wrong-doing properly or to investigate most Christians who were clipping coins and, contrary to religious prohibition, also involved in money-lending.

Not only were many hundreds of Jewish men imprisoned for clipping in November 1278, but wives were as well. In comparison, only a small number of Christians were arrested. When it came to hanging, the trials were no better than kangaroo courts. Although the total number is debated, almost three hundred Jewish men and women were certainly hanged in London alone and far more in other parts of the country. Eight from the Oxford Jewish community were executed, including one woman. Contemporary records suggest between thirty and forty Christians were hanged. Most of them got off with fines, also known as bribes.

The speed with which people were arrested (in swift night raids over two days) and the perfunctory nature of the judicial reviews suggest that a few of the executed were probably innocent. As was discovered in early 1279, some of the hanged were convicted on planted evidence. That this should happen in the reign of a man, whom many claim was passionate about law, is an especial tragedy.

But Edward always needed money and coin-clipping was considered treason. All possessions of the convicted, from houses to goblets, were confiscated, sold, and the proceeds deposited in the king's accounts. When the message finally got through to the king in May 1279 that people were planting evidence of treason in Jewish households to avoid paying back loans, out of revenge or even religious fervor, he stopped the executions. Instead of releasing the remaining prisoners, or demanding proper trials, he ordered them to pay a fine if they wished to be released. Those who could not were left in prison until the community could get the money together to free them or they died. An interesting approach from a man praised as the English Justinian.

◇◇◇

Edward I, following one of the few popular practices of his father, did what he could to get the Jewish community to switch faiths. During the reign of Henry III, all converts had to surrender every possession after baptism to the king's coffers. Since they were now poverty-stricken, Henry III established a place in London where these converts could live, receive a small weekly allowance, spend their days studying the new faith, and survive in monastic simplicity. At least families were apparently not separated, unless sent to religious houses to live. The residence was called *Domus Conversorum* or House of Converts. King Edward, slightly more generous than his father, eventually required the convert to hand over only half of all his property to the king. This price for conversion did include the guarantee that families could live without persecution or the extreme taxation they had previously suffered. Nonetheless, very few ever took up the deal.

◇◇◇

Queen Eleanor's reputation has swung from villain to saint but rarely fluttered in the middle. From records left, she seems to have been a ruthless (often brutal) business woman, a scholar, a duplicitous manipulator of useful people, a generous and kind friend, a wise (albeit subtle) advisor to her husband in matters of diplomacy, and a skillful administrator with great personal charm who won over men and women alike.

No one really knows what she looked like, since portraiture was not common in her time, but details left suggest she was attractive (but not an era beauty), probably not blond (since her favored colors were autumnal reds and rich greens), with an oval face, possibly hooded eyes, and a long, straight nose. Despite about sixteen pregnancies in around twenty years, she seemed to have remained remarkably slender, due to her extraordinary energy and avid hunting.

In her personal affairs, she did not get along with her mother-in-law but was careful to avoid open conflict. She did not repeat Eleanor of Provence's mistakes by importing and enriching relatives. Instead, Eleanor of Castile made sure the relatives she enriched were born in England. Since she had learned administration, image-building, and the art of winning peace after a successful war from her father (the well-regarded Ferdinand III of Castile), Edward I probably sought her advice, but the couple was wise enough to hide the extent of her influence. When the children or families of her attendants, servants, and other retainers were in need, she was generous with time, money, and gifts. All that said, her business practices would make the robber barons of late nineteenth-century America look like newborn lambs, and her subjects disliked her for her ruthless acquisition of property and rents. It wasn't until the Victorian Age that she was painted as a retiring and modest queen, an image that would have horrified her Archbishop of Canterbury, John Pecham, who berated her for not being the gentle lady she should be.

On the surface, her dealings with the Jewish community seemed more enlightened than those of her husband. (Her father, Ferdinand III, had supported the practice of *convivencia* in which the three major religions were encouraged to interact with greater, albeit never perfect, ease to promote a more productive society.) She had even been unsuccessfully rebuked by Archbishop Pecham for her financial dealings with the community, but, when Jewish economic usefulness ended and the community was expelled from England in 1290, she remained silent, even on behalf of those who had helped her so much. Her health was poor, and she died a month after the deadline for obeying the expulsion order. Some point to that as the reason for her seeming heartlessness. I am not quite so forgiving. The plans for the order of expulsion would have been discussed long before issuance in July 1290. Had she wanted to protect a few individuals, or at least grant them a better deal under the expulsion edict, her wishes would have been respected.

In a different aspect of her life, she was one of the few men or women to own a personal scriptorium where books she liked could be copied. Her fondness for fruit was legendary. She imported olive oil, figs, oranges, lemons, saffron, and other items from Spain. The hollyhock is alleged to have been her gift to English gardens. The carpet was another present, initially greeted with derision but later adopted to the relief of many cold feet. She was not a clotheshorse, although her attire was quietly fashionable, but she made sure her husband put on the bling when required to impress. Edward was far happier in hunting attire and had to be forced into the medieval equivalent of white tie.

As a final observation, Eleanor of Castile was the great-great-granddaughter of Eleanor of Aquitaine. That fact alone may say more about her personality, intelligence, and talents than any transient theories developed over the centuries, even if she did not always put those qualities to the same use.

◇◇◇

Woodstock Manor no longer exists, razed by Sarah, the Duchess of Marlborough, in 1720 when she decided to change the look of the land, build a lake, and find a more attractive use for all those stones. Its former glory is now represented by a plinth on the Blenheim estate.

But the manor had a long history before it crumbled into an offensive ruin. It was built by Henry I as a hunting lodge with an attached park for his exotic animals, became a palace under Henry II who kept his beloved Rosamund nearby, and was fortified by Henry III after his wife's lady foiled an assassination attempt against him in 1238. Elizabeth I was held captive there for a year under Queen Mary, although the palace had deteriorated significantly by then. It never regained its former glory, and Queen Anne gave it to the hero of the Battle of Blenheim, along with a dukedom and enough money to build a more suitable palace.

◇◇◇

Alan FitzRoald is the real name of the High Sheriff of Berkshire (which included Oxfordshire from 1248-1566) during the time this book took place. Other than his name, I have been unable to find out anything about him. Trying to avoid too much fictional license, I gave him a family (likely), portrayed him as an honest man (probable since King Edward had dismissed three-quarters of the sheriffs for corruption in 1274), and one who wanted to render fair justice (always possible).

◇◇◇

Confession time! In this book, I added a bit more imagination than usual to known facts by including the spaniel, El Acebo. There was no El Acebo (Spanish for *Holly*), and we do not know that the queen owned a spaniel.

There is much debate about when spaniels of any size and appearance were introduced to England, ranging from the first paw on the shore at Cornwall in the 900s BCE to the time of Julius Caesar. There is also disagreement over whether spaniels even came from Spain, which their name suggests. Although they did exist in medieval Spain, they might have originated in the Middle East or China.

The early dogs were prized for their ability to retrieve prey, flush fowl for hunters, and were good at swimming and burrowing. They were also infamous for being easily distracted and chasing local chickens instead of the desired partridge. By the 17th century, the breed had evolved into two types: water or land dogs. The now-extinct English water spaniel was probably the one called a "water rug" in *Macbeth*. The cocker, a land dog, developed from the springing or pointing spaniel.

Edward II included spaniels of some variety in his hunting pack, so it would not surprise me if he got the idea from his mother. Eleanor of Castile loved hunting dogs and certainly could have had some in her packs. Although not impossible, I lack any proof.

My reason for including the scenes with El Acebo, apart from the hoped amusement, is to honor a particular spaniel. Since her ancestors have a long and storied history in the British Isles, I thought she might enjoy the cameo appearance, especially because it included the theft of a choice bit of venison.

Bibliography

Because the histories of King Edward's reign usually deal with the vast canvas, his decisions are most often discussed in terms of monetary policy, war planning, political maneuvers, legal reform, and the reactions of the large, primary groups affected. The individual stories—the innocents condemned with the guilty; the consequences suffered by fathers, mothers, and children from his wars; implementation of laws; fiscal problems; or treatment of the Jewish community—are rarely addressed in depth.

Enter the historical novelist...

But I have made little out of whole cloth, except for the specific characters and the mystery tale. Once again, I urge the reading of several academic books that deal with the events of this book in greater detail. Several selected are more focused on the experiences of the Jewish community as it struggled to survive under Edward's rule.

Mints and Money in Medieval England, by Martin Allen, Cambridge University Press, 2012.

Licoricia of Winchester: Marriage, Motherhood and Murder in the Medieval Anglo-Jewish Community, by Suzanne Bartlet (edited for publication by Patricia Skinner), Vallentine Mitchell, 2009.

Eleanor of Castile: the Shadow Queen, by Sara Cockerill, Amberley Publishing, 2014.

The Hound and the Hawk: the Art of Medieval Hunting, by John Cummins, Phoenix Press, 1988.

Eleanor of Provence: Queenship in Thirteenth Century England, by Margaret Howell, Blackwell Publishers, 1998.

Expulsion: England's Jewish Solution, by Richard Huscroft, Tempus Publishing, 2006.

England's Jewish Solution: Experiment and Expulsion, 1262-1290, by Robin R. Mundill, Cambridge University Press, 1998.

The King's Jews: Money, Massacre and Exodus in Medieval England, by Robin R. Mundill, Continuum, 2010.

Eleanor of Castile: Queen and Society in Thirteenth-Century England, by John Carmi Parsons, 1998.